THE
ORPHAN'S
TESTIMONY

By Morgan Keyes

ISBN: 979-8-9999867-2-6

Book design by Morris Lowery Jr.

"Bad men need nothing more to compass their ends, than that good men should look on and do nothing".

- John Stuart Mill (1867)

"For God hath not given us the spirit of fear; but of power, and of love, and of a sound mind."

- 2 Timothy 1:7 King James Bible

Principle characters

Damion Jackson, Chief Master-At-Arms, U.S. Navy
Reverend Jeremiah Coburn
Delilah Parsons
Sebastion Donovan
Jacob Hicks

Bishops Creek Law Enforcement (BCLE)

Sheriff J.T. Douglas (Callsigns Sheriff-1; 6-Lincoln-1)
Deputy Delbert Jamison (Callsign 1-Adam-12; North Sector Patrol)
Deputy Linda Mack (Callsign 2-Adam-7; East Sector Patrol)
Deputy Percy Johnson (Callsign 3-Baker-21; South Sector Patrol)
Deputy Paul Alvarez (Callsign 4-Charles-9; West Sector Patrol)
Detective Brandy Phillips (Callsign Delta-5; Homicide)
Deputy Tony Bass (Callsign Echo-6; Evidence/Coroner Liaison)

BCLE radio brevity codes

10-4: Acknowledged
10-20: Location
10-76: En route
10-97: On scene
Code 3: Lights and sirens
Signal 7: Dead on arrival
Signal 13: Officer in trouble

Chapter 1 – Once Upon A Time

Jonah Wilde was a happy man. For about as long as he could remember, he had never been as happy as he was tonight.

The charcoal-gray 1998 Peterbilt 379 T/A Sleeper semi-truck – affectionately named *Betty Sue* - purred beneath him, steady and low, like a sleeping beast content in its own skin. The hum of the engine reverberated softly in his bones, a comforting vibration that put him at ease with every subtle bump in the road. The steering wheel, thick and well-worn, fit perfectly in his strong, calloused hands, while the driver's seat had been conditioned over time to fit his massive 5x-sized frame. A man and his machine. There was nothing else better in the world than that.

The cool night air blew through the open windows, flowing over Jonah's cheeks and tugging gently at the strands of his scraggly, dirty-blond beard. The faint scent of pine rode on the breeze, reminding him how much he loved doing what he does. The idling engine grumbled as he coasted slowly down the winding off-ramp toward the truck rest area. Crickets chirped as if they were trying to outdo each other, while mosquitoes buzzed angrily past his ears in and out of the neon-lit cab. Jonah didn't care.

He mused on how these younger truckers rode with their windows rolled up, sealed tight in their cozy little worlds, and using air conditioning to block out the natural world. But not him. He was a *real* trucker. An old-school road warrior. He loved the feel of the night air, the rustling trees as he drove by, even the steady splattering of bugs against his windshield. The rawness of it all made him feel alive.

A big grin crept across his face as he thought about the imminent meeting—his big five-o. Tonight marked his 50th run. He chuckled to himself, barely believing his luck. Not only did he get to do what he loved more than anything else in the world—driving his rig—but he got paid to do it.

His regular route took him across several of the southern states, and he was thankful for that. He never did care much for those Yankees up north. Always zipping about in a hurry, going nowhere, and thinking they were better than good southern folk. He was on the road away from home at least two days a week, but that was just fine by him. A man had to provide for his family, and he did what he needed to do to bring in the cash and support his kin. He loved his wife and seven kids, of course, but the constant yelling, running, and fighting—it could wear a man down. Out here, with nothing but blacktop and the sky, Jonah always found his peace.

He shifted the gears smoothly, and *Betty Sue* responded with a contented growl in return. The feel of the gearstick in his hand was like shaking hands with an old drinking buddy. The dash lights glowed faintly orange, casting soft shadows over his weathered face. Every sound from the truck was familiar and reassuring—the soft whirr of the turbocharger to his powerful turbodiesel engine, the subtle creak of the cab shifting as he took a turn, even the sharp hiss of the airbrakes when he tapped the pedal gently. Only a *real* trucker could appreciate the personal moments like these on the road.

His wife, Dee-Dee, didn't understand his need for time alone. She never had. She would often nag that she wanted him around the house more, but Jonah felt that all she mostly did was stay at home and spend his hard-earned money. He couldn't stomach being there and seeing that happen every single day. She seemed to always be complaining about what the kids needed, and how they would grow up and leave home before he knew it. As far as Jonah was concerned about that last part - he would never say it out loud - but the idea didn't exactly upset him that much.

She had even started in on him again just before this run. She said she needed a break and some time to herself. Jonah hadn't wanted to fight, so he'd shrugged and told her she could leave the kids with their oldest daughter and go do her stuff. Dee-Dee fired back that a ten-year-old shouldn't be watching six younger kids. He had laughed while taking a sip of his bourbon and told her that his older brother used to watch him and his four siblings growing up, and they'd turned out just fine, at least until their late teenage years.

The memories drifted in like smoke. Jonah, his brothers, and their one sister. The Wilde Bunch, the locals called them, comparing the mischievous family to a 1969 western with the same name, minus the 'e' in Wilde. Fighting, vandalizing mailboxes, setting off fire extinguishers in school hallways, and busting car windows with slingshots. They thought they were invincible, and they wore that nickname like a crown, even though it wasn't meant kindly.

But life has a way of humbling even the wildest of the wild.

In the span of one year, the Wilde Bunch fell apart. Two brothers overdosed on some new street drug that found its way into their small town. One was stabbed to death in a "friendly" poker game that got out of hand. Another was shot in the head while drunk and playing Russian Roulette with a cousin. And their sister...just gone. One day she was there, and the next she wasn't. There were rumors, of course. The most popular being that she ran off with a traveling preacher in town around that time. Jonah never knew for sure, but he didn't believe it.

And now, it was just him.

At least he still had Dee-Dee. She had been his anchor after all of that drama. A local girl from a neighboring town, they had attended the same district high school. She was a petite, sandy-blonde cheerleader who loved to brag that her boyfriend was the largest guy on the football team. She would've been his high school sweetheart the entire senior year, too, if he'd stayed in high school. But she didn't care about diplomas or fancy stuff. They got married right after she graduated, and the kids came fast—like dominoes falling. She was a good woman, a real country girl, but she just didn't get it. A man needed his space sometimes to relax and have a little peace and quiet. And *Betty Sue* was his sanctuary.

He rounded the last curve of the off-ramp and rolled into the lot. The Peterbilt coasted over the gravel, each bump and crunch sending up a satisfying hum through the floorboard. A few trucks were parked here and there.

Several hulking shadows stood under buzzing halogen lamp poles, while a few others were parked in lesser illuminated areas of the parking lot. He pulled into a spot near the back, under a single light that flickered slightly, like it was struggling to stay awake.

Jonah killed the engine, and *Betty Sue* gave one last sigh before settling into silence. He sat there for a long moment, basking in the stillness. Then he reached into his shirt pocket and pulled out a tight knot of hundred-dollar bills. He thumbed through it slowly. Fifty runs. And all of them had gone off without a hitch.

He thought about the electronics company he was driving for now. They weren't the best-paying outfit, and a little stingy on benefits. Most of the other companies he'd worked for paid at least twenty-five percent more—but these folks were the only ones that would take him on, especially after the unfortunate incident with Mandy.

Mandy, like candy, she'd said. Red hair, long legs, and lots of perfume. Perfect. Except she wasn't.

He'd been driving for a big-name clothing distributor back then. The pay and benefits were good. One night, he stopped at a secluded truck stop for some food and rest. Mandy had approached him, said that she wanted some company, and that if he paid for a room and dinner, they could spend some time together. Jonah had quickly agreed, and they got a room. The moment they were inside, and he had given her the cash for herself, the door flew open. Several large men in masks rushed in, tackled him to the floor, and cuffed him. Undercover cops, and he was busted. But he had had the last laugh on those pigs.

He remembered the courtroom as if it were yesterday. The judge, a good old boy and old-timer, threw out the charges. Jonah's lawyer had called his arrest entrapment and argued that the police had tricked him while he was exhausted from driving his rig. Said Jonah was a good family man with a wife and kids, and just happened to be in the wrong place at the wrong time.

The judge agreed, and the charges were dismissed. However, the damage was already done. His employers dropped him the day after he was freed. They said their brand was family-oriented and that they couldn't be perceived as promoting or associating with anything that could lead to a scandal.

Word spread fast, and he couldn't find work after that. Nobody wanted to hire a guy with that kind of stain on his record.

Then he heard about a new electronics company looking for experienced drivers, with no questions asked. He walked in for an interview, was hired on the spot, and was driving the same day.

He had been working steadily for a couple of weeks when one day, a man wearing a cowboy Stetson hat and spurs, riding a red Harley-Davidson motorcycle with gold stripes, approached him and asked if he would like to make some extra money. He said that there was no risk and all he had to do was drive. Jonah was initially skeptical, but when the guy promised to start him off with $1,000 after five successful runs, he agreed.

Jonah shook his head at how easy making the money had been. They said that the packages would be just like the rest of his cargo and blend right in. Nothing illegal-looking, so that if he were stopped and inspected—which had happened five times—there would not be any issues. The money had rolled in. A thousand to start. Then two thousand for every five successful runs. And tonight was number fifty.

And the best part? Dee-Dee didn't know anything about it. She never saw the extra money. Whenever he got his regular paycheck, she was already waiting and complaining that it wasn't enough, talking about bills and groceries. He got annoyed sometimes, but he wasn't a total jerk; he convinced himself. He would occasionally give her a little extra from his side job, saying it was a bonus from the electronics company for doing a good job. But the rest? That was his. Bourbon. Lottery scratch-offs. A few gun shows. No, he wasn't being selfish. *He* was the one who earned it.

The radio crackled as it tried to tune in on a good signal, but it was usually static-filled and patchy in this part of West Virginia. A brief sports report, some weather. Then, a strange story about a group of campers finding a burned bear carcass in the woods. Jonah shook his head.

"This world's full of strange people," he muttered. "What a waste of good meat."

Leaning back in his seat and letting the worn leather embrace him, he stared through the windshield at the stars above. Jonah placed his money back inside his pocket, interlaced his hands behind his head, and closed his eyes. He was a happy man. And tonight, the road would be especially good to him.

Chapter 2 – Jonah and the Whale

The sound of crickets and the gentle night wind caused Jonah to nod off into a deep sleep - a dream world where beautiful women with beach balls and bikinis surrounded him in a swimming pool filled with whiskey and colorful, peeled fruit. One of the women, a tall redhead with freckles and long legs, was pouring him a shot glass and whispering something to him, but he couldn't hear her. He leaned closer as she spoke again, her voice sounding as if it came from some dark, sultry pit.

"Hello, Jonah," she said again.

He slowly turned his head to face her, looking straight into a pair of dark, soulless eyes that were only a foot away from him. Jonah almost wet his favorite jeans as he jumped up from his comfortable seat.

"Oh Christ Almighty!" he yelped, as he focused on the full-bearded image staring at him from the darkness.

"Not exactly, Hoss," replied the man while stepping down off the truck's side running board. His weather-beaten mask of a face cracked a thin smile, having achieved the desired effect from his 'employee'.

Jonah, catching his breath, slowly climbed down out of the truck and stood in front of his 'boss'.

"Jeez! You nearly scared the bejeebers outta' me. You shouldn't go creepin' up on a fella like that. You nextan' gave me a heart attack," he said after taking a deep breath.

The man's smile disappeared, replaced by a dark, ominous expression. When he spoke, his voice was cold and devoid of all emotion.

"Maybe you should be more alert when you are transporting our goods. We don't pay you to sleep while someone else could be taking what is ours. This is unacceptable, Jonah. You will not get another warning."

"Yes, sir, I mean no, sir!" Jonah replied nervously. "It won't happen again, sir. I swear, sir!"

The darkness in the man's eyes made Jonah shudder as a cold chill ran down his back, but he dared not look away. Jonah's subconscious screamed at him that if he broke eye contact for even a second, this wild animal disguised as a human would attack. After what seemed like an eternity, the man's cold smile returned as he extended his gloved hand towards Jonah, holding a familiar brown envelope.

"Congratulations. This is your fiftieth run with zero incidents. I must admit, we were a little skeptical about you at first, but you proved us wrong. We are happy that we decided to take a chance on you." Turning his head slightly to the side with an exaggerated wink, he added, "Now Jonah, don't go spending it all in one place."

Jonah held his breath. This is the moment he had been waiting for, for what seemed like forever. With trembling hands, Jonah reached out and took the large envelope as his eyes began to tear up. He had made it. He had finally made it and was getting the recognition that he deserved. Jonah slowly opened the envelope and gasped. He had never seen so much money in one place before, and it was all in his hands. A tear ran down his cheek, leaving a dirty, wet trail from his eyes to his chin, and dropping down onto his gray flannel shirt. The man continued to speak as if the money was as common as leaves on a tree.

"That's fifty grand in there. You can count it if you like. Our way of showing our appreciation for a job well done."

Jonah was so choked up that he couldn't find the words to speak. He just nodded as tears ran down his face, staring at his newly gotten fortune. He became vaguely aware of the man removing his other hand from behind his back and pointing a large, black object at him. Wiping his eyes with the sleeve of his shirt, he strained to focus on the dark object in the low light of the parking lot lamp. When he realized what it was, his eyes grew wide in shock as his hand flew over his mouth.

"No," he whispered to himself, followed by more tears.

Jonah visibly shook as the man gestured for him to take the carton containing a bottle of West Virginia Black Draft Straight Bourbon: 96-proof. Jonah had often looked from a distance at the expensive, sixty-dollar-a-bottle liquor locked in a glass case behind the counter of his favorite liquor store. He never would have dreamed that one day he would get some of his own. A slamming door at the back of his truck startled him as he turned and saw two men finishing loading several boxes into the back of a dark pickup truck. Jonah had been so preoccupied with his 'boss' that he hadn't noticed the other men were present or that they had entered the back of his truck.

"Okay, Jonah," the man started, drawing his attention back to him. "Time for you to get going. I think you and that fine, little wife of yours have some celebrating to do. And don't be drinking that while you are on the road. We wouldn't want you getting pulled over for a DUI or getting in an accident now, would we?" he said with a wink and a smile. Jonah nodded, thanked him several times, and climbed up in his truck. After wiping his eyes again, he turned the key, and *Betty Sue* roared to life once more. Five minutes later, he was heading down the highway towards the Virginia state line with an envelope full of cash and a new friend riding shotgun in the passenger's seat next to him. Setting the cruise control at 55 miles per hour, he inhaled a deep breath of the fresh night air while glancing at the beautiful, custom-made box sitting in the seat.

"What a beautiful piece of work," he said out loud. "They musta' had some of them artist folks paint that box 'cuz it is dang right purdy."

He began to think about what he would spend his money on first. Buy a stack of scratch-off tickets and win a million dollars, or head over to the backroom casino in Botetourt County? Or maybe he could go find him some "friendly" company before heading back to his zoo of a home. Then, another thought hit him. It's his money, why not just do all three? Yeah, that sounded like a good plan.

As he continued down the road, fairly lit up by the clear night sky, traffic was almost non-existent. The only other motorist he could see came from a vehicle about a mile behind him, and they were keeping their distance. Probably not in any hurry either, he thought to himself. As he drove further, he couldn't keep from glancing at the black box resting quietly in the passenger's seat. After several minutes of deep thoughts and smacking his lips, he decided that it didn't make much sense for him to have to wait until he got home to taste this fine product. It wasn't like he was going to have a couple of glasses full, just a little taste. Visibility tonight was very good; he could see clearly for a distance in both directions, and there was only one vehicle far away.

Keeping one hand on the wheel and grabbing the box with the other, he quickly managed to remove and open the bottle of bourbon. The cab of the truck immediately filled with the scent of bourbon, vanilla, toasted oak, and cinnamon. Jonah took a deep breath and then a small sip. He had never tasted anything so good in his life. He turned the bottle up and took another, longer pull of the bourbon. The dark liquid slid down his parched throat with a steady burn that eased into smooth warmth, leaving a rich sweetness behind that settled deep in his chest and made him feel alive.

"Whoo-whee! That's some good stuff!"

Shaking his head with a big smile on his face, Jonah placed the bottle back in the box. He was getting even more excited now, and his heart was beating faster. He could hardly wait to get back and really turn that bottle up. Too bad Dee-Dee didn't care much for bourbon.

"Oh, well," he thought. "More for me."

As he drove a little further, the dashboard lights suddenly grew brighter, and little stars began appearing in the truck.

"What in tarnation?" he mumbled as a warm sensation flowed over his body and the steering wheel started feeling like a soft, round marshmallow. A wave of euphoria gently lifted him from his driver's seat as he saw himself floating in the cab of the truck, as if looking from outside a house through a bedroom window. The highway blurred into a smear of black and white lines, and the world outside his windshield dissolved as the mirror above him cracked open like a stage curtain.

The fuzzy dice tumbled down first, sprouting spindly legs and translucent wings that buzzed with an angry hum, circling his head like vultures drunk on neon light. Then came the eight-ball, rolling forward on its own, its glossy black shell rippling until it stretched into the pale, freckled face of the red-haired Mandy, her lips moving soundlessly as though whispering a secret he could never quite catch. The laughing dice kicked her face across the floor of the cab, a grotesque soccer match unfolding to the sound of a hollow stadium roar growling from the engine beneath his feet.

Exactly one mile behind Jonah, two men in a dark pickup glanced at each other as they slowly increased speed behind the swerving semi-truck. The big rig zig-zagged back and forth over the highway for half a mile before running off the road and slamming into a ditch on its side.

The pickup slowed to a stop thirty feet from the wrecked truck - smoke pouring from the idling engine and the wheels still spinning. The camouflage-clad men exited the pickup and waited a full minute before approaching the semi, looking for any signs of fuel leakage or sparks that could set it on fire. Satisfied that there was no immediate danger, they casually approached the front of the overturned truck. A large red spot marked the cracked windshield where Jonah had impacted when the truck crashed.

"The boss was right; the old coot couldn't wait to take a sip. And he must've forgotten to put on his seatbelt," one of the men remarked dryly as they each took out flashlights and examined the interior of the truck.

"I see it," said the other man. "I'm going in."

"Don't forget your gloves," said the other.

"Right."

After sliding down through the open window, the man retrieved the large envelope and passed it out to his partner.

"Make sure the cash doesn't touch the outside of the envelope when you take it out," he told him.

"Not my first rodeo, dude," came the sharp reply.

"Might be your last, though," mumbled the man in the truck.

After a few moments, the outside man called out again.

"Hey! Check if he has any smokes. I'm out."

"Okay." The man patted Jonah's clothing until he hit a bump in his shirt pocket. Grinning to himself, he called out to his partner.

"No smokes, but he had this," he said while holding up the roll of hundred-dollar bills.

The outside man's smile lit up like a spotlight.

"Sweet!" he replied.

After checking the rest of Jonah's clothing, the man picked up the unbroken bottle of bourbon, opened it, and inhaled the dark liquor's aromatic scent. He then poured the remaining contents of the bottle all over Jonah's lifeless body and took one last look at the bottle before tossing it back on the floor of the truck.

"What a waste of good liquor," he remarked as he climbed out through the truck's open window.

"Don't forget the pill," his partner called out.

"Got it right here," he replied while taking out a small plastic container from his pocket. He removed the single white pill and dropped it into the truck, where it stuck to Jonah's bourbon-soaked shirt.

"Icing on the cake," he said to no one in particular, before hopping down and rejoining his partner.

The two men stood still, listening and surveying the area for a full minute, before casually walking back to their pickup truck. Taking one last look and satisfied that no one else was in the area, they started the engine and drove back in the direction they came from.

After several minutes of nervously tapping his fingers on his knee, the man riding passenger turned towards the solemn-looking driver with a serious expression on his face.

"Hey. I know we have to get back with the envelope and all, but do ya think we got time to hit up the Outback?"

The driver, focused on the dark road ahead, glanced over at his partner as the big grin lit up his face once again.

"Dude, we *always* got time to hit up the Outback.

The passenger interlaced his fingers behind his head and reclined his seat with a smile on his face, thinking of all the side orders he was going to choose from the menu.

Without saying a word between them, both men separately entertained the same thought:

"What a good night this was turning out to be."

Chapter 3 – The Road Taken

North Carolina Highway 903 was not what Damion had expected. There was no hard crunching of dirt and rocks followed by a massive cloud of dust in his wake. No sudden potholes or rough bumps to challenge the car's sport-tuned suspension system. Not even trash or roadkill for him to swerve around. Instead, the 1970 Ford Mustang Boss 429 glided smoothly down the paved, well-maintained road, with the only audible sounds coming from the 430-horsepower engine as it breathed through its massive, black hood scoop on the "Grabber Orange" muscle car.

Housed in a garage for nearly its entire "life", the vehicle was immaculate and affectionately maintained from the roof to the chassis. With 95% of its original parts still installed and fully functional, the only significant changes to it over the years had been the tires and the high-tech alarm and engine-immobilizing system installed later.

Damion smiled to himself as he thought about the day he took possession of the keys to the sleek American classic.

His next-door neighbor, a retired steelworker at Sparrows Point Shipyard in Baltimore, had bought the car for his own fortieth birthday in 1970 for $4,500 when the model first rolled off the assembly line. When he turned ninety and was no longer able to drive due to medical reasons, he offered to sell the car to Damion for what he had purchased it for in 1970. Stunned, Damion had hesitated, and his neighbor quickly offered to re-negotiate the price if it was too much for him to pay.

Damion had tried to convince him to accept a higher price, saying that the car was worth much, much more than what he was asking. Still, the kind old man refused, saying that he had no family to leave the car to and had gotten his use out of it anyway. He felt that Damion had always been good to him, and knowing he had the car would make him feel much better, as he would continue to take good care of it. So, after sneaking in an extra $500 while his neighbor wasn't looking, Damion paid for the car and took him for one last ride around the city.

Now, after a rather interesting overseas deployment where he was involved in events that were *highly suggested* he forget ever happened, he was back home and three weeks into his thirty-day permanent change of station (PCS) transfer to a new duty station.

Upon returning from deployment to Naval Station Mayport, Damion had immediately booked the first available flight to San Juan, Puerto Rico. He and Salina had corresponded regularly after she had returned stateside due to her injuries, and plans were made to get together as soon as possible when he returned. When the time came, Damion had said his goodbyes and checked off the USS Daniel Shaw (DDG-148) on his PCS leave. Taking advantage of a 1-month half-price promotion by a self-storage facility, he rented their smallest storage unit. He placed his duffel bag, along with all of his other belongings from the ship, in it for temporary storage.

The plan was to fly first to Puerto Rico for a week with Salina, then fly home to Baltimore for two weeks with his family. There, he would retrieve his car from the old family garage and drive down to his new duty station at Naval Air Station Key West, Florida. A stop along the way to retrieve his stored belongings would have to happen, and only take him slightly out of his way. The days seemed to creep by as slowly as time would allow without coming to a complete stop, but finally, he was on his way to visit and create new memories with Salina and, hopefully, a lasting relationship.

The sun had already begun to set when his plane finally touched down in San Juan. The rich Puerto Rican sky was brushed with deep oranges and dusky purples as palm trees danced gently in the wind just outside the terminal. The warm air hit Damion like a welcome hug as he stepped out into the open, rolling his small duffel bag behind him. There, standing beside a weathered Jeep with faded green paint and chrome mirrors that caught the last light of the day, was Salina. She waved with that smile, the one that reached all the way to her eyes.

They stayed at her family's home nestled in the quieter, rural outskirts of the city, a small concrete house painted pale green, with iron bars on the windows and the smell of simmering sofrito floating from the open kitchen. There was a modest vegetable garden out back full of an assortment of vegetables, peppers, and green bananas. A rooster crowed unnecessarily each morning as if it were his sworn duty to ensure no one slept past sunrise. Two Beagles, one old and sleepy, the other endlessly excited, followed Damion around from room to room as if he were the new alpha male of their little dog pack.

Salina's parents were gracious hosts. Her father was a wiry man with permanent grease under his fingernails and a firm handshake. He grilled oxtails over an open flame and served them with a homemade sweet and sour sauce almost every day; a routine that nearly made Damion laugh at the vivid memory of an earlier conversation during his previous visit to Spain. He briefly thought about sending a picture to QMC Valentino as an inside joke, but he held back. Her mother, full of warmth and smiles, gave him *the look*. The subtle, suggestive one that whispered, *"This one will give us beautiful grandchildren."*

Salina's brother, a mixed martial artist with cauliflower ears and a jaw like granite, was less subtle. He sized Damion up immediately and invited him to spar nearly every afternoon. Damion, to his own surprise, accepted. But it was always Salina who put an end to the sessions before anyone left with more than a bruise.

Damion and Salina spent the days venturing through the cobblestone streets of Old San Juan, exploring vibrant murals, ducking into tiny cafés for café con leche and buttery mallorcas - a Puerto Rican sweet bread also known as Pan De Mallorca. They hiked El Yunque, where the dense rainforest swallowed the sun, and the only sounds were coqui frogs and the rush of distant waterfalls. Some places they visited weren't on any tourist maps - hidden beaches, overgrown ruins, places the locals only spoke about in hushed tones.

At night, the air cooled slightly, just enough to make walking along the moonlit shore feel like a dream. Hand in hand, they wandered beneath the soft glow of string lights hung across open patios, music drifting from local bars, the ocean a constant hush behind them.

On one of the more humid afternoons, they decided to go swimming. In the room, as Salina casually undressed to change into her swimsuit, Damion saw the scar. The gunshot wound – now, a puckered blemish on her back shoulder. It was the first time he'd actually seen it without bandages.

The memory hit him like a freight train. That night. The gunfire. The panic.

He froze.

Salina noticed the shift in his demeanor and slowly stepped toward him, taking his hand in hers. Her fingers were warm and firm, grounding him like a lightning rod.

"This was not your fault," she said, her voice softer than the breeze that floated in from the open window.

"Torres had planned to do this long before we got to that point, so stop blaming yourself for it and just be thankful that it wasn't worse. Another inch or two, and it would most definitely have been much worse."

He nodded, but the pain still lingered on his face.

With a light punch to his arm, she added playfully, "Besides, guys dig chicks with scars."

She kissed him gently on the forehead and turned away, sauntering back across the room to finish dressing. Her body swayed just enough to make her point. When she glanced back and saw that he was still sitting on the bed like a small, wounded bird, she turned up the charm.

"*So*...are you going to change into your swimming trunks, or just sit there naked, staring all googly-eyed?"

Had anyone been nearby, they might have heard Salina's hysterical laughter moments later, as Damion tossed her back onto the bed and launched a merciless tickle assault that had her breathless in tears.

The rest of the week felt like a series of stolen moments. Beautiful, fleeting, and drenched in a kind of bittersweet magic. They did their best to find time alone - to talk about things they couldn't tell anyone else. *The* classified mission. Friends who didn't come back. Warnings that weren't spoken but understood.

On the final night before he flew back to Baltimore, they sat side by side on a blanket on a small hill behind her house. Fireworks cracked in the distance, little explosions of red, blue, and gold reflecting in both their eyes. The air was heavy with tropical warmth, and the occasional firefly that floated past like a drifting ember.

"That message you got..." she started.

"Yeah. *'Do the right thing,'* he finished. "I think it was Stephanie. Or someone like her."

They were quiet for a while. The kind of quiet that always preceded deep contemplations and unpopular decisions.

"We always knew," Salina said, her head resting against his shoulder. "This can't last forever. Not unless one of us leaves the service."

He nodded.

"So," she said, lifting her head and giving him a solemn, but beautiful smile, "let's make this the most amicable breakup ever."

They kissed then, with the kind of tenderness that only two warriors who understood each other's pain could share. No anger. No regrets. Just gratitude for the time they had, and the peace in knowing they'd found something real - even if only for a moment.

———

A small, energetic dog chasing a bright, blue ball across the unfenced lawn of an old, sun-washed brick house snapped Damion's attention back to the present. The dog caught the ball well before reaching the road and turned to run back to a small child, who clapped her hands and laughed. The drive along NC-903 was quiet, peaceful, and totally uneventful. A public utilities facility here, a Baptist church there; lots of trailers with both cheap and expensive cars beside them. There were even some with polished, decorated semi-trucks, which he guessed were owned by independent truck drivers. And, of course, there was lots of flat, fertile land for growing all kinds of vegetables. He thought about stopping for a stretch and taking in some of the fresh, country air at one point, but then a childhood memory of him and his brothers watching a film about some children standing in a cornfield convinced him to roll down the windows instead and press on until he reached a well-populated town. He was, after all, still a city boy.

Continuing down the two-laned road, the scenery and action didn't change much, but then he saw a sign up ahead reducing the speed limit from 55 to 35 miles per hour, along with a small green and white sign that read:

Bishops Creek City Limit.

Taking the slight curve past the City Limits sign, he passed small and large brick houses with long driveways, large, well-manicured lawns, and tall pine and pecan trees with branches swaying as if they were waving him into town. With the car's windows down, he could hear the melody of a lone wind chime tapping softly in the late afternoon air.

Coming to a stop sign with a convenience store on his left, he saw that he was at the intersection of East 12th Street, West 12th Street, and Main Street. Looking left, he saw what appeared to be some type of clinic for emergency home health care, a large church, a sports field, and several other older buildings. The street also appeared to be heading into another residential area. To his right were several brick buildings – some with American flags flying – that looked like small businesses, and a moderate number of cars were parked. Turning right, he headed into what he hoped was the center of town and would lead him to someplace decent to eat. He passed the typical small-town establishments - a thrift store, a laundromat, and a place advertising mobile phones and internet service. A Post Office, pharmacy, small bank, and, of course, in a far corner of the "city", a steel water tower with the town's name painted on it in large black letters.

He smiled to himself as he drove a little further down the two-lane street, which could have easily accommodated four lanes if not for the parking spaces for vehicles in the center of the road. The cars, parked perpendicular to the traffic lanes, served as a "natural" median separating traffic while also increasing the number of parking spaces.

A little further, just past the gas station and a Family Dollar store, stood the kind of establishment he was looking for - Del's Diner.

Chapter 4 – Welcome to Bishops Creek

The building was a low-slung, one-story structure painted in off-white, with a trim of soft coral around the windows. A silver-framed screen door creaked slightly on its hinges, and through it drifted the scent of coffee, cinnamon, and something frying on a griddle. The linoleum tiles visible inside were checkerboard black-and-white, with worn smooth at the edges, like something out of an old, drive-in styled café. A neon *Open* sign buzzed faintly in the window, glowing pink against the glass like a memory that refused to dim.

It felt like a place out of time—like something Salina would have loved.

Damion felt his stomach rumble as he stepped over the threshold, and the scent of pancakes and bacon attacked his nostrils. He barely registered the soft creak of the door closing behind him before a voice, gentle as a lullaby but laced with a southern twang, met his ears.

"Go on now, hon. Grab yourself a seat wherever you like."

Damion looked up at the source of the twang and froze.

Bright, emerald green eyes latched onto him with a touch of amusement. Her hair was a cascade of copper waves pulled into a loose knot, and the smile playing on her lips was all slyness and charm. She wore a pale blue uniform, the sleeves cuffed neatly, and a nametag that read "DEL."

The voice came again, coaxing but patient. "You alright there, hon?"

He blinked twice as his tongue stuck to the roof of his mouth. He pulled himself together enough to slide into a booth by the window. The vinyl seat hissed softly as he settled in.

"Y-yeah. I'm good, thanks."

Del approached with a steaming coffee pot in one hand and a menu in the other. "Rough day?" she asked, pouring him a cup without waiting for an answer.

He nodded, watching the dark liquid swirl in the mug. "You could say that."

"Well," she said, flipping the menu open for him and placing it gently on the table, "my name's Del – short for *Delilah* – and you're in the right place. The griddle's hot, the biscuits are fluffy, and if you're lucky, Mrs. Charlene might have some of her custard pie left."

He met her eyes again, trying to steady himself. Something about her was familiar, like a forgotten song.

"I think I'm already feeling lucky," he said, surprising himself.

Del chuckled low in her throat and gave him a wink. "We'll see about that."

And with that, she glided away, the scent of cinnamon trailing behind her.

Damion watched her walk away, as though she moved not for speed but to be watched. Her steps were soft but confident, each one trailing just a whisper of sound across the linoleum. The sunlight through the window bounced off the copper strands of her hair, turning them briefly into the color of a bright flame.

His head swirled, thoughts tangling, as Salina's face flickered in his mind, half-formed, like a dream you try to hold onto just before waking up. Then, his stomach reminded him why he was there. He looked down at the menu. "Grits, eggs, bacon, toast, orange juice, and a side of pancakes," he muttered under his breath. As he continued browsing the menu, he heard the small bell jingle as new customers entered the diner.

Damion looked up into the face of a tough-looking Sheriff wearing a brown Stetson hat and a name tag that read 'J.T. Douglas'. His deputy also had a matching hat and tag that only read 'Jamison'. They looked around the diner, gave him a quick, cursory glance, then moved on to the counter to order their food. Damion heard the door open again, but this time he didn't look up until two pairs of sandaled feet slowed as they passed his booth.

"Heyyy Boo. You ain't from around here," came a heavy, high-pitched southern accent, followed by a second one, only slightly lower in pitch.

"Mm-mm. Gurrl, he sho' is fine."

Damion hesitantly looked up into the small, round faces of two teenage girls, who couldn't have been more than sixteen years old. One African American and the other, Caucasian. He was so shocked by their boldness that he was utterly at a loss for words, but fortunately, he got help.

Del had returned, her presence felt before it was seen, like a change in air pressure.

"Shouldn't you girls be in school or *somewhere else?*" she asked, with the tone of a disapproving adult.

"Aww, Ms. Del, you know there ain't no school on Friday night," came the darker girl's reply.

"Well, then stop gawkin' at grown men and tell me what ya'll doin' in here."

"My mama want to order one 'o dem catfish dinners with bisquits and gravy. She said to ask if you could put some extra gravy on the side, too."

"Okay, but tell Sadie-Mae that I want the works when I come over to the salon later."

"Yes, Ma'am," the teenager replied respectfully.

"All right then, ya'll git on outta here, and I'll send her plate over when it's done."

The two girls turned and smiled at Damion, "*Bye, Boo,*" they sang in unison.

Del watched with a concerned smirk on her face as the two girls left the diner.

"They grow up way too fast around here. Idle hands are the devil's work," she remarked to herself.

Damion felt that there could be an interesting story behind the long stare at the closed door, but he had no right or interest in knowing what it was. Then, abruptly, Del turned to face him. Her smile wasn't wide - it was something more dangerous. It curved slowly, like she had secrets she'd never tell unless you asked the right questions. Her eyes met his again, green like tidepools, still and deep and impossible to look away from. She stood by the table with the confidence of a woman who knew she was in control, as her voice came out smooth with a tone more welcoming than what she had used on the girls.

"Got somethin' in mind, sweetheart?"

Damion cleared his throat, fighting to sound casual.

"Yeah. I'll have grits, two eggs, four slices of bacon, toast, orange juice…and a side of pancakes. Please." Then, after a thought, "And a glass of milk."

Del tilted her head, amused by his formality. "Classic choice for a workin' fella," she said, scribbling quickly on her notepad. "You must be a man of strict habits," she commented.

"Used to be," he said, not meaning to say it aloud.

Her smile deepened - like she understood - and she didn't press; just turned, slow and graceful, and headed towards the kitchen to place his order.

His meal arrived in good time, and Damion was momentarily stunned by how good it looked. The eggs were perfectly over-easy, yolks still golden and trembling. The bacon was crispy, and the toast was thick-cut and buttered with a shine that caught the morning light. The orange juice, pulpy and deep orange, sat in a frosted glass beading with condensation. The grits were served in a miniature bowl, separated from the rest of the food, and the pancakes were light and fluffy. Maybe it was just that he was starving, or perhaps the food really was that good. Either way, it felt like a small miracle had been laid out before him.

"Almost forgot this," Del said, placing a large glass of milk on the table before leaving to wait on other customers.

Damion picked up his fork and took a bite of the eggs first. Rich, warm, perfectly seasoned. He let out a soft breath through his nose, nodding to himself. Then the bacon—a satisfying crunch, smoky with just a hint of what he thought was sage. Toast followed, warm and buttery, grounding him with each bite. Then the rest.

Out of the corner of his eye, he saw Del watching.

She leaned against the counter with the grace of a lounging cat; arms crossed just loosely enough to give the impression of casualness, but her eyes were sharp, observing everything that happened in the room. When he met her gaze, she gave a satisfied tilt of her head with a slight smile tugging at the corners of her lips. It was a smile of pride, as though his enjoyment meant something more to her than just a well-done meal.

"Good?" she called lightly over the low murmur of the diner. Damion, with a mouth full of pancakes, lifted his glass in quiet salute.

The diner had begun to hum with new life. The door creaked open again and again as regulars and newcomers wandered in. A couple of older men settled at the corner booth with newspapers and black coffee. A young family slid into a window seat—two kids giggling as they played with jelly packets. Somewhere, a baby babbled. The smells thickened: butter sizzling, sausages browning, pancakes rising on the griddle, as conversations overlapped like a quilt of sound.

Between bites, Damion watched Del move through it all like a conductor in a slow, joyful symphony. She greeted each customer with that same electric charm, but she adapted it—her voice a little warmer for the older gentlemen, more teasing with the teenagers, soft and bright with the children. And always, always, like the person she was speaking to was the only soul that mattered in that moment.

Damion had been halfway through his bacon when he felt another presence—small, still, and watching. He turned slightly and caught sight of her.

A little girl, maybe six years old, stood beside a nearby booth, arms hugging a plush rabbit worn from love. Her hair was auburn and fell in soft, uneven waves around her face. Hazel eyes—green with flecks of gold—met his. She didn't say anything. Just stood there, observing him with wide-eyed curiosity and a kind of fearless innocence that only children have. He smiled.

She smiled back, shy at first, then fully, like a sunrise cracking through the clouds.

A voice cut in, low and firm, yet careful not to scold too hard. "Don't disturb the man, honey. Let him eat in peace."

The girl didn't flinch, but her smile faltered. Damion held up a hand.

"It's okay," he said softly, glancing toward the parent without quite seeing them. "She's not bothering me."

He turned back to his plate, but now Del was beside him, as if she'd materialized from thin air. A trait that quickly reminded him of someone else with that ability.

He startled just slightly, enough for her to notice. His fork hovered in midair. She was close now — close enough for him to smell the subtle mix of coffee and her warm, intoxicating perfume.

He looked up at her and found those emerald eyes again, bright with mischief, but softened with something even kinder.

"You've got fans already," she said, nodding toward the girl, her tone teasing but warm.

Damion chuckled, lowering his fork. "I guess your food has that effect."

Del smiled slowly, leaning just a fraction closer. "Mm. I think it's the company, hon."

His heart gave a slight, unexpected stutter. He looked away, cheeks warming, and returned to his toast with a quiet grin as she walked away again.

Damion sat back in the booth, his plate empty except for a smear of yolk and a lone crust of toast. His stomach was full, but not heavy.

Across the diner, a small boy was stacking creamers into a tower while his dad scrolled through his phone. An older woman in a wide-brimmed hat sat alone by the window, methodically stirring sugar into her tea, gaze distant, as if watching something only she could see. The young family who had come in earlier was mid-laugh, the mother trying to clean syrup from her daughter's chin as the father sneakily stole bites of her pancake. The whole diner buzzed with an energy both quiet and alive.

And then, there was Del.

She appeared once more, this time with a wipe of her towel over the table's edge and a devilish twinkle in her eye.

"Now the question is," she said, resting her hand lightly on the back of the booth, "do you want dessert?"

Damion looked up, drawn instantly again by the sultry quality of her voice, the way she leaned just slightly in, like they were sharing a secret.

"What's on the menu?" he asked, though his mind was only half on the question.

"Well," Del began, ticking off with her fingers, "we've got warm custard pie, peach cobbler if you're lucky—and today's your lucky day, sugar—banana pudding with homemade whipped cream, and chocolate cake that'll make you forget your mama's name." She grinned. "And then, of course, there's me."

Damion nodded absently. "Sounds amazing…"

Then it hit him. His eyebrows lifted, and he blinked, eyes suddenly wide as her words replayed in his head.

"Wait, what?" he said, sitting a little straighter.

Del's smile spread slowly and wide, but there was no mockery in it - only amusement, and maybe a little bit of something else.

"I said, 'and then there's me,'" she repeated, one eyebrow raised in perfect mischief.

Damion's face flushed instantly, a vivid, unmistakable red. He looked down, scratching the back of his neck. "Oh. I, uh—I didn't... I didn't realize you said that. Sorry."

Del chuckled, "Honey, you don't need to be sorry. I'm not offended. Just making sure you're still awake under all that bacon and charm."

He laughed nervously, running a hand through his hair. "Guess I should skip dessert and get going before I really make a fool of myself."

"Suit yourself," Del said, stepping back with that same graceful sway. "But if you promise to come back this way one day soon, then the meal is on me."

Damion stared at her, surprised. "You serious?"

"As a heart attack," she said with a wink as she slid a folded piece of paper with her name and phone number on it. "But only if you promise."

He smiled, still blushing, but more at ease now. "Alright. Deal."

He stood, grabbed his jacket, and gave her one last glance before pushing open the door. The buzz of the neon sign was behind him now, but it still lingered in his ears like a tune he couldn't shake.

Outside, the air seemed cleaner than it had seemed when he arrived. He walked away from the diner feeling lighter, invigorated, as if the visit had filled more than just his stomach.

As he crossed the parking lot, he saw two figures stooped down beside his car; one was positioned directly in front, and the other was beside the driver's side, front fender. Damion slowed his pace and maneuvered quietly between two parked cars until he had a clearer view of the men, whom he now identified as the Sheriff and his deputy. Not wanting to spook the two gun-wielding lawmen, he called out to them in a non-threatening voice.

"Is there a problem, Officers?"

The two men glanced over their shoulders at him, then slowly stood up while still looking at the vehicle.

"Is this your car, son?" the Sheriff asked.

"Yes, sir. Is there a problem?"

"No, we just checkin' her out," he replied while leaning closer to the fender.

The deputy joined in the conversation. "Man, this thing's prettier than my wife. What's she got – 300-horsepower?"

"Actually, it's closer to 430," Damion replied with a slight hint of pride.

This elicited a long, low whistle from the deputy. The Sheriff then looked at Damion, sizing him up.

"Military?"

"Yes, sir. Navy Chief Master-at-Arms."

The deputy looked a little confused and was about to say something when the Sheriff cut in.

"That's sorta like a military police, Delbert," he said to the deputy, surprising Damion.

"Well, she sure is a beauty. Just make sure to keep it under the speed limit."

Damion nodded, "Thanks, will do."

After taking one last envious look at the impressive muscle car, they went to their vehicles and drove off in separate directions.

After they were out of sight, Damion turned and glanced at the diner, and caught sight of Del standing by the window, her hand resting lightly against the glass. She was watching him with that same curious warmth she had carried all afternoon. When he lifted his hand in a casual wave, she answered with a smile so bright it made his chest tighten. She waved back, and for a fleeting second, he wished he could scrap the road ahead and spend another night here. Maybe he'd circle back sooner than expected. Perhaps fate would drag him this way again. Who knew?

Sliding into the Mustang's soft, white leather seats, he turned the key, and the engine answered with a throaty roar that rolled through the evening air. The low growl of power under the hood steadied him as he eased back onto NC-903. The sun was slipping lower now, its orange fire dripping over the horizon. The smell of warm pine and freshly cut grass filtered through the open vent as he thought about how strange life was. How something as irritating as a six-hour traffic jam could steer you toward something that made you feel alive again. If not for that accident near Emporia and the GPS's insistence on rerouting him through two-lane country highways, he never would've walked into that diner, never would've met Del.

Sometimes...strange could be good.

Chapter 5 – Whispers From the Shadows

Bishops Creek shrank in his rearview mirror, its small cluster of buildings fading into the line of trees behind him. The road stretched forward, weaving its way past darkening fields, sleepy farms, and patches of woodland that smelled of damp earth. Damion let his thoughts linger on Del a little longer before reaching down to switch on the radio. His fingers brushed over the trunk-mounted CD rack controls until the speakers filled the cabin with the relaxing sounds of Smooth Jazz. Saxophone and rhythmic piano melodies seamlessly blended with the background hum of the Mustang's engine.

He had driven a good twenty miles when the road gradually curved long and lazy through a corridor of tall pines. Glancing down at the radio to adjust the volume, a flicker of movement flashed at the edge of his vision. His head snapped up as every muscle fired at once.

The world appeared to scroll by in slow motion. His right foot slammed down hard on the brake, jolting the Mustang forward as the tires screeched against the asphalt. His hands clenched the wheel and wrenched it left, the car lurching violently into the oncoming lane. The nose of the Mustang dipped as the rear swung wide, fishtailing, throwing up the sharp stench of burning rubber.

The figure didn't move.

Damion's pulse thundered in his ears as the car slid closer, headlights spilling over what was unmistakably a girl—

small, thin, her hair hanging like a curtain over her face. He could see her now, frozen in place, and for one breathless second, he was certain he wasn't going to stop in time.

The Mustang's hood seemed to reach out for her.

He sharply turned the wheel back in the opposite direction, reversing the car's fishtail so hard that it rattled his teeth. The front bumper whipped past her so close that her tangled hair flew up and over her shoulders in the rushing wind.

The world contracted into sounds and sensations: the shriek of tortured tires, the thunderous pounding of his heart, the jolt of the steering wheel biting against his palms. The car skidded across the lane, angled toward the ditch, the headlights slicing through grass and brush just inches away. Damion eased the wheel to the left, feathered off the brake, and coaxed the Mustang back in the lane, feeling the car buck and settle beneath him.

Then, silence.

He came to a complete stop on the shoulder, the engine rumbling low as if catching its breath along with him. For a moment, he sat frozen with both hands locked on the steering wheel and staring in the rearview mirror.

She was still there and unharmed, standing exactly where she had been; her small frame silhouetted against the fading glow of sunset and staring at his car with an eerie calmness.

Damion killed the engine and flicked on the hazard lights. The rhythmic blink cast a red glow across the asphalt as he opened the door and stepped out into the cooling evening air. The sharp scent of scorched rubber mingled with the country air as cicadas screamed angrily in the bushes, filling the silence he carried with him as he walked slowly towards her.

As he approached, her outline sharpened. She wasn't a blur anymore - she was a girl, maybe ten, barefoot and dirt-covered with hair so matted and filthy he couldn't make out its actual color. Her dress was nothing more than a potato sack, hanging loosely from her small frame. In her hand, a battered little notebook.

Damion stopped a few feet short of her, crouching and keeping his voice calm and low.

"You okay, kid?"

Her eyes lifted to meet his. Sad, trance-like, unblinking. No answer.

"What's your name? You live nearby?"

Still nothing. Just silence.

Damion glanced around – nothing but empty highway and dense woods on both sides. No houses, no lights, no sound except the cicadas and the faint whisper of wind in the trees. An unsettling thought crept up inside him. *Had she travelled through those woods alone? Or worse - had she been abandoned?*

Either way, he couldn't leave her here.

He extended a hand, palm up, but expecting her to shy away. To his surprise, she didn't hesitate. Her small, grimy fingers wrapped tightly around his, gripping like she'd been waiting for someone to reach out all along.

Together, they walked back to the Mustang. When he opened the passenger-side door, she froze, glancing down at her clothes, then back up at him with shame flickering in her eyes.

Damion knelt again, softened his expression, and gave her a nod that said *it's okay.*

The girl climbed in carefully, settling upright in the seat. Damion pulled the seatbelt across her and clicked it into place, then closed the door gently. He lingered for a second, staring down the empty stretch of highway, the evening sky bleeding from gold into violet. His mind raced with what to do next.

Then his hand brushed his front pocket. The folded piece of paper was still there. He pulled it free, staring at the name and numbers scrawled across it.

"Looks like I'll be seeing you a little sooner than expected," he muttered, closing his hand tightly around the paper before sliding behind the wheel.

The Mustang roared back to life, its engine growling deep and steady. Instead of pressing forward, he eased the car into a tight three-point turn. The tires crunched against side road gravel before straightening out in the opposite direction - back towards Bishops Creek as the sharp trill of a ringing phone filled the cabin from the Mustang's Kardon Harman speakers. After four rings, the sound suddenly cut off abruptly, replaced by a familiar, easy drawl:

"Hey ya'll, this is Del."

"Hello, Del. This is Damion," he started, but didn't get any further before she interrupted him.

"Hey, hon! You miss me already? Maybe you shoulda' stayed in town."

"Actually, I'm on my way back to you now."

"Okay, then, but I don't get off work for another hour."

"Unfortunately, it's not for a social visit," he replied while glancing at the quiet girl seated next to him, looking out the window.

Damion explained to her what had happened and asked that she call the Sheriff to meet him at the diner to take custody of the girl. He didn't know who else to contact in the area and thought it best to leave her with the authorities as soon as possible. When they finished discussing the arrangements, he ended the Bluetooth connection and glanced at the girl, who was looking directly at him. He wasn't sure if he was only imagining it, but she did not look as sad and hopeless as when they first met. Her face was more relaxed – peaceful. Maybe he should try again. He reached over to her with an open hand and waited.

"My name is Damion. Would you like to tell me yours?"

The girl looked at his hand, but this time she didn't take it. She just looked down at the floor of the car. Damion pulled back his hand and placed it on his leg.

"That's okay, you don't have to say anything." He paused, then continued. "I'm taking you to a friend of mine who will get you something to eat, and then someone will come to pick you up and take you someplace safe, okay?"

For a moment, the girl just sat there quietly looking down. Then, as if she had come to an important decision, she sat up straight and looked at him with the beginning of a smile. She grabbed hold of his hand, turned her face towards the window, and closed her eyes. They drove for about another five minutes before her grip loosened in Damion's hand as she fell into a deep, exhausted sleep.

When they arrived at the diner, the girl was still in a deep sleep, and Damion was able to quietly slip out of the car without waking her. Del was standing outside, and when they locked eyes, a warm smile spread across her face. She glanced at the car with a look of concern as he got closer.

"Poor thing, she looks exhausted," she said.

"Yeah. She's out like a light. I didn't dare wake her yet, but I want to make sure she eats before the Sheriff takes her."

"He won't be taking her," Del said to his surprise. "He's sending one of his deputies to pick her up."

"Okay," Damion replied, relaxing a bit. "Well, I guess we had better get some food in her before then. Give her whatever she wants. I'll pay for it."

"No, hon. I got this," Del answered back. "You've already done enough for this girl, probably saved her life. Besides, you can pay me back later," she added with a wink and a smile.

Damion opened the door and lightly tapped the girl on the shoulder. She woke up startled, her eyes filled with fear, but relaxed when she saw Damion. She glanced at Del, then quickly back at him.

"It's okay. This is the friend I told you about," he assured her.

She then relaxed and allowed Del to help her from the car and into the diner.

Del slipped her arm gently around the girl's shoulders, speaking softly as if she'd known her for years.

"Come on, sugar, let's freshen you up a bit."

With a quick glance back at Damion, she gave him one of those universal, reassuring smiles that always seemed to settle the edges of a tense moment.

Inside the diner, the smell of fried bacon and fresh coffee lingered in the air, but Del steered the girl straight toward the bathroom. The sound of running water and a soothing voice carried faintly through the thin walls. A few minutes later, Del returned with the girl. Her hair was slightly damp where Del had washed out most of the dirt and dried it with paper towels, her cheeks were scrubbed pink, and her hands and face were cleaner than when she'd first stepped out of the car. The girl looked younger now, though still haunted around the eyes.

"Better?" Del asked her kindly. The girl gave the slightest nod.

Del guided her to a booth and slid a plate in front of her with country-fried potatoes, scrambled eggs, toast, and bacon. The girl hesitated at first, glancing between Damion and Del, then suddenly dug in with a hunger that was almost too painful to watch. She ate as if she hadn't seen a meal in days, with each bite faster and larger than the last. The orange juice glass was drained in a matter of seconds before Del quietly refilled it.

Damion sat across from her with his elbows resting on the table, eyes focused and full of concern. He didn't disturb her or try to get answers to the growing number of questions forming in his head. He just watched. Del leaned against the booth, arms crossed, her expression a mirror of his unease.

The time passed quietly, broken only by the scrape of her fork against the plate and the gulping of a third glass of orange juice. The sound of tires crunching on gravel outside drew their attention to the diner window. A black-and-gold Sheriff's Deputy car rolled in, headlights briefly washing across the glass before it came to a stop.

The diner's door creaked open, and in stepped a figure who nearly filled the doorway. Damion estimated that the deputy stood around six feet five inches tall, two hundred and thirty pounds, with shoulders like a football linebacker, and arms that could have pulled a small tree from the ground by its roots. The black and tan, short-sleeved uniform was spotless, and the spit-shined shoes and badge glinted under the diner's fluorescent lights.

Damion blinked, caught between awe and disbelief.

"Linda Mack!" Del announced warmly as she went to greet her. "But most folks 'round here just call her *the Mack truck.*"

Deputy Mack was a towering woman whose presence alone silenced the few local regulars sipping coffee at the counter. Her handshake swallowed Damion's with a grip firm enough to test his knuckles, and her voice, *much* softer than her grip, was official and no-nonsense. She got right down to business.

"You the one who found the girl?"

"Yes, Ma'am," Damion answered.

"Okay. Tell me everything that occurred from the time you met her until now. Every detail, no matter how small."

Damion related everything that happened: how he'd left the diner and come around the curve on the highway, how she'd been standing there alone, and how he'd brought her here instead of leaving her alone by the roadside. Deputy Mack listened and wrote down notes on a digital tablet without interrupting, her stern gaze flicking now and then toward the girl, who was still working over the last of her toast.

When Damion had finished, she asked a few questions of her own, including his contact information.

"Alright," Mack said finally, nodding. "You did right. I'll be taking her with me, but let her finish up first." She then reached into her pocket and pulled out a small wallet.

"Here's my card. If you think of anything else, call me or the station. We'll contact you if we have any follow-up questions."

Damion took the business card with the county Sheriff's Department logo on it and put it in his pocket next to Del's folded paper.

True to her word, Deputy Mack didn't rush the child. She stood by the door, watchful, until the girl had eaten every crumb Del had placed in front of her. When it was time, Del crouched beside the booth, brushing the girl's hair back with one last tender touch before stepping aside.

The girl hesitated, looking to Damion one last time for approval. His nod was steady, though his chest tightened at the sight of her small hand slipping into Deputy Mack's massive one. Together they walked out, the door jingling behind them.

Through the diner's front window, Damion watched as Mack opened the rear door of her cruiser and helped the girl climb in. The engine rumbled to life as the red taillights glowed against the gravel lot. As the car began to roll away, the girl turned in her seat, pressing her hand to the back window. Her eyes locked onto Damion's - wide, sad, and full of something he couldn't identify as the cruiser disappeared down the dark road.

The silence that followed sat heavy in the diner until Del spoke softly by his side.

"Hard part's done, hon. But I got a suspicious feelin' this ain't the end of that girl's story."

Damion was silent as he stared at nothing, wondering if he should have tried to do more for the girl. At least she was with the cops now, and hopefully they would take good care of her and maybe even find out if she has any family. He was still lost in his thoughts when Del's voice smoothly parted the fog in his head.

"You know, there's another gal that could really use some freshening up," she said matter-of-factly.

Damion turned and looked at her, his face blushing slightly as he did.

Del shook her head with a crooked smile on her face.

"I'm talking about *her*," she said, pointing at his Mustang.

"That little girl, as sweet as she is, was kinda' filthy. I'm sure those white seats of yours could use some cleaning up, too. I'll get you something to take away that crud that won't mess up that pretty leather, hon." She then turned and headed towards another room, leaving Damion feeling a little embarrassed.

"Thanks, Del, for everything," he said as she glided away.

"*Anytime, hon,*" she sang, disappearing behind the closed door.

Chapter 6 – Pictures Worth a Thousand Words

Damion squeezed out the dirty sponge into the bucket of warm, soapy water, watching the gray suds swirl and settle with lazy bubbles on the surface. His forearm ached from scrubbing, but he didn't stop. Five passes with the sponge and the dark spots where the girl had sat in his car were finally fading, though not as quickly as he wanted. Dirt had a way of sinking into white leather like a bad habit that won't leave you alone. It was taking him longer than he'd expected, but what was time compared to what he'd gained? The girl was alive. That was what mattered. He had no illusions that he had more than likely saved her life, and tonight she was at least someplace safer than being alone, standing barefoot in the middle of a rural asphalt road.

He rinsed the sponge again, the water sloshing against the bucket's sides. As he wrung it out, something caught his eye - a corner of paper wedged upright between the open door and the passenger seat. He frowned and leaned down, fishing it out carefully.

A notebook.

No, not just a notebook - *her* notebook.

Damion froze with it in his hand, remembering the way she had clutched it in her grimy fingers, pressed against her chest as though it were the only thing she owned in this world. His chest tightened as he turned it over. The little book was in bad shape - front cover ragged, back cover completely missing, pages curled and yellowed at the edges as though they'd been handled a thousand times.

Perhaps he could leave it with Del, or if the deputies cared enough, they could return it to the girl.

But curiosity tugged at him.

He opened it slowly, half expecting to find nothing more than a child's scribbles. What greeted him instead brought an involuntary smile to his lips.

The first pages bloomed with trees and flowers while shaky lines colored in with uneven pressure. On the next page were drawings of crude animals - a cow, or maybe a horse, lopsided and charming. Insects with too many legs, a sun with rays like knives. He chuckled softly. She was an artist in her own way, a little storyteller painting the world as she saw it.

He turned the page again.

And stopped.

The smile faded from his face as a knot formed in his throat.

Two pages, front and back, were nothing but chaos. Scribbled, dark lines. Stick figures piled over one another, lying flat, their eyes crossed out with heavy "X" marks. Open mouths, oblong and hollow, sketched with frantic circles. Above them stood other figures, their mouths huge black O's, angry eyes slanted like slashes, long sticks protruding from their hands.

Guns.

He didn't need sharp details to recognize the messages in the sketches.

Damion swallowed hard, his thumb rough against the paper as he turned the page.

This one was worse. Figures hanging from trees, their stick bodies swaying on jagged lines of rope. Around them stood more of the wide-mouthed figures, silent witnesses with sticks and angry eyes.

The girl had seen something. Something atrocious.

Her notebook wasn't art; it was a testimony.

Each turn of the page revealed more. Buildings, crude and crooked, smoke curling from their roofs. Faces warped in grotesque exaggerations. Words scrawled phonetically, painfully misspelled: *raat, eeel, batcher, golfer*. A child who is reaching for a vocabulary she didn't fully possess to name things too dark to describe.

Damion's chest tightened until he could barely breathe. What horrors had she witnessed?

The crunch of gravel behind him snapped him back in focus. He turned.

Del was coming towards him. Her copper-colored hair, now in a ponytail, swayed in the evening breeze as she carried a steaming cup of coffee in one hand. Her face was bright and radiating that familiar warmth she always seemed to have in reserve.

"You gonna' be out here all night, hon?" she teased lightly.

Her smile faded as soon as she saw his expression. She slowed, eyes narrowing with concern.

"What's wrong?" she asked quietly.

Damion held out the open notebook.

"This is hers," he answered in a low voice.

Del took it carefully, her other hand covering her mouth as she stared down at the child's nightmare-scrawled pages.

"Oh, dear Lord." Her voice trembled. "Did that poor little thing see all of this?"

"Looks like it," Damion murmured.

Together, they flipped through the rest. More crude images. More misspelled words. Oddities scattered between the horrors. A dancing elephant, a fat bird with round, staring eyes, and a crooked orange beak that stretched across its face. The bird clutched a dinner fork with jagged teeth drawn along its edge, a water gun under its wing, stars flying wildly around it. On the final page, a crooked "T" stood alone above looping lines that touched nothing at all.

Del exhaled sharply, shaking her head.

"It doesn't make sense," she whispered.

"Maybe it's not supposed to." Damion closed the book, his jaw tight. "We need to get this to the Sheriff."

"First thing tomorrow morning," Del answered, firm now. "Nothing they'll do tonight anyway."

Damion nodded reluctantly, slipping the notebook into the glove compartment as though tucking away a live grenade. He looked around the empty lot, shadows stretching long under the yellow glow of the diner's lights.

"There wouldn't happen to be a motel in town, would there?" he asked.

"Sure is," Del replied, then hesitated. "But you don't have to stay there. I got a trailer on the other side of town with two bedrooms - one for me, one for my boy. There's a sofa bed you can take. It's sturdy and cheaper than that motel."

Damion blinked, taken off guard. "Del, you don't even know me."

She smiled faintly. "Hon, I know enough. I saw the way you were with that little girl. I think I can trust you in my home for one night. Just let me give you my address."

Her certainty disarmed him, but he managed a smile and nodded, choosing not to argue.

————

When Damion drove up Del's driveway, he was pleasantly surprised as his previous misconceptions of her trailer home quickly faded away. The two-bedroom structure sat neat and orderly at the end of a finely graveled driveway, its aluminum siding gleaming softly beneath the porch light fixed above the screen door. The fresh coat of pale blue paint caught in the glow, its edges crisp and clean where the trim had been carefully done in white. The steps leading up to the door were sturdy, the boards sanded smooth, their stain rich and dark against the light. Even the handrail looked freshly coated, no hint of flaking, rust, or wear left to show.

Along the porch railing, flower boxes overflowed with color—marigolds, petunias, and bright geraniums tended with care. Their blooms swayed gently in the evening breeze, fragrant against the hum of night air. A hammock hung stretched between two small trees, its canvas taut and clean, swinging slightly as though still holding the shape of someone's weight.

The yard spread out in every direction: grass neatly trimmed, gravel raked evenly along the drive, no clutter or trash anywhere to be seen. A small wooden playhouse stood off to the side, shutters straight, and a little door perfectly square on its hinges. The toy shovel leaning nearby in a square sandbox looked more like it had been set in its place than forgotten. A line of laundry stretched between two pine trees, clothes pinned in a straight row, catching the porch light in the soft folds of fabric.

Through the screen door's mesh, the glow of the porch lamp pooled inside, bathing Del's son where he sat cross-legged on the spotless floor. A sheet of paper lay pinned beneath his knee, his crayon moving in hard, deliberate strokes. The intensity on his face made the act of coloring look as if an artwork of extraordinary significance was being created. Every few moments, he reached into a tidy tin box at his side to switch colors, the clink of crayons sharp against the hush of the night.

Inside, the trailer's interior reflected the same care as the outside—walls clean, trim polished, surfaces free of clutter.

The faint aroma of a recent meal drifted through the open windows along with the smell of fresh coffee brewing. The whole place radiated a quiet sense of pride, a sanctuary maintained not out of duty, but out of love. Each detail was a small piece of a life carefully cultivated, that separated itself from the rough edges of the world beyond the fence line.

Del watched him without saying a word, as Damion admiringly looked around the trailer, until his eyes finally settled back on her.

"Wow, Del. You have a really nice place."

"And here you thought I lived in one of those *duck-boy* trailers," she joked as she left to get him a sheet and blanket.

The sofa bed wasn't kind to his back, but Damion didn't complain. Del's hospitality more than made up for the aches. The morning sunlight beamed through the thin curtains, painting pale stripes across the trailer's modest living room. Del's son, a lively five-year-old, had already pulled Damion onto the floor before his mother was awake, to show him his toy cars, before being hustled off to a babysitter.

By the time they arrived at the diner, two Sheriff's cruisers were already parked out front.

Inside, Sheriff Douglas sat at a booth with Deputy Jamison, their gazes sharp as knives when Damion walked in. The temperature in the room seemed to drop ten degrees.

"Mornin', Sheriff. Deputy," Damion greeted.

An uncomfortable pause stretched before Douglas finally replied. "Mornin'. I hear you've got something for me."

Damion stepped forward, pulling the notebook from his jacket and placing it in the Sheriff's outstretched hand.

"The little girl left this in my car. Some of the drawings..." he hesitated, "they might be evidence of criminal activity. Or at the very least, maybe tell you something about why the girl is reluctant to speak."

Douglas and Jamison bent over the pages, their brows knitting deeper with every turn. Neither spoke until they reached the end. Then the Sheriff snapped it shut and stood.

"We'll look into it," he said curtly.

Damion rose as well. "What about the girl? Is she still here? I'd like to see her – see how she's doing."

Douglas's jaw tightened. "She's fine. At the station. Child Protective Services will take her on Monday."

"You've got her in a jail cell?" Damion asked, disbelief sharpening his tone, which didn't go well with the Sheriff.

"She's in *protective custody*," the Sheriff replied coolly. "We'll take care of her. You may have found her, but you're not a relative. So no, you can't see her. *We'll* handle it."

His irritation was palpable. Without another word, Sheriff Douglas turned and strode out with Jamison hot on his heels. Both cruisers pulled away from the lot faster than necessary, thought Damion, with loose gravel spitting behind their tires.

Damion exchanged a glance with Del.

"That was...intense," he commented.

Del nodded, unsettled. "Yeah. I've known J.T. for fifteen years. Never seen him rattled like that. Something's not right."

"Hmm," Damion grunted, thinking to himself. "There's another thing I don't get. How does this place have a Sheriff? I thought they covered counties, not small towns."

"That's right, they normally do. He's been covering as the Chief of Police until the regular one returns from sick leave. He was injured in a boating accident. J.T. was the police chief before he transferred to the county. That's why he's here."

"Okay. So, what's the J.T. stand for?"

"Oh, his mama had a thing for that Captain Kirk fella from *Star Trek.* Named her boy after him. When he learned about that, he started using only J.T.," Del replied, walking away.

Damion slid back into his booth, jaw set. He pulled out his phone, cycling through the photos he'd taken of the notebook before handing it over. The crude drawings weren't random. They were memories. A child's testimony rendered in crayon and pencil.

Del came by with his breakfast, pausing to glance at his phone. Her brows rose.

"You took pictures?"

Damion gave her a wink. "Never hand over evidence without a backup copy."

She grunted. "Smart."

He ate in silence, studying the photos until a voice from another booth cut through.

"You some kind of cop?"

Damion looked up. The man wore a ball cap with his back to Damion, facing the door. The voice was raspy, with a twangy edge and a hint of disdain.

"You talking to me?" Damion asked.

"You're the only one sittin' there, ain't cha?"

"No. I'm not a cop."

"Then maybe you should do what the Sheriff told ya - mind your own business. Better for everyone that way."

Damion's eyes narrowed. "What do you mean?"

"Just leave it alone, stranger. Nobody wants to know about the *shadows*. Folks that go lookin'…they don't come back. Go back to where you came from and leave it be."

The man pushed up from his booth and left quickly, his boots thudding against the floor.

Damion sat there and stared for a moment, then went after him. But when he stepped outside, the lot was empty. No man, no car. Gone.

He scanned the road in both directions. Nothing.

When he returned inside, Del was refilling his coffee cup.

"You know that guy?" he asked.

She frowned. "What guy?"

"The one that was sitting right there."

"Didn't see him," she said, frowning.

Damion relayed the warning as Del's expression darkened.

"Sugar, I really don't like the sound of this," she said softly.

"Yeah. Me neither." Damion sat back down, jaw tightening. "I don't like people threatening me, either. This town's small. I'll start asking questions."

Del's eyes searched his, concern flickering beneath her calm.

"Just...be careful, hon," she whispered. "If he was trying to scare you off, he might not be the only one involved."

Damion leaned back, gaze hardening as he watched the road through the diner's front window. The Sheriff was spooked. A stranger was warning him away. And somewhere in the middle of it all was a helpless little girl with a notebook filled with horrors that couldn't have sprung from her imagination.

Something was very wrong in Bishops Creek.

And Damion wasn't leaving until he knew what.

Chapter 7 – Shadows On River Road

Damion didn't bother talking with the Sheriff's office. He was sure that he had already worn out his welcome with local law enforcement. Instead, he would start with the locals, in places where eyes and ears recorded everything, and information intended to be hidden became unhidden. His first stop was the gas station in the middle of town. The morning sun had burned off the dew, leaving the asphalt smelling like sun-warmed oil and old rubber. A couple of pickups idled by the kerosene tank, while a small mutt lay flopped under the shade of a lounge chair, tail thumping lazily at flies.

A bell on a spring gave a half-hearted jingle as he pushed through the door. The air inside was warmer, with that universal convenience-store perfume: machine-brewed coffee, cheap grilled hot dogs, and disinfectant. A man behind the counter with half-moon reading glasses, a receding hairline, and an old shirt with *Cletus* stitched on it, looked up from a lottery scratcher. Without a word, he scrutinized Damion with a slow, unblinking glance.

"Mornin'," Damion said.

The man tipped his chin. "Help ya?"

"Looking for directions," Damion started – neutral but friendly. "And maybe a little local wisdom."

The man smiled with only one side of his mouth. "We're rich in both, dependin' on who's askin'" he replied while continuing to work on his ticket.

Damion wandered to a souvenir rack, pretending to study a group of keychains shaped like watermelons and bass fish, letting the moment settle in. On the wall behind the counter hung a pegboard with flyers: a church fish fry, a missing cat, a yard sale, and one glossy handout advertising a "grand reopening" that he wouldn't have noticed if not for the drawing in the notebook that was still poking in the back of his mind.

The flyer showed a cartoon bird - fat, round, eyes too wide, beak too long. Orange. The bird grinned around a comically large dinner fork. "Freeman's Feather & Fork - New Ownership! Family Night Specials!"

Damion's pulse kicked once. Almost right, but not quite. In the girl's notebook, the bird had been grotesque, most likely exaggerated through a child's fear. Here it was softened, smiling. A family business' brand.

He nodded at the flyer. "That place any good?"

The man behind the counter watched him longer than the question needed. "I guess so. Folks go. Kids love the mascot. Wings're decent."

"Where is it?"

"Used to be on River Road. They're talkin' about a new spot closer to town. Food truck's out on the highway till then." He paused. "You ain't from around here, are ya?"

"Just passing through." Damion turned back, resting his elbows on the counter. "Had a bit of excitement on 903 yesterday evening. Little girl standing alone in the middle of the road barefoot and starving. I took her over to the diner, and the Sheriff's got her now." He paused and watched for any reaction from the stoic faced man. When he didn't get a response, Damion continued.

"You hear anything about kids out late alone, or folks messin' 'round where they shouldn't?"

The man's fingers drummed the lottery scratcher without looking at it. He didn't blink much.

"Lotta kids. Lotta folks."

"Any trouble out by the river?" Damion asked. "Late-night trucks, generators, lights where they shouldn't be?"

The man's eyes flicked towards the bell over the door, as if expecting it to ring.

"River's always busy with fishermen and fellas wit' their expensive toys. You want a good catfish hole, I can oblige. Trouble? Not my department." He scratched once, hard, and little silver flakes fell to the counter.

Damion smiled a bit too pleasantly, paid for a coffee he didn't want, and left the man in peace to continue the work of scratching his lottery ticket, and himself. Outside, he stood by the pumps and let the cup warm his palm while his eyes took a lazy tour of the lot.

There was one pickup next to the gas pumps, and a camouflage painted, older model Ford Bronco SUV idling near the propane cage with tinted windows rolled up. Damion could see several silhouettes inside and feel their eyes on him, but he could not make out their faces. He made a show of peering at the oil-stained concrete, took a sip of the coffee, and then set the cup on the outside icebox. When he pulled out from the parking lot, the Bronco stayed put, but he watched his mirrors anyway.

Damion went to the post office next, because Del had said, "If you want to know what's happening in a small town, ask the woman who hands you your bills." The postal worker in charge of the facility was a lean, middle-aged woman with a perfect bun and a name tag that said 'Sally'. She moved with the speed and efficiency of someone who knew exactly where every envelope in the building lived.

"Help you?" she asked, sliding a stack of mail into a P.O. box without looking up.

"Just inquiring about local businesses - who's hiring, who's not. Passing time while I'm here." He gave her the same charm he would use as an incoming Chief to a new command when he needed a serious favor but hadn't earned it yet.

She looked him over, registering his posture, his haircut, the way he stood square. "Recruiter?" she guessed.

"Not today." He smiled. "Just standard-issue curiosity."

"Uh-huh." She slid another stack into a numbered slot. "Freeman's Feather & Fork's always hiring. Personnel turnover's a killer in the fast-food industry. Not enough positives versus the negatives, I suppose. They're always moving trucks in and out like they're relocating."

"From where?"

"River Road. Old poultry processing plant situated out that way. Not within the town limits, so we only hear so much." She paused, then added, almost as an afterthought, "Sheriff was in here earlier this morning, askin' somethin' akin to the plant also – if I had heard anything strange around town. Plus, he was not very happy that the department's mail didn't come in on time. He wasn't very patient at all, which ain't like him."

"Did he say anything in particular about what he was looking for?"

Sally eased a drawer shut with a click that sounded like a line being drawn. "Gossip ain't my business, mister." Then, more softly, "But if you're askin' because of that little girl at the station, you'd best mind the Sheriff's temper. He don't rattle easy, but when he does, he bites. *Hard.*" Then, in a more pleasant tone, she added, "You have a blessed day, now."

He took his not-quite-dismissal and went to the library, located one block off of the main street. The librarian, an older woman with another precise bun in a different shade of gray, smiled politely.

"Local newspaper archives?" he asked. "Industrial permits, county board minutes? Anything public."

"We keep the Standard in bound volumes. County records are digital over here." She tapped a public computer. "What are you looking for?"

"River Road," he said. "Poultry plant. Any closures, incidents, ownership changes."

She nodded and led him to a cabinet. Damion skimmed through detailed documents, looking for patterns and dates. Any notices about Freeman Poultry or the

surrounding land property. One particular item caught his attention. There was a tax lien for an unspecified amount three years ago, and then a sudden "transfer of assets" to a holding company with an unremarkable name. Zoning permits had been approved and were written in a plain little paragraph no one would read unless they were paid to do so.

He made notes, eyes moving fast. The image of the bird popped up in his mind again, along with the upside-down T. The looping line not touching anything. What if the T wasn't a letter at all? What if it was a shape? A shovel or a garden hoe? The loop could be a hose or water from a pressure washer spray arcing without touching anything. In the eyes of a kid, a stream of water could be drawn as anything, including a wiggly, disconnected line.

The librarian reappeared with a thin stack of old clippings. "There was a fire out on River Road last fall," she said in a careful tone. "No injuries. Electrical. The report was two lines." She set the clippings down and lowered her voice. "We don't get many fires. We get a lot of 'electrical.' That make sense to you?"

"It does," he said. "Thank you."

She studied him, then added, "Be careful, young man. Curiosity's a virtue…until it isn't."

When he stepped outside, the air had warmed up a little more, hinting towards a humid afternoon in the small town. Across the street, a deputy he recognized as Jamison sat in a patrol cruiser, sunglasses on, face impassive.

Damion didn't give him the privilege of a stare and walked on like the day was empty and his time was cheap.

Heading towards the church he had seen earlier, he saw an elderly African-American man with salt-and-pepper hair sweeping pine needles off the front steps. He was dressed for outside work in jeans and a dark T-shirt and had the kind of eyes that looked as if they could peer straight into one's soul.

"You the man that helped that little migrant girl?" the man asked without preamble or looking up. Del's town apparently moved news like stormy weather.

"I am," Damion answered with a nod.

"Bless you, son." The broom stopped as he stood up straight and extended his hand. "Reverend Jeremiah Coburn. *No relation to the actor, James Coburn,*" he added with a playful smile. "I'm the church Pastor. Sheriff says she's safe. Is that true?"

Damion reached out and shook the man's firm grip before answering. "Damion. She's alive. *'Safe'* is not a word I'm ready to say out loud just yet." Then, after a brief pause, "Why did you call her a *migrant girl?*" he asked, with a curious look.

Pastor Coburn paused for a moment, as if he were sizing up Damion before making a decision. "People pass through here quite often. Not many hang around…too long. If you're askin' me whether I've seen things I wish I hadn't, the answer is yes. If you're askin' whether I can prove any of it, the answer is no. Men do what men do in the dark and call it honest business." He set the broom aside. "You ain't from around here, so I'll tell you somethin' the locals don't want to acknowledge - this is a part of the country where favors are currency and the *unwanted* are a commodity. Sometimes the bill comes due, and when it does, no one wants to be seen standing in the path of the collectors."

Damion nodded slowly, thinking. "And where would one go or send someone to make a *bill payment*?" he asked while glancing around for any curious bystanders.

Pastor Coburn's mouth ticked. "River Road - east," he said softly. "And the old ferry landing. Be careful if you plan on headin' out that way. Folks out there aren't always the most *hospitable*."

"Thank you," Damion replied. Then, looking up at the large brick structure, "This is a beautiful church."

"You should see the inside…come by tomorrow for service. Everyone is welcome."

"Maybe I will, if I'm still in town," Damion replied.

As he was walking away, Pastor Coburn called out to him.

"Did you say your name was *Damion?*"

"Yes, I did. Why? Have you heard someone asking or saying something about me?"

"No…just thinking. You *know* that they made a movie about a little boy named Damion, right?" replied Pastor Coburn with a big grin on his face.

With an amused look, Damion replied, "I guess my parents either like a good joke, or they were expecting me to turn

into someone else." He gave a half-wave then continued walking down the street.

The ferry landing faced the Roanoke River, wide brown water moving slowly along the banks crowded with cottonwood and willow. When Damion pulled up, two men stood hip-deep near the shore, working a fishing net with slow, practiced hands. A pile of catfish twitched in a cooler as the air carried the smell of fish, mud, and algae.

He walked along the bank, eyes scanning the opposite shore. An old dock sat half-collapsed, sun-bleached posts leaning like bad teeth. A hundred yards upriver, a square-shouldered structure squatted behind the trees, half-hidden with a corrugated metal roof glinting dull through the leaves.

A generator coughed once, then chugged long like an old locomotive. The sound was faint, but once you heard it, you couldn't un-hear it. The wind brought the stench of a chemical he couldn't identify, which caused the inside of his nose to sting. The men working the nets apparently were used to it.

The fisherman closest to him spoke without glancing over. "You're the fella from Del's, ain't ya?"

"I am."

"That girl got folks?"

"I don't know. Maybe, but the Sheriff's not sharing any info." He paused. "You fish at night?"

"Sometimes. Depends, if the law ain't chasing us home over nothin'." He finally looked up: a face that held more

years than his skin admitted, eyes that had known what it meant to pick truth up, weigh it, and set it back down. "You see them lights up yonder? You best stay away and mind your own. Big fellows with long sticks don't like company."

"Long sticks?" Damion repeated.

The fisherman's mouth didn't smile, but it changed shape. "Call 'em what you like. I call 'em a reason to stay over here and go home when I'm done."

"Anybody who hasn't gone home?" Damion asked. "In the last few weeks?"

The man studied the current. "Folks come and go. Boys get in trouble, men get drunk, women take their babies and run. That what you mean?"

"I mean missing, disappearing," Damion said softly. "Not leaving because they want to."

The man's jaw moved side to side, working an invisible gristle. "I ain't sayin' it, because I didn't see it. I'm just sayin' there's places where bad things look like honest work on paper." He then turned and went back to working on his net as if Damion was not even there. Conversation over.

Damion stood there longer than he needed to, letting the shape of the river settle against the shape of the notebook images in his head. Hanging figures. Angry-eyed men with sticks. Buildings and trees. The upside-down 'T' which could be a hoist beam or a crossbar with a vertical support, would look just like that, if you were a child looking up from the floor. The loop could be the line, a strap, or a tether. If you'd never seen a processing line, you might draw it the only way your mind knew how to translate it.

He drove to River Road in daylight, with the windows down, letting the hot wind rush through the car and force the smell of the chemicals from the landing out of his nose. The old poultry plant gradually came into view. Through a break in the tree line, he saw a gravel lot spiked with weeds, and a series of low buildings with metal siding, each one about as welcoming as an outhouse in the middle of the woods. The main gate had been mended recently and was secured with a new chain and a bright padlock. A white, metal sign wired to the fence announced, in bold letters:

"PRIVATE PROPERTY — RENOVATIONS IN PROGRESS."

While a smaller, separate sign with a yellow background and stenciled black paint read:

NO TRESPASSING. NO PHOTOS. VIOLATORS WILL BE PROSECUTED.

Mounted to the side of the main building was the cartoon bird with the orange beak.

Damion pulled off onto the shoulder and pretended to check a map. His eyes moved, counting. Cameras - two at the gate and one on the corner. A loading dock with fresh tire cuts in the gravel. A dumpster tucked into a shadow where cool air breathed out through several louvers. A strong odor of bleach, laced with the tang of something coppery buried under it.

A white pickup rolled out from behind the building and stopped inside the fence. The driver sat with the engine running, elbow resting on the window ledge. He wore a cap and a beard that had been trimmed with thought. The kind of thought that meant you had reason to want your face to be favorably remembered less, and misremembered more.

"Help you?" he called, voice flat with no hint of giving any actual assistance.

"Looking for Freeman's Feather & Fork," Damion said, dumb-tourist bright. "Sign says renovations. That mean you're hiring?"

"Online," the man said. "We ain't takin' walk-ins."

"Food truck out on the highway yours?"

The man's silence was his answer.

Damion nodded and put the car in gear. "Appreciate it," he called back. He pulled away casually, like he'd found the wrong driveway and suddenly remembered an important appointment elsewhere. In the mirror, the pickup idled, then crept forward and turned the other way. Nothing obvious stood out. Nothing you could tell a judge that was suspicious. But everything about it said: *we see you*.

Chapter 8 – Stop Asking the Silence

Back at the diner, Del had a pot of coffee ready and a frown that projected the worry she'd been enduring while he was away.

"Well? Did you see anything that looked familiar from her book?"

"Maybe the bird, but River Road smells like a janitor's closet exploded," Damion said. "Heavy chemical odors, warning signs, and way too many cameras for a place that claims to be mostly dead."

Del exhaled slowly through her nose. "I hate that bird," she said into the pot. "I didn't know I hated it until just now, but I do."

Damion sat in a corner booth where he had a clear line of sight to the front door, the restaurant, and the kitchen. Del brought him a plate he hadn't ordered and slid into the seat opposite without a word.

He showed her the job postings he'd pulled up on his phone - vague descriptions for 'line techs,' 'sanitation associates,' and 'overnight logistics specialists.' He showed her the holding company's name, a paper umbrella casting shade over several small outfits along the river. He told her about the fisherman and the not-quite-smell of bleach that clung to his clothes even after he'd returned to the diner.

Del rubbed her temples. "So, what is it? They doing something bad or just doing it ugly?"

"I don't know yet," Damion said. "But the girl's notebook says she saw something worse than ugly."

Del chewed on that for a second. "You try the Sheriff?"

"Not yet."

"You gonna?"

"Eventually. Maybe. Right now, I want to look at this from another angle."

Del stared out the window toward Main Street, the bright reflection in her eyes floating over the road. "You know who might talk? Sally, at the post office. She knows what everybody pays for bulk stamps and where they ship to. But you didn't hear me say that."

"I already saw her. She warned me about The Sheriff's temper."

Del's eyebrows shot up. "Wow. Then she likes you. She doesn't warn everybody. Some folks, she just lets them find out the hard way."

The bell over the door gave its tired jingle. Damion's gaze flicked up. Ballcap, beard, sunglasses, jeans. *The man from the other booth with the not-so-subtle warning?* Hard to tell. People wear camouflage like a second skin in towns like this.

The man took a seat at the counter, asked for coffee without looking around, fingers tapping a steady rhythm. Del poured. He didn't say thanks. He didn't say anything, but he watched the mirror behind the register. And in that mirror, Damion saw himself reflected, and in that clear reflection, he saw the man watching him. There are ways to be obvious without moving at all.

Damion smiled and ate. He showed Del the photos from the notebook again, not because she needed to see them, but because he did. He needed to spend time with them and let the shapes reveal their story to him. On one page, the dancing elephant made no sense. On another, the bird did. And, on another, the hanging stick figures. He imagined the girl's silence as a desperate cry for help that only he could hear.

"Look here," he said softly. "Those trees - the ones with the hangings? The trunks are drawn in dark, almost black tones. The kid pressed hard. That's a memory that hurt." He traced a line in the air above the page on his phone. "And these—those aren't houses. Those are square buildings with big doors. Loading bays. She drew the doors taller than the people."

Del swallowed. "You're making me sick."

"Me too," he said. "But sick doesn't help her or whoever she might have left behind."

Damion swiped through the following pages, his thumb slowing as the shapes grew darker, stranger.

"See this?" he said - jagged, heavy pencil marks. A crude outline of a truck filled the page, its wheels nothing more than lopsided circles, the box a square with stick figures crammed inside. Arms were drawn as dark, straight lines reaching upward, pressed against the walls as if trying to push through; no faces, no eyes, just empty heads like hollow balloons.

Del leaned closer, "They're in the back of the truck," she whispered.

He nodded. "Yeah. Cargo, not passengers."

He swiped to the image of stick figures scattered across the bottom of the page, drawn low, as if sunk into the ground. A pit. Some arms stretched upward, others were half-formed, fading into the scribbled earth as though being swallowed whole. Above them, a square tower stood at an angle, spitting out a crooked stream of gray lines that draped over the figures like rain.

Del's voice was low, barely audible. "Is that a machine?"

"Looks like it." The girl had pressed down so hard that the paper tore in places. "She saw this happen. Up close."

Del wrapped her arms around herself. "Dear God."

Damion closed the photo application, as if that would stop the darkness flowing out of the images from the notebook.

"If she drew it," he said absently, "then somewhere out there, it's real. People being kidnapped and hauled away in trucks, digging machines, and a mass grave.

Damion finished his meal, then returned to the streets looking for clues. He spent the rest of the afternoon walking, visiting the barbershop, hardware store, and the discount dollar store. He asked questions like he was new and nosy but harmless. He listened more than he spoke, as most of the people said a lot without saying anything. A retired mechanic told him he'd seen 'ferry trucks' out by the landing after midnight two nights ago while he was crabbing. A teenage cashier said her cousin went to work at the Feather & Fork and quit after one shift because of "the smell." A woman stacking shelves said the Sheriff looked as though he hadn't slept well, and added her opinion that *when a man looks like that, he's either falling out of love or falling into debt.*

Near dusk, he decided to take a chance and stopped in the Sheriff's office. A handful of official vehicles, both marked and unmarked sedans, sat crooked in their slots like tired horses. When he entered the building, a front desk deputy gave him a lazy, disinterested look when he asked to see the girl.

"You the fella that found her," she stated, not asked.

With an easy smile, he replied, "Yes, I am. I want to check on her if possible."

"She's sleeping," the deputy said, her voice a firm *do-not-disturb sign.* "CPS is on it."

"It's Saturday," Damion replied. "They won't be here until Monday, I was told."

The deputy's expression didn't soften an inch. "*CPS is on it,*" she repeated. "Come back Monday before they pick her up."

Seeing that this was going nowhere, he tried something else. "Can you give her something? A message? Tell her that the man who found her was here asking about her, to see if she is okay?"

The deputy's eyes slowly rolled up towards the ceiling as she let out a loud, impatient sigh. "We don't pass notes around here," she said flatly. "*Good evening, sir.*"

Damion grudgingly left before his temper tested the hinges of the conversation, and he was *invited* to occupy one of the cells in the small building. Outside, twilight peeked over the horizon as crickets began their evening serenade, and fireflies took to the approaching darkness.

The Ford Bronco had returned, a few slots down, windows dark. It eased out of its space when he did, followed him a block, then turned away, clever enough to be seen and not seen in the same motion.

He drove without a destination until he found himself again at the old ferry landing. The river in the evening light looked like a smooth, silk sheet. Bats flitted, stitching the air as a soft wind carried the scent of damp earth and wood smoke from somewhere upriver. The landing was empty; no fishermen or other evening visitors were present.

He sat in the idling Mustang, the low rumbling of the engine soothing his mind, as he sorted through the day's events and the pieces of a puzzle he had yet to decipher. The bird. The fork. The loop. The T. The Sheriff's indifference and temper stretched tight as a drum. The stranger in the diner with a voice like a worn fan belt. An unusual number of *words of caution* from the townspeople. The old processing plant.

His thoughts were interrupted as his phone buzzed. He looked down, expecting to see Del's name, wondering where he was.

Unknown number.

He didn't move for a moment, just stared at the words. Then he swiped.

STOP ASKING ABOUT THE BIRD, the text read.

A second came in, like a finger pressed against a bruise.

SOME THINGS GET CLEANED. SOME THINGS GET BURIED.

He looked up, scanning the shadows of trees, the slope of the access road, the slow glide of the river. Whoever had sent it wanted him to know, or feel, that he was being watched. They wanted the sensation of breath at his neck and eyes at his back. 'Fear' came to the door and knocked, but he didn't open it.

He texted back, not because he hoped for a conversation, but because he wanted to gauge the person on the other end of this conversation.

WHO IS THIS???

A long pause. Then:

A FRIEND OF YOURS, the reply said. GO HOME.

He typed quickly, thumbs steady.

CAN'T. I LEFT SOMETHING HERE.

No answer.

WHO ARE YOU…FRIEND?

….GO HOME

Sensing that the conversation had ended, Damion placed the phone in the dash-mounted holder. After staring at it long enough for the mosquitoes to notice him and make

their presence known, he rolled up the windows and drove to Del's trailer.

"You look like you've been chewing gravel," Del said, her forehead creased with concern as she poured a glass of lemonade instead of coffee.

Damion filled her in on his activities after he left the diner: his visits and discussions with the townspeople, his attempt to see the girl and the deputy's refusal, how he ended up at the old ferry landing, and receipt of the anonymous text from a *friend*. She listened, one hand covering her mouth, the same way she had when she first saw the notebook.

"You and the Sheriff's office are the only ones that have my cellphone number," he said thoughtfully.

"I don't like this, Damion," she said. "I don't like any of it. And I especially don't like the look that was on J.T.'s face this morning, like he bit into something that bit him back."

"I think he either knows or suspects what's really going on, and he's in over his head," Damion said. "Or…he's holding it behind his back for some reason."

"You *can* just say that you think he's dirty," she said, a hint of disappointment laced in her voice.

"I think he's scared. *Scared* makes men sloppy, mean, or both."

She leaned on the counter with both palms, knuckles going white. "So, what do you need to be certain?"

He thought for a moment. "I need a place to start where *they* wouldn't expect me. Something the girl saw that isn't on their radar because it's not too significant. Something dumb or silly that a child would latch onto."

Del stared past him, eyes going thin. "The elephant," she said.

"What?"

"The dancing elephant. It didn't fit, right?" She moved to a drawer and came back with a folded fair brochure. "These are handed out every summer - Halifax County Fair. Last year's mascot theme was some fool in an elephant suit. He danced and hopped around like an idiot in ninety-five-degree heat until he collapsed from heat exhaustion. He recovered, but the paramedics said his blood alcohol level was high, and he was dehydrated. *Go figure.* The fairgrounds also rent out for off-season events. It's down by the old grain silos. They sometimes run catering through the Feather & Fork using food trucks and booths. Look at the sponsor list." She tapped the tri-fold, where the smiling bird grinned under a row of logos.

The upside-down 'T'. The loop in the air. In one of the brochure photos, a portable hoist and a tangle of hoses arced across a demo area for farm equipment. If a child had stood by the edge of the grounds looking through the fence at night—if something had happened there, after the lights were off and the public had gone home—the pictures in her mind might have grabbed whatever images they could find to anchor terror to memory. An elephant. A bird. A fork. Stars.

"I'll go look," he said.

"Tonight?"

"They told me to go home," he said, followed by a smile that didn't match the seriousness of the situation. "That's as good as a ticketed invitation."

She started to protest, then closed her mouth. "Take my spare," she said finally, and held up a key on a gold and black keychain. "Old Chevy. Quieter than your baby. Less noticeable."

"You sure?"

"Yep. Your car's unmistakable 'round here and pretty. Pretty things get remembered. Take the ugly one."

He accepted the key with a nod that felt heavier than it should have.

Damion knew that his reconnaissance would require stealth, so he changed into his Maritime Interdiction Operations (MIO) gear, which he had packed into his Big Oxx Expedition hybrid duffel bag/backpack.

Military boots, black tactical clothing, a balaclava (also known as a tactical face mask for protecting one's identity), a flashlight with a green night lens, a backlit compass, a digital voice recorder, a pen, and a small green notebook (known as a *wheelbook* to sailors everywhere) for making notes in silence.

Not willing to be caught lacking if he ran into the stick figures from the little girl's notebook, he also carried his personal SIG Sauer P320 10mm pistol and a Kershaw

Fringe Carbon Fiber tactical survival knife. Using a tactical shoulder holster to *open carry* the pistol should keep him from getting a concealed weapons charge if a deputy confronted him, figured Damion, but he wouldn't be so lucky if they found his knife. Still, as the old saying goes, *'better to have it and not need it, than to need it and not have it.'*

Lastly, he grabbed his ATN Thor 5 XD LRF thermal scope, which had a detection range of up to thirty-six hundred yards. He would be able to identify any heat-producing objects —human, animal, or equipment — in or around the fairgrounds when making his approach.

When he was ready, he turned and gave Del a serious look.

"Lock the door and keep your son close. And if you see an old camouflaged Ford Bronco hanging around outside for too long, call the police."

"I will," she replied uneasily.

"And Del?" He paused.

"Yeah, hon?"

"If I'm not back in three hours, call Pastor Coburn. Then the Sheriff."

She nodded and steadied her breathing. "Are all you Navy boys this crazy?"

He gave her a half-hearted smile, *"You should see some of the ones I work with."*

Crickets worked the dark like a thousand tiny hand saws, and mosquitoes buzzed by like miniature electric razors. The car, a dark green Chevrolet Chavelle, started on the second crank and idled like a man clearing his throat. He rolled without headlights down the lane until he reached the main road, then headed west for about a mile before turning on the headlights.

Chapter 9 – Every Bird Has a Grave

The fairgrounds lay quiet. Quiet like an old western ghost town, with the passing whisper of a rolling sage brush the only sign of life. Damion shut off the lights and eased off onto the grass approximately fifty yards from the grain silos, then killed the engine. Beyond the chain-link fence, the main pavilion sat dark, its corrugated sides reflecting silver under the moon. A banner with curling corners still hung above the gate:

THANK YOU TO OUR SPONSORS.

Damion exited the car and conducted a full 360-degree scan with the thermal scope for any heat sources that might be lurking nearby. He pivoted slowly, as the scope cut through the moonlit darkness, identifying two small foxes approximately thirty yards away, and an owl that had perched itself in one of the nearby trees.

He moved along the fence line until he found what he was looking for, a spot where someone else had made an opening between the fence connections. The fence parted with the tired sigh of a thing that had been asked more than once to pretend it was still new. He slid through, letting the chain links close silently behind him.

The grounds smelled like mildew, old fertilizer, and damp hay. He stopped twice, listening with his whole body, reading the breeze. No voices, no machines thruming, but at the far end of the pavilion, a soft rectangular glow leaked from a door someone had forgotten to close all the way.

Damion circled wide, staying in the shadows cast by old game booths and stalled rides. A cutout of a cartoon elephant waved a four-fingered hand at nothing, its painted smile cracked as it stood on one foot, while the bird mascot grinned from a sandwich board near a food stall, fork upraised, and eyes too dull. Crouching by a trash barrel next to a raised performance stage, Damion watched the flickering seam of light closely.

Bootsteps. One pair, then another. The door opened wider, spilling more light onto the pavilion. Two men stepped out wearing camouflaged clothing, slowly glancing around at the night—silhouettes and conversation in low tones. One handed the other a clipboard, who used a flashlight to read it in a way that said he didn't want to turn on any more light than was necessary. Damion strained to hear what they were saying, but they were too far away for him to hear the entire conversation.

"—by morning," one said. "Truck at four. Wash it down afterwards."

"Business as usual," the other replied, and Damion heard the words not as instructions, but as a doctrine. The men talked more about the morning activities before returning inside the building.

Damion stayed in the shadows but now leaned against the base of the raised stage. He had heard the words "river" and "load-out," heard a number that could have been weights or could have been headcount. He heard nothing about a child. *Of course, he didn't.* Men doing things in the dark don't say the details of a plan that you want them to say, just because you wish it.

After whispering his notes into the digital voice recorder, he started to move closer to the pavilion to see if there was a window where he could gather more information about the men, when he heard a soft creak right above him. The armed man must have been behind a building when Damion did his scan with the thermal scope and missed him. The man was tall and wiry, standing right above him and staring out into the darkness, his rifle slung over his shoulder.

The man started to pivot, when his eyes dropped — catching the faint outline of Damion's dark-clad form crouched in the shadows below. He hesitated, brow creasing, head tilting as if trying to make sense of what he was looking at. That moment was all Damion needed. He exploded upward, hands snapping around the man's ankles and yanking hard. The man's legs shot forward, his body folding back unnaturally before he crashed onto the wooden stage with a violent crack, skull bouncing against the boards.

Damion flowed with the motion, rolling up onto the platform in one fluid surge. He came down low and drove his elbow across the side of the man's head, the strike landing with brutal precision. The man's body jerked once, then went slack, as consciousness faded away in an instant. The only sound left was the echo of the impact reverberating through the empty stage.

The night became quiet again, but soon the silence was broken by the sound of cautious steps drawing nearer—deliberate and too controlled to be panic.

"Jeb?" a low voice whispered from the dark. "Jeb, you good?"

Damion pressed tight to the corner of the wall, every muscle coiled. The first thing he saw was steel—the black muzzle of a rifle sliding past the edge—then the man's head easing into view. Damion struck like a shadow uncoiling, fist slicing forward in a perfect arc meant to end the fight before it began.

But the man wasn't there. Whether it was instinct, a stumble, or some trick of the dark, Damion's punch cut only air. The man's eyes widened at the sudden appearance of the black-masked figure lunging at him, and he reacted fast—ramming the butt of the rifle into Damion's chest. The impact thundered through him, driving him back several steps, ribs screaming.

Damion staggered but held his ground, teeth gritted. The man advanced, swinging again with the rifle, but Damion slipped the blow and drove his knuckles across the man's jaw. The crack echoed, but the stranger barely faltered—he came back with a wild right hand that clipped Damion's cheek, snapping his head to the side.

The two men battled in the shadows, trading blows like two rabid wolves locked in a mad frenzy. Damion's fists thudded into ribs and shoulder; the man answered with elbows and desperate punches, each one jarring. The rifle clattered to the ground, forgotten, as the fight tightened to raw brutality—grunts, the scuff of boots, the smack of flesh against flesh.

A hard hook from the man split Damion's lip, copper flooding his mouth. Damion spat red and drove forward, catching the man with a vicious knee to the gut. The air rushed from him in a wheeze, but still he clawed back, swinging wide.

Damion ducked, came up inside the arc, and slammed a short, brutal uppercut that snapped the man's head back. He staggered, dazed, but not finished—until Damion pivoted on his heel and delivered a final crushing elbow to his temple. The man went down hard, body sprawling across the boards next to his fellow guard.

The night swallowed the sound again, leaving only Damion standing in the silence, chest heaving and fists throbbing.

Damion stood still for a moment, his breath fogging in the cool night air and his ears straining for movement. The echo of the fight lingered in his head, but the area remained quiet. No shouts, no boots pounding towards him. Just the low buzz of insects passing by. He gave the shadows one last hard look, then proceeded quietly away from the stage and slipped through the fence the same way he'd come in, the metal edges tugging at his clothes as if reluctant to let him go. On the other side, he crouched low, moving quietly through the darkness.

The car was still where he'd left it, half-swallowed by the brush alongside the road. He slid behind the wheel, eyes on the rearview and side mirrors as he started the engine.

Every instinct was screaming at him that he'd pushed his luck far enough for one night. If there were more secrets buried inside the fairgrounds, they would stay buried—for now. He eased onto the road, headlights off until he finally rounded a curve and the fairgrounds were no longer in his mirrors.

As he drove, he decided to text Del. It hadn't been three hours, but he felt obligated to let her know that he was okay. As he headed down the dark road, there was enough moonlight for him to see a small road coming up where he could pull off. Damion drove the car entirely onto the side road, partially obscured by several small trees, killed the engine, and took out his phone.

He texted Del: ALL QUIET. THEN NOT QUIET. ALIVE.

The reply came fast. GOOD. COME BACK.

A faint smile formed on Damion's mouth as he glanced down at the message glowing on his phone. Suddenly, the night erupted as blue strobe lights washed across the trees, pulsing against the windshield like fire. A Sheriff's cruiser roared past the side road, engine howling, heading in the direction of the fairgrounds.

Damion went rigid, his breath caught in his chest. Cold sweat slicked down his back as the weight of the moment pinned him to the seat. He didn't move, didn't breathe, just stared into the darkness as another set of flashing lights flared to life. A second cruiser screamed past, chasing the first one, its siren slicing through the quiet night.

The silence that followed was even more unsettling than the siren. He sat frozen, counting the seconds, each one dragging like a dull blade. Then, exactly one minute later, his nerves decided for him. He twisted the key, and the engine rumbled to life.

The Chevelle's ugly green frame shuddered, then leapt forward, tires clawing at the blacktop. Damion sank into the wheel, man and machine blurring into one. The car tore into the night with a desperate urgency, as if it carried its own destiny, its own fear, or because to stop could mean death. When he arrived, the neighborhood appeared eerily quiet. Eyes alert, and senses sharp, he drove slowly down the sleepy road and crept up into Del's driveway. As soon as he turned off the engine, his phone buzzed—same unknown number.

YOU DON'T LISTEN.

He typed while scanning the surroundings.

YOU DON'T SCARE ME.

Three dots appeared, then vanished, the universal pause of someone deciding whether speaking is worth what speaking costs.

ASK DEL WHAT HAPPENED LAST TIME SOMEONE WOULDN'T LET IT GO.

A lump formed in his stomach as he stared into the dark rearview mirror at the long, empty space behind him, and into his own reflection. The message sat there, glaring at him like a hot branding iron, as if the words were daring him to answer back.

Del opened the trailer door, breaking his concentration, as if she'd been standing there listening for the sound of the little green beast the entire time.

"What?" she asked, seeing his face as he walked up to her.

He held up the phone. She read. The blood went out of her cheeks, then surged back, leaving her green eyes bright and angry.

"I'm not afraid of those men," she said, her voice too loud for the small room. "I was, once. I'm not now."

"Tell me," he said gently.

She looked past him, toward the room where her son slept, then back to the phone, then to Damion. She nodded once, her shoulders sinking as if she had the weight of the world on them.

"Fine," she said. "But you lock that door. And when I'm done, you're gonna' wish you'd never seen a bird with a fork."

He slid the bolt home as the night pressed its ear to the windows. Del grabbed a cup of tea she had been nursing while waiting for him to return, and sat at the small kitchen table. She took a slow, deep breath, and in the little diner town that began as a relaxing pause with good food, the story leaned forward and picked up speed.

Del's eyes drifted down to her hands as she spoke, fingers folding and unfolding the way people do when they're trying to keep something steady inside of them.

"He wasn't a bad man, Damion. Not by a long shot. He worked the fairs, doing whatever needed doing—hauling lumber, fixing the wiring in the tents, tightening bolts on the rides when they rattled loose, even security after closing sometimes. It wasn't glamorous, but it was steady, and steady counted for a lot back then. We were gettin' by."

She took a slow breath, her voice tightening as the memory pressed its weight against her.

"Then the gang moved in. Not the kind that roared in on bikes or sprayed their colors on the walls—no, these men wore clean clothes and kept their shoes polished. They brought in crates, tools, and presses. They said that it was just cheap jewelry, knockoff handbags, designer sneakers, and shirts with the wrong stitching. Counterfeit. Trash, but harmless. They told him to look the other way, gave him cash—almost as much as his regular pay—and said that their stay was only temporary. He told me that he didn't like it. I told him I didn't either. But money has a way of talking louder than either of us did, and with a baby in diapers..." She trailed off.

Damion stayed quiet, watching the tremor in her hands.

"One night he forgot his tools," she went on. "Went back to the fairgrounds. That's when he saw it—boxes stacked differently, heavier. He asked about them, and they didn't hesitate. They opened one up." Her pain filled eyes flicked sadly to Damion's. "Pills with different colors and shapes, in small plastic bags. He didn't know what kind, but the look in those men's eyes, and the guns they carried... he knew not to ask about them again."

Her voice dropped to a whisper. "He came home that night and told me everything. Said he was going to the Sheriff. I begged him not to. Told him men with guns don't give second warnings. He promised me he'd think about it. But every night after that, he'd come home from work with it written on his face—that guilt, that weight. He said that it felt wrong and that he couldn't keep quiet about it."

Del swallowed hard, eyes glassy now. "We fought about it. He stormed out, angry at me for telling him to stay quiet. Later, we went to the Feather & Fork. Sat down, tried to pretend that things were normal. Then he saw two of them there, sitting across the room. They came over uninvited, smiling like a pair of snakes, and introduced themselves to me without giving their names. Not friendly. Not at all. After they walked away, I begged him again to forget about the drugs and let it go. He wouldn't. The next day, he went to the Sheriff."

Her shoulders stiffened as though bracing against the cold, haunting memory. "Two days later, he was under a stage at the fairgrounds, checking the supports. The whole thing came down on him. Everybody said it was an accident. Lots of witnesses, they said. The Sheriff said the same thing as everyone else, but he would investigate it. Afterwards, he swore up and down that there was no evidence of drugs, no proof of anything. And so, the investigation was closed."

She stopped there, the silence filling in around her words like water around a sinking stone. When she spoke again her voice was softer, bordering on the edge of hopelessness.

"That was it. Just me and my boy after that. He never really got to know his daddy. And nobody came after me, not directly. But I always felt like eyes were on me. Always."

Damion nodded quietly, letting her steady herself. Then he leaned forward, his voice even.

"I may have run into two of those men tonight. We didn't exactly exchange names, but let's just say that I think they'll be extra cautious at the fairgrounds from now on. Maybe they'll even consider moving to a new location if they think that someone is on to them and about to shut down their operation."

Del blinked, looking at him closer under the dim light. *"I thought your face looked a little swollen."*

A grin tugged at the corner of Damion's mouth. "You should see the other two."

Her laugh was soft, but it cracked a little something in the heaviness between them. She got some water and retrieved a first aid kit, pulling out gauze and antiseptic. She fussed over his cuts like she would do to her son, while he just sat there, his eyes scanning through the window as though he were expecting flashing blue lights to roll up at any second.

"Get some rest," he told her when she was done, voice low but firm. "I'll be up anyway. Still running on adrenaline. If anyone decides to drop by, I'll handle it."

Del leaned in, pressed a kiss to his cheek—quick, but lingering just long enough.

"Thank you, Damion. For everything."

She disappeared down the hall, leaving him alone in the stillness of the trailer, as the night pressed against the thin walls with the weight of old ghosts closing in around him.

Chapter 10 – Caught Between Grace and Vengeance

Damion woke to the sound of giggling. It came light and airy through the trailer walls, carried by the steady hiss of bacon on the stove. The smell of it pulled him upright before the laughter did, sharp and familiar, cutting through the remnants of restless dreams. He washed his face in the small bathroom sink, the cold water waking him fully, and followed the sounds toward the kitchen.

The morning light slipped through the light green linen curtains, softening the linoleum floor and catching on the chrome trim of the counter. Del stood at the stove in a faded blue blouse with the ends tied in a knot across her stomach, spatula in one hand, and hip cocked against the counter as she worked the pan. Her son perched on a chair pulled up to the table, both hands wrapped around a whisk too big for him, beating eggs in a steel bowl like he was chasing a runaway train. Yellow froth splattered over the tabletop, but he didn't notice—his laughter bubbled up each time the whisk clanged.

"Mornin'," Del sang, glancing over her shoulder with a warm smile. "I kept him from waking you. Figured you could use the sleep."

Damion rubbed the back of his neck, smirking. "Thanks. Yes, I did." Then, glancing out the window, "That makes two nights in a row, now. You know, your neighbors might start whispering about this."

She slid a strip of bacon onto a plate and set it on the counter, arching a brow. "Let 'em. They need something new to wag their tongues about, anyway. Besides, I don't mind giving them a little excitement."

Her son piped up, proud of his work. "I'm helping, Mama!"

"You sure are, sweetheart," Del answered, kissing the top of his head before turning back to the stove.

They sat down together to glass plates stacked with bacon, scrambled eggs, and buttered toast. Her son dug in with both hands, crumbs scattering across the table. Damion leaned forward in his chair with fork and knife in hand. The sight and smell of the warm food in front of him was almost enough to ease the thoughts that had chased him through the night.

"So," Del began, sipping her coffee, "what's the plan?"

Damion started cutting into his eggs. "Reconnaissance is done, so now we review, refine, and respond. Continue to kick over the cans and see what falls out. Try and come up with a plan for whatever we find, and if it doesn't pan out, then we circle back and start from square one." He shoved a forkful of eggs into his mouth, then continued. "As for today, Pastor Coburn invited me to attend the morning service. I think I'll take him up on it."

She nodded, her expression neutral. "Good. He'll be glad to see you there."

"You should come too," Damion suggested.

"I haven't been to church since..." She went silent, glancing at her son.

Damion nodded in understanding while also glancing at the happy little boy. They continued talking, mostly about local town events, while skipping over the more serious happenings of the moment, eating, laughing, and enjoying some everyday morning conversation.

The meal ended with the scrape of chairs and the clink of dishes washed in quick succession. Damion changed into clean clothes, thanked Del for breakfast, and made his way out to his car parked on the side of the driveway.

The morning air was crisp, and the ground was still damp with dew as he headed down the two-lane road. Most of the businesses were closed, and he counted only two of the locals walking down the street, each one holding a leash attached to their canine companion.

Halfway to the church, bright blue flashing strobe lights abruptly lit up his rearview mirror. Damion pulled over onto the shoulder, rolled down the window, and turned off the engine as gravel cracked under the weight of a police cruiser easing up behind him. Deputy Jamison stepped out, boots crunching and hat low over sunglass-covered eyes. He came up slow, leaned on the edge of the Mustang, and held out his hand.

"License and registration."

Damion passed them over, slowly. "You already know who I am, Deputy Jamison. What's the problem?"

Deputy Jamison studied the cards longer than necessary. "Where were you last night?"

"At Del's place," Damion answered. "She let me crash on the sofa. Kind of a *thank you* after everything that happened with the girl."

Jamison's mouth twitched, but didn't quite move into a smile. *"Not at the fairgrounds?"*

"No," Damion said flatly. "Haven't been to a fair since I was a kid."

The deputy's gaze lingered, searching. "There was some vandalism out there. Spray paint, a lot of busted locks, and some damaged...equipment."

Damion shook his head. "I'm too old for childish pranks, Deputy. My car was parked over at Del's all night. Her neighbors can tell you that much."

After a pause, "They already did," replied Jamison, his tone sharpening. "One of them said she saw your car there last night—and still there this morning when she went out for her walk."

Damion let the silence hang before answering. "Then you've got your answer. Like I said, Del let me crash for the night on her couch."

Jamison leaned in closer, forearm on the roof of the pristine Mustang, his shadow cutting across the driver's seat. The scent of too much aftershave that smelled of sandalwood and musk was beginning to sting Damion's eyes.

"Funny thing, though," he said in a low voice. "Lately, every time trouble seems to kick up, you're somewhere nearby. Doesn't look good."

Damion stared at his reflection in the sunglasses without blinking. "Is that a question or a statement?"

The deputy didn't move for a long moment, the silence stretching well past the comfortable limit as Jamison's gaze lingered, heavy with suspicion.

"Where are you headed?"

"Church. Pastor Coburn invited me to the morning service, so that's where I'm going."

After a cynical glance, Jamison pushed off from the car, taking the license and registration back to his cruiser. He sat down in the driver's seat, staring at the back of the Mustang, and let the minutes grind down. The flashing lights kept burning in Damion's mirrors, washing the Mustang's interior in blue strobe lights, the air in the car thickening with every passing second. When Jamison finally returned, he bent down low again, voice just above a whisper.

"You keep out of our way, Jackson. We'll find out what happened to that girl. And when we do, we'll take care of whoever is responsible, along with anyone else screwing around with this investigation." He tapped the license against the door to emphasize his point.

He handed the credentials back, straightened, and walked to his cruiser without another word. The tires spat gravel as he reversed, swung wide, and rolled away, lights cutting off as he disappeared around the bend.

Damion sat in the Mustang, thinking, with the steering wheel tight in his grip as the morning sun reflected brightly across the hood. *They were grasping at straws.* The police suspected that it was him at the fairgrounds last night, but they had no proof. If they did, he would be in cuffs and on his way to a jail cell right now. Instead, they had given him a warning, or a veiled threat, depending on who you asked. One thought was a little troubling, though. If the Sheriff wasn't involved, why would gun-carrying men shipping drugs out of a closed amusement park call the police?

As Damion started the car and steered back onto the road, he knew that he would also need to be just as cautious as those men at the fairground would most certainly be now.

The glass doors silently opened, bathing Damion with cool, conditioned air as he stepped inside. The church didn't smell of dust and wood polish, but of fresh fabric, clean carpet, and a faint trace of lavender from an unseen vent. Instead of hard pews lined shoulder to shoulder, rows of cushioned blue/gray chairs curved toward the front. Three aisles—one through the center and two along the sides— allowed attendees to move easily throughout the spacious room.

The air was hushed, not with the heavy silence of old sanctuaries, but with a calm that settled over him like a warm shower. The carpet beneath his shoes was thick, muting each step as recessed lights above glowed warmly.

Soft shafts of daylight poured through the glass, so that the entire sanctuary felt alive with a spirit of its own.

At the front of the church, Pastor Coburn stood behind a simple pulpit of polished wood and fiberglass, his voice steady, carrying across the space without strain.

"For God so loved the world, that he gave his only begotten Son," the Pastor read, his hand resting on the open Bible. "That whosoever believeth in Him should not perish, but have everlasting life."

The words from John 3:16 echoed not with fire and judgment, but with warmth, as though they were stitched into the very air. The people listened, some nodding, some with eyes closed, their hands resting easily in their laps.

Damion slipped into a chair near the back, letting his body and mind relax for the first time in what felt like days. Still, as he listened to Pastor Coburn begin to preach about forgiveness, his chest tightened. Forgive? How was he supposed to forgive men who'd kidnapped a young girl? Men who saw suffering as profit? His jaw clenched as the sermon progressed, the tension beneath his skin rising in sharp contrast to the calm around him.

Pastor Coburn continued, shifting to Hebrews 10. He spoke about priests of the Old Testament, offering sacrifice after sacrifice, endless motions that could never erase sin. "But Christ," the Pastor said, his voice lifting now, "by God's will, gave Himself once for all. It is finished. We are made holy, not by what we do, but by what was already done."

The sermon shifted again, weaving its way through the expectations of daily life as a believer. "We are not just to receive forgiveness," Pastor Coburn said, leaning on the pulpit with both hands, "but to carry it into the world. Love others. Show mercy. Be a hand to the broken. This is the work we are called to."

Damion sat stiff as a board, the words sliding under his skin like splinters. *Show mercy*. He thought of the girl and her notebook; of her silence. Mercy wasn't the word he wanted. *Justice* was.

However, Damion felt it was challenging to focus on getting even while sitting in the church. Everything about the place felt intentional—calm, soothing, and peaceful. Not like the churches in Damion's memory, where preachers shouted and sweat dripped from the pulpits as if salvation came by force.

Here, even the words felt different. And yet, for Damion, forgiveness still hung out of reach, a shape just beyond the light.

When the service ended, whispered conversations filled the sanctuary, as voices blended with the soft hum of music and community. Pastor Coburn stepped down from the pulpit, his eyes finding Damion in the back row.

"I'm glad you came," he said, extending his hand and a big smile. "What did you think?"

Damion rose, shifting uneasily. "It was... different. The only two times I remember going to church as a kid, the preacher yelled a lot about fire and brimstone. Everyone was going to hell for something. We didn't go back."

The Pastor gave a knowing chuckle. "And now? Are you a believer?"

"I don't know." Damion's eyes flicked to the stained-glass cross glowing in the light. "I've seen things I can't explain. I just figured they happened by chance or coincidence. My family isn't full of bad people—we just didn't go to church that much."

Damion paused for a moment, then looked Pastor Coburn square in the eyes. "I've visited different parts of the world, and have seen people do some terrible things to others, and even to themselves. I used to wonder about something, but gave up on trying to find an answer - why does God allow bad things to happen in the world?"

Pastor Coburn's expression didn't change, as if he had been expecting the question. He folded his arms and shifted his stance, his voice taking on a philosophical tone.

"Do you mean, why does *mankind* allow bad things to happen?"

Damion cocked his head and looked at him curiously as Pastor Coburn continued.

"Let me ask you this: if a parent gives their child a new car for their 18th birthday, full of gas, oil, and all the works. Perfect condition, everything in place. Now, the child drives the car until it's empty, never fills up the tank, or never changes the oil. When it breaks down, whose fault is it? The parent? Or the child?"

Damion absorbs the words, jaw tight and eyes focused.

"God gave mankind the earth full of everything we needed, and also gave us an assignment to take care of it," the Pastor went on. "But from the start, man has been blaming Him for all of the bad stuff that happens. Do you recall Adam's words after he realized he was naked? The woman *You gave me* - gave me the fruit." He tilted his head, giving Damion a profound look.

"If I were a betting man, I would bet that most problems here on earth that need solving reside solely in man's hands to do so."

The words sank deep into Damion's consciousness as he nodded slowly to himself. After a few moments, Damion shifted the conversation and spoke about the girl, what Del had said about her son's father, and about the fairgrounds.

Pastor Coburn nodded gravely, then recited a quote that cut through the silence like a hot knife.

"When bad men combine, the good must associate; else they will fall, one by one, an unpitied sacrifice in a contemptible struggle."

Damion looked up in surprise. "Edmund Burke," he replied, his voice filled with astonishment.

Pastor Coburn's gaze locked onto him. "It doesn't take a philosopher or a preacher to understand common sense."

Damion nodded slowly. "I would be lying if I said that I don't want to seriously hurt someone for what they've done; they need to be stopped. But, right now, I've got no hard evidence and the Sheriff—it seems like he doesn't want to touch it."

"Then listen to your heart and let God guide your actions."

"And how do I know which is God, and which is me?"

The Pastor's smile was a warm support under the soft light. "I'm sure you've heard that *God works in mysterious ways?* Well, sometimes, we don't actually see His hand in things until long after the moment has passed."

As Damion stood thinking, Pastor Coburn placed a hand on his shoulder. "If you don't mind, I would like to say a short prayer for you."

The words of the prayer were simple, asking God to show Damion the path and to give him strength. The air seemed to thicken with each word, as if the sanctuary itself leaned in closer to listen. When Pastor Coburn finished, his tone carried quiet conviction.

"Everyone has an assignment in this life. Some fulfill it. Others never even seek it. Trust God. Do the right thing with a clean heart. In return, you may receive some much needed help in your mission."

With that said, Pastor Coburn moved on toward the small crowd waiting to shake his hand, leaving Damion standing alone, thinking about their conversation.

The glass doors eased shut behind him, and the calm of the sanctuary bled away as Damion stepped into the gray light of day. Noon, but the sun was nowhere to be seen — clouds pressed low and heavy, the low-hanging cumulus streaked in darker shades that promised rain.

The church's brick facade stood clean and steady against the dim sky, its exterior lights glowing faintly under the overhang, washed pale in the daylight. The parking lot was nearly empty, just a handful of cars parked in neat lines, their windshields glossed with the sheen of gathering moisture.

Damion paused at the edge of the lot, the Pastor's words still echoing in his chest: *Do the right thing with a clean heart.* Inside, surrounded by warmth and color, the idea had felt almost possible. Out here, with the horizon darkening and the storm crowding in, it felt heavier, harder.

He crossed the lot in silence. A breeze carried the smell of rain and the restless rustle of trees beyond the parking lot. He slid into the driver's seat and caught his reflection in the mirror; he had seen better looking days. Eyes shadowed, jaw bruised, a man pulled between the light and darkness.

The engine rumbled to life, and as he shifted into gear, the first drops fell—spattering against the windshield in soft, deliberate taps. One drop became many, with streaks soon running down the glass as the sky opened wider. The wipers swept across, clearing his view, but the road ahead looked less certain; just a strip of asphalt leading into a horizon blurred by rain.

Behind him, the church stood like a quiet sentinel against the storm. Ahead, shadows and rainwater blurred together, challenging him to go forward.

Chapter 11 – Pressure Points

The steady downpour of rain outside his window reflected the mood of Sheriff James Tiberius Douglas as he slouched in his recliner, one hand loosely holding a half-empty beer and the other resting on the armrest like it carried too much weight to lift. The living room was quiet except for the low murmur coming from the television, where two sports commentators were locked in their usual shouting match—this time over the greatest receiver in football history. One had the statistics for Jerry Rice memorized down to the decimal. The other argued for Randy Moss and his athletic brilliance as if it were a holy crusade. The argument rolled on, numbers and passions thrown back and forth like the punches of heavyweight boxers, but J.T. barely heard any of it. The noise had become background static, drowned out by a single, relentless thought.

Blackmail.

The word alone made his gut twist. He should've seen it coming. Men like him—men with a badge, a reputation, a family—were prime targets. He'd read the case studies, the cautionary memos, the training briefs warning officers to watch for subtle entrapments. He'd given those warnings to his deputies, too. "Don't get comfortable," he'd said more than once. "No one offers you easy money without having a hidden agenda."

But all the warnings in the world hadn't saved him. He'd let his guard down.

It had started with a handshake and a smile.

Mr. Donovan came into town with a clean suit, clean shoes, and clean intentions—or so it seemed. He introduced himself as the new owner of *Freedman's Feather & Fork*. He said he was investing in renovations, hiring locals, and giving the town a fresh boost. The kind of talk that always sounded good in a place that hadn't seen much new life in years.

Donovan's visit to the Sheriff's office had seemed routine.

"I'll be needing a bit of extra security," he'd said in a smooth, even tone. "I don't want any of that new equipment walking off, and would prefer to keep things local. It would save me a significant amount of money on transportation, housing, food, and other expenses if I didn't have to ship in outside security. Perhaps some of your deputies would like to earn a little extra cash on the side during their off-duty hours, compensation for their time with no paperwork headaches."

J.T. remembered hesitating, just for a second. But Donovan had been polite and businesslike, and said that the Sheriff himself would also get a small supervisor's allowance for managing it, off the books, of course. No one would ever need to know.

His deputies jumped at the offer. They already knew the plant, already drove by it on patrol. "Heck," one of them said, "we're protecting the place anyway." The first envelope of cash had come a week later. The second was thicker than expected. Donovan called it *"gratitude for a job well done."*

Soon enough, everyone was smiling. Bills got paid faster. Christmas came early. J.T. even treated his wife to a weekend in Raleigh, bought his grandkids a new playset, and tucked away a little for a Florida vacation.

Then one day, Donovan's smile changed.

It was a phone call first. Calm, quiet, polite—yet with something sharp beneath.

"One of your deputies stopped a truck of mine today," he said. "I thought we had an understanding."

J.T. had played dumb, promised to look into it. It turned out to be Jamison—good deputy but still a little too *by-the-book*. He'd pulled over a truck with "workers" riding in the back, no seatbelts, no IDs. The driver claimed their bus had broken down and they were just trying to get them to the plant.

"Next time," Donovan said, "maybe your men could try and not be so observant."

And J.T., against every instinct he'd ever trusted, agreed. He held a morning meeting the very next day, but was careful not to name names or events.

"Let's not bite the hand that feeds us our dessert," he'd said. "Feather & Fork's been good to this department and wants to keep it that way." Everyone nodded; no one had asked questions.

Things stayed calm for a while—until one of Donovan's men got himself arrested for assault after a night of heavy drinking and attacking a hostess at the local strip club. J.T.

had personally locked the man up. Thirty minutes later, his office phone rang.

"I'm disappointed in you, Sheriff. Apparently, I wasn't very clear," Donovan said, hanging up before J.T. could respond.

Two days later, a package arrived on his desk. No return label. Just his name written neatly on top.

Inside was a custom-made, black and gold coffee mug, the kind that catches the light regardless of where it is placed. It was beautiful—heavy, expensive, and too nice for the type of man who drank gas-station coffee by habit. On one side, the official Sheriff's Office badge, proud and glossy, with all the details. On the other side, a full-color photo that sucked the air out of him.

His daughter. Her smile was caught in mid-laughter, and her hair was pulled back in a loose ponytail as she stood near a park bench. And his granddaughters—two of them—playing on a bright red seesaw, sunlight glinting off their hair. One leaned forward, eyes squeezed shut in laughter; the other kicked her small legs toward the sky. The scene was perfect—too perfect. It radiated peace, innocence, joy. A moment suspended in golden daylight. Family.

Beneath it, in etched gold lettering, were the words:

Thank you for protecting us every day, Grandpa.

His hands trembled before he even finished reading. His throat went dry. The mug slipped slightly in his grip, forcing him to set it down before he dropped it. To anyone else, the coffee mug would have appeared to be a nice, thoughtful gift from a loving family. But to J.T., it was a message written in a language he couldn't afford to misunderstand.

He didn't need to call his daughter to thank her for the gift. She hadn't sent it—he knew that without question. The photo had been taken in *Marion, South Carolina*. Nearly two hundred miles away, where she and her little family lived, across state lines and well out of his jurisdiction. The sunlight, the park, the position of the seesaw—it was a place he'd never seen before. Someone had located and followed them. Someone had stood there, close enough to hear their laughter, and captured it through a lens.

Then, the phone rang.

Donovan.

"Did you like your gift?" The voice was calm. Pleasant. Then, "I trust that we will not have any more misunderstandings."

J.T. had sat frozen, staring at the mug until his pulse became the only sound in the room.

That was the day he stopped being Sheriff and started being property.

Now, sitting in his recliner, he could still see their faces every time he closed his eyes—the little one's toothy grin, the sunlight in her hair, the carefree tilt of his daughter's head as she watched her children play. He wanted to remember it for what it was: happiness. But now, even that memory had been poisoned.

He thought about the recent commotion at the fairgrounds: the official report and the hushed rumors at the station. Someone had stirred things up there, big time—someone with military-like precision, according to the witnesses. Could've been this Jackson fella, who'd found the girl, or maybe someone else entirely. J.T. didn't know for sure, but if someone was moving against Donovan, a part of him hoped they'd succeed. However, another part feared what that might bring down on everyone else if they didn't.

He was still lost in a spiral of thoughts when his wife's voice broke the silence.

"I don't know what's bothering you, J.T., but here's some freshly baked pecan pie and a glass of milk."

She came in smiling, her hair tied back, carrying a small tray that smelled of sugar and cinnamon.

He blinked, forcing a smile as she set it down beside him.

"Thanks, hon."

The pie glistened under the light—a golden crust, warm with caramelized edges, the kind of simple sweetness that made everything else fade for a while. He looked around their living room—neat, comfortable, modest. A good home, built from years of honest work. Or at least, it used to be.

He took a slow bite. The sweetness filled his mouth, cutting through the bitterness that had settled in him for longer than he cared to remember. For just a moment, he let the taste carry him away—back to a time before Donovan, before the mug, before the fear.

The storm in his body, unlike the one outside, had quieted, if only for a breath.

He leaned back in the recliner, swallowed, and stared at nothing. Maybe fate would finally throw him a lifeline, along with one clean chance to set things right.

If not, then he'd have to find a solution himself, one way or another.

The last bite of pecan pie lingered on J.T.'s tongue—sweet, rich, and just warm enough to feel like home—when the doorbell rang.

His wife wiped her hands on a dish towel as she passed him, her soft steps fading down the hallway. The low murmur of voices followed a moment later, polite but cautious, then the sound of approaching footsteps on tile.

Deputy Jamison stepped into the living room, hat in hand, looking like a man who'd rather be anywhere else on a Sunday afternoon.

"Sorry to bother you, Sheriff," he said. "But I figured you'd want an update."

J.T. straightened a little in his recliner, setting his empty plate aside. "You're fine, son. What's going on?"

Before Jamison could answer, J.T.'s wife reappeared from the kitchen with another tray—pecan pie and a glass of milk balanced neatly on it.

"You look like you could use something sweet," she said with a warm smile.

Jamison smiled back, "Thank you, ma'am. That's mighty kind of you."

As she disappeared again, he took a seat across from the Sheriff, resting his hat on his knee while clearing his throat.

"I went back out to the fairgrounds this morning. Figured I'd take another look during daylight before the rain washed any evidence away, to see if we missed anything from last night." He leaned forward slightly, his voice dropping lower. "Found a splatter of blood on the stage where the fight happened. Whoever tangled with those guards got hit hard – hard enough to draw blood. I took a sample and thought I'd send it to the state lab to see if we can get a DNA match - maybe the assailant is in their database. With your approval, of course."

J.T. nodded slowly, eyes narrowing. "Continue."

"There's something else," Jamison continued. "Whoever he was, he didn't take any of their weapons or ammo. Both guards still had everything on them. Makes no sense. Those rifles could fetch quick cash at a flea market or gun show, no serial number checks, no questions asked."

The Sheriff rubbed his jaw, the faint rasp of his stubble filling the silence. "Strange," he said quietly. "Anything else?"

Jamison hesitated, shifting in his seat. "I, uh… did a *courtesy* traffic stop this morning on that Navy man—Jackson. Asked where he was last night."

J.T.'s eyes lifted, steady. "And?"

"He said that he was at Del's. Stayed overnight." Jamison looked faintly uneasy. "I checked with her neighbor. They confirmed it."

The Sheriff gave a slow nod. "All right."

Jamison waited, expecting more of a response, but none came.

"That all?" J.T. finally asked.

"Yes, sir."

"Good work," J.T. said. Then, as the younger man stood to leave, he added, "Hold off on sending that blood to the lab."

Jamison froze halfway to the door. "Sir?"

J.T.'s voice stayed level, casual even, but his eyes stayed fixed on the dim reflection in the TV screen.

"The only thing that happened out there last night was a trespasser getting into a fist-fight with two armed guards and living to walk away from it. No one died, nothing was stolen, and no property was damaged. You know as well as I do—sending a sample like that means it comes out of our budget. And for what? A scuffle?"

Jamison nodded after a moment, understanding registering across his face. "Yes, sir. You're right. Wasn't thinking about the cost, with no real potential benefit."

The Sheriff offered a faint, tired smile. "You are just doing your job, Delbert. I appreciate that."

Deputy Jamison nodded, thanked the Sheriff's wife again on the way out, and closed the door behind him.

For a moment, the house was silent again.

J.T. exhaled slowly and leaned back, staring at the flickering television without seeing it. His mind wasn't on the game, or the deputies, or even Donovan. It was on the man who'd left that blood behind—the stranger who had walked into Donovan's lion's den and walked out again.

Whoever he was, he wasn't ordinary, and he wasn't afraid.

J.T. felt something he hadn't felt in a long time—hope. Quiet, dangerous hope. Maybe that stranger would come back, stir the hornet's nest again, and poke the bear that is Mr. Donovan. And if he did, maybe J.T. could find a way—quietly, carefully—to sharpen the spears waiting for him to use.

He reached for his beer, the glass cool against his fingers, and let the thought settle like a whisper in the back of his mind.

If the devil is coming for Donovan, maybe, just this once, J.T. would hold the door open for him.

The late afternoon light had shifted by the time Jamison stepped out onto the porch again. The dark rain clouds, thick and heavy, hovered over him like a menacing giant waiting for him to come out far enough to be stepped on. He paused for a moment at the edge of the steps, his hat in hand, replaying the conversation in his head.

The Sheriff's reasoning had sounded right enough on the surface, not wanting to spend budgeted funds

unnecessarily, but something in his tone didn't match his words. It wasn't what J.T. had said; it was what he hadn't.

Jamison adjusted his hat, eyes glancing over at the Sheriff's cruiser parked by the gravel drive. He'd worked under Douglas for almost five years now and had the utmost respect for him. Sometimes, the man was a stickler for procedure, but he was always honest, fair, and he took care of his people. The one thing that he didn't do was ignore evidence. Not ever.

And yet, a blood sample—something that could possibly identify a suspect connected to an assault—was being shelved, just like that. It didn't make sense.

Deputy Jamison climbed into his cruiser, closed the door, and sat there with the engine idling, watching the rain bounce off the hood. He thought about the fairgrounds—the blood, and the imprints in the dirt where someone may have hidden before attacking the two men. He thought about the way the guards had acted when questioned, their eyes darting, and their stories not completely adding up. Something was off with this whole situation.

He shifted in his seat, glancing back toward the Sheriff's house. The curtains in the living room were drawn, but he could still see the faint flicker of the television inside. For the first time, Jamison felt like there were things going on in Bishops Creek that he didn't understand, and worse, that someone wanted to keep it that way.

He pulled onto the road, as deep puddles of rainwater splashed under the patrol cruiser's tires. Nodding to himself, he decided that he'd keep that blood sample a little longer. The Sheriff may not want to send it now, but it may become relevant if the stranger shows up again and they catch him.

Inside the house, J.T. stood by the window, watching the cruiser's taillights disappear down the road. His reflection stared back at him from the glass—older, heavier, the weight of too many compromises in his eyes.

He knew Jamison had questions; he could see it in his face. The man was too smart not to. But too much curiosity in a small town could be dangerous and a liability.

As thunder rolled low in the distance, J.T. turned away from the window and picked up the empty glasses and pie plates from the table. He carried them to the kitchen sink, where the air smelled faintly of sugar and dish liquid. But, underneath it, he swore that he could still smell the cold metal of that coffee mug on his desk—the one with the picture of his daughter and granddaughters' faces smiling happily, oblivious to the danger close by them.

The storm outside was moving away, but not the one he could no longer avoid. He washed the dishes, dried his hands, turned off the kitchen light, and stared at the dim reflection in the window one last time.

If Jamison were smart, he'd stop digging. If he weren't, then Sheriff J.T. Douglas would have another kind of problem on his hands.

Chapter 12 – *After the Storm, Before the Flood*

The Sunday thunderstorm pummeled the small town of Bishops Creek and its surrounding areas. Damion had watched most of it from Del's trailer window the night before, the rain beating like a fist against the thin window panes while gusting winds rattled the aluminum siding. He had planned to drive by the Feather & Fork processing plant after the church service, but the storm had rapidly strengthened and the roads had become a moving question mark. Damion decided not to push his luck, getting caught in the harsh weather, and returned to Del's trailer instead.

They had spent the rest of Sunday inside with the trailer lights dimmed low, playing board games sprawled on the living room floor and watching movies while the wind moaned and the rain hammered the roof. Del's son's laughter had been a continuous happy reprieve from the gray, howling weather outside. Damion had quickly fallen into a rhythm of small kindnesses—making coffee, fixing a broken shelf, and reading to the little boy until his eyelids drooped.

By Monday morning, the full toll of the storm's wrath was visible—strewn branches, piles of leaves plastered across yards like confetti, and the occasional flutter of insulation clinging to lower tree limbs. In Del's yard, it looked like every tree had lost an argument with the wind; yet by some minor miracle, no trees lay toppled across roofs or porches, and her rain gutters were not clogged with debris. Del turned on her battery-powered storm radio while they ate breakfast, and they listened to the monotonous, battered voice of the local reporter as he called off road closures and damage assessments.

Power lines were down everywhere, leaving half of the town without electricity, while the other half struggled with gas-powered generators. Emergency vehicles were out in full force, attempting to clean up the area, but it would take some time before regular services would be restored. Heading south on US-258 towards Tarboro, trees were down in the road just past the tractor equipment store. The storm had hit harder than expected, and several ditches dug on the side of the road to keep water from overflowing had not functioned fully as intended. Now, the road was impassable due to the overflow of runoff water. Somehow, the cell towers had sustained only minor damage but were functioning, allowing good communication between people and emergency crews.

Damion helped clear the table when they were finished, and was out the door before Del started on the dishes. The yard needed a lot of work. He started in one corner, hauling branches into neat piles, dragging twigs away, and righting a plastic lawn tractor. Del's son, clad in his yellow duck rain boots, came out to join the 'fun', running back and forth and jumping into piles of leaves. Del soon slipped outside, and they worked beneath the clear blue sky, thankful that there hadn't been more damage. Del's son got tired of the leaves and went back inside to play, only to come out again around noon to let her know that he was hungry.

Del said that she had called the diner; the building had sustained some minor damage from flying debris but had otherwise remained intact. "They're open," she told Damion, with a suggestive smile. "Peaches said they're doing lunch and coffee, and a few folks from town have been pitching in."

"I'm on it," he replied, returning the smile.

Damion got cleaned up, changed his shirt, and took the Chevelle down Main Street. People were out—neighbors with brooms and shovels, shop owners sweeping grit from entryways, and utility crews moving with a dedicated purpose. The sight carried him back to the Daniel Shaw in an odd, familiar way: men and women working together in unison, faces set, practical gestures exchanged without fanfare. The communal effort towards a common goal warmed him; it was an echo of discipline and purpose, the kind of thing sailors felt etched into their bones.

When he arrived at the diner, he was surprised at the number of people inside. Every booth and counter seat was occupied, and there were a few customers ahead of him waiting to place their orders. He stood in line by the counter for about five minutes before a vibrant, dark-skinned waitress with a name tag that read 'PEACHES' approached him.

"Damion?" She asked with a bright smile and cheerful voice.

He nodded, returning the smile.

"Del called ahead with her order. She described you *perfectly*," she said, handing him a large, paper food bag while eyeing him up and down.

"Thanks, I think," he replied.

"Oh yeah, sugar. That she did. You have a good day now," she sang, as she spun around and hurried off to a waiting customer.

As he headed towards the exit, the entry bell announced the arrival of several new customers: Sheriff J.T. Douglas and a man in a white suit at his side. As they made eye contact, the Sheriff paused uncomfortably, as if someone had placed a knife to his chest. Damion gave a slight nod while trying to keep his face neutral.

"Afternoon, Sheriff," Damion said.

"Jackson. What are you still doing here? Thought you were passing through," J.T. said, voice threaded with suspicion.

"Just grabbing lunch," Damion replied, raising the bag. I've been helping Del clean up around her place. The plan was to head out this morning, but the radio said the roads are blocked, so I don't know when I'll be leaving. I guess it all depends on whether or not another storm blows across the horizon."

Sheriff Douglas' face carried a look that was hard to read: a mixture of warning, hope, and something like resignation. He grunted with a sound that came off as an effort to manage his own unease.

"Stay off the back roads," the Sheriff said finally, his eyes cutting quickly over at the man standing next to him before returning to Damion. "They don't drain as quickly as in town. They can be…treacherous." He then continued walking, followed by the overly dressed man, to a reserved booth in the back of the diner.

Damion watched the two men as they walked away. The scene resembled something from an old 1980s movie. A man in a white suit, the Sheriff, and a small town in need of help while recovering from a near-disaster. *What a cliché that would be if he were actually the bad guy*, thought Damion with a chuckle. He probably was the town's mayor, dressed like that. As he turned to continue out of the diner, he bumped into Peaches, who had silently strolled up right behind him.

"Oh, I'm sorry," he said.

"I'm not," she replied with a smile that didn't quite reach her eyes. "If you're wondering who the man in the suit is—that's Sebastian Donovan. He's the owner of the Feather & Fork. Most of the folks around here think he's some kind of saint. Me? I think he's a dirtbag. Something about him just makes my skin crawl."

She glided away without another word, as Damion looked at the man again, then at the Sheriff, who was nervously tapping his fingers against his leg. The Sheriff looked over at Damion hard, then focused back on the conversation with *the man that made Peaches' skin crawl* as Damion headed out the door.

Inside the diner booth, J.T. Douglas was uncomfortable. No, not uncomfortable; he was *very uncomfortable*. Sebastian Donovan's presence in Bishops Creek had been totally unexpected. He usually informed the Sheriff when he would be visiting the production plant and, therefore, the town. That way, J.T. could bring the local business owners together and host their usual gathering to show their full appreciation for everything he had done for them. For him to show up like this out of the blue could not be a good sign. If he weren't a religious man, J.T. would swear that yesterday's storm had been a premonition of this devil's return.

A chill ran down his back as he thought about how he had been sitting in his office working this morning, and when he looked up, Donovan was standing there as if he had materialized out of thin air. His presence had startled J.T., and Donovan had smiled like the predator he was, totally amused by his reaction. The man had closed the door, sat down, and asked about the girl. The Sheriff had explained that Child Protective Services would be coming to pick her up today and place her into state custody, but they were probably delayed due to the weather. Donovan had then asked about the girl's notebook. The Sheriff said that it was logged as possible evidence and would be turned over to the Department of Justice, a comment that did not appear to sit well with his current visitor. Donovan then abruptly suggested that they should get something to eat.

Now, they were sitting here in the crowded diner, as J.T. watched him blow over the surface of his hot tea before taking a sip. He stared into the cup as he spoke; his voice low and sinister.

"Do you know why we are here, Sheriff?" Donovan asked, his voice as smooth as coarse gravel. "Because of the girl."

The Sheriff's leg bounced to an unconscious rhythm as his eyes swept the room. He caught sight of Damion looking at them, and tried to cast a look that said, *"Leave"*, without saying it, and Damion had left. A slightly, strained relief passed across J.T.'s face, like someone blowing out a candle they didn't want anyone to notice.

"What about the girl, Mr. Donovan?" J.T. asked, each word spoken with an attempt to keep his voice from breaking.

"She needs to disappear," Donovan said flatly.

Silence enveloped the booth like a dark cloud as J.T. looked around the room of oblivious patrons and employees. He felt the words hit him, as if they had landed on his chest like a ton of bricks.

"That is why I chose this spot to tell you, Sheriff," Donovan continued, leaning forward, "so that you would understand the gravity of the situation. Granted, there are no witnesses to our conversation, but make no mistake, I am completely serious. She has seen too much, and I can't afford to have her inviting unwanted guests poking around my property and causing unnecessary interruptions to production."

J.T. swallowed hard. He thought about the small notebook, the childish drawings that mapped unspeakable horrors— the wide-open mouths, people drawn in boxes, and words that made no immediate sense, but pointed to a darker tale. The Sheriff had intended to file it with the Department of Justice if he felt that there was any substance to the girl's drawings, but now, he was beginning to understand that there was. And, there was nothing he could do about it.

"So, all those drawings in her notebook…"

"Do you really want to know, Sheriff?" he replied, making a slurping sound with his tea. "But, if it will make you feel better, not all of her drawings are accurate."

J.T. felt his heart beating faster as beads of sweat formed on his forehead. *This can't be happening*, he thought, trying to make sense of everything, as Donovan continued.

"Of course, nothing can happen while she is at the station. It's not uncommon for runaways to…run *away*", he said, smirking at his use of words. "Maybe she escapes when she's allowed to use the bathroom. Maybe when they take her out to buy clothes or candy. Migrants don't trust police anyway—everybody knows that. You'll let her slip away, and no one will know the difference."

J.T.'s head was spinning now. What Donovan was asking was unthinkable and criminal. He had to find a way out of what this lunatic was suggesting.

"The girl is in our custody," he said eventually, voice low. "If anything happens to her before CPS picks her up, we're opening the door to State and federal attention. We have procedures we must follow."

For a long moment, Donovan said nothing - his face a mask that could have been either an expression of amusement or one of contempt. Then, a slight, menacing smile formed.

"We will intercept the girl after CPS takes custody, outside of your jurisdiction. You give us their vehicle type, plate number, and departure time. We'll take care of the rest," he replied in a cold, flat tone.

The room seemed to tilt again. J.T.'s stomach did a sick little flip while his pulse pounded loudly in his head.

"You're asking me to—look away while you hurt the kid?"

"I'm *telling* you to be practical," Donovan countered back, standing and buttoning the cuff on his pristine suit.

"Eat something, Sheriff. It's not good to work on an empty stomach."

Donovan let the words hang like a mockery of comfort, then drifted from the booth like a ghost leaving the grave.

J.T. watched him go, feeling the cold chill in the air that always followed the man's departure. He sat in the booth, his mind racing, as the sounds of the diner faded into the background. Donovan was going to kill the girl and the CPS worker, then make it look like an accident. He couldn't let that happen. He admitted to himself that it had been wrong for him to have taken the extra money on the side while looking the other way now and then on some minor infractions by Donovan's men, but he was not a murderer.

He took an oath to serve and to protect, and Donovan was trying to force him to break it. He needed to figure out a solution to this problem and possibly seek some additional help. He also had to find a way to keep his family safe before he considered moving against Donovan. The man was pure evil and had access to resources, making him one of the most formidable kinds of enemies.

The phone in J.T.'s pocket buzzed, snapping him back to the present. The caller ID showed it was Deputy Jamison. He answered, his voice careful and low.

"Sheriff, there's been a delay in reinitializing power to the station," Jamison said. "The transformer part is two days out. I told the crews it was a priority—said they could drive to Virginia, if they located another part, to fetch it. The backup generator is holding, so we are still functioning, just a little bit less than optimal, though."

"Okay," J.T. said, fingers tightening around the receiver. "Keep me posted."

He ended the call and began rubbing his temples while the diner's sounds morphed into muffled echoes in the back of his head. As he sat there, deep in thought, Peaches came over with a plate of food and coffee and placed them on the table.

"Here you go, Sheriff. Sorry it took a while, but this'll get you movin' in the right direction," she said in a cheerful voice. "Can I get you anything else?"

J.T. sat there staring at the plate for a moment, then all of a sudden, his head snapped up as he looked at the smiling waitress. He suddenly grabbed her hand and kissed the back of it, startling her.

"Bless you, Peaches!" he said while fumbling to take his phone out of his pocket.

She laughed, uneasily, then drifted back to the counter as he quickly scrolled through a list of names until he found the one he was looking for. As he dialed the number, he thought of the girl and her notebook, and of the three faces in a photograph on a coffee mug that had arrived on his desk. The phone on the other end rang three times before a professional-sounding female voice answered.

"Child Protective Services, how may I direct your call?"

J.T. steadied his voice into something less than a quake.

"This is Sheriff Douglas over in Bishops Creek. I need to inform the case worker that the migrant girl we have for transport today has become very ill. Our doctor here says that she may have come down with a touch of pneumonia, due to her being exposed to the cold and all. She has a high fever and is not feeling well right now, but the doc is sure she will be okay in a couple of days. He recommends that we not transport her until she is feeling better. Is it possible to delay the transport until, say, Thursday? See how she is doing then? We are already providing her care, and there's no need to expose the case worker to this also."

The woman's voice was businesslike, but compassionate, and J.T. felt a spark of hope in the sterile competence on the other end.

"Well, of course, Sheriff. I will notify the case worker immediately. We can reschedule the pickup for Thursday, and if she still isn't feeling better, please feel free to inform us before then."

J.T. breathed in the diner's air, smelling the sizzling bacon for the first time since he entered the crowded room.

"Yes, Ma'am. Will do," he answered a little more upbeat than he intended.

"Bishops Creek must be proud to have a Sheriff like you who cares," the woman on the phone said. "Have a good day." Then, the line went dead.

He then scrolled to another name in his phone as his pulse raced. The phone on the other end rang once before being answered.

"Deputy Mack."

Sheriff Douglas spoke in a low, rapid tone, giving the deputy very specific instructions for an assignment that she alone would be responsible for handling. After ensuring that all of his instructions were understood, he ended the call.

J.T. sat in the booth, his mind racing through his decisions. He had struck back at Donovan by delaying the girl's transfer and thus stopping his hit on the transport. And, if his plan worked, then he might be able to get rid of this Donovan altogether. J.T. was resolved that he would not willingly let a child die on his watch, and he would not be the man who let a child's life be traded like a backroom secret. Yet, Donovan's reach was a thing to be feared - made of expensive suits, white collars, and black-leathered fists. It had already touched the Sheriff's life - a reminder sitting in his office like a metallic nightmare. But it was high time that he remembered why he had put on his badge in the first place.

J.T. picked up the fork and quickly ate while gulping down the cup of coffee. He slipped out of the booth, paid his bill with trembling fingers, and walked briskly towards the door. Stepping out under the afternoon sky, he felt the increasing humidity that usually followed an intense rainstorm. The storms would return someday. They had a tendency to break things down, then wash them away, forcing everyone to pick up the pieces and start again. J.T. looked back towards the diner where life continued, and felt the thin, raw edge of a plan forming like a bruise under his skin. He had to protect the child, protect his family, and find the lifeline that would allow him to become a sheriff again, not the lost man who'd sold out his soul. And if he had to cross a line to do it, then so be it.

Chapter 13 – The River Cries Foul

Sheriff Douglas sat in his patrol car as the warmth of the sun beamed through the windshield. His hands rested on the steering wheel, while his mind juggled the list of dangerous steps he'd have to take if he wanted to turn the tide on Donovan. Each one, if not done correctly, could be the final nail in a coffin of his own making.

The sky was bright, and the last storm cell had moved out over the Atlantic Ocean, but the dark clouds rumbling in his mind hadn't yet made their peace with the earth. They hung low and heavy, as if a downpour of misery and pain could come again at any moment.

Snapping out of the depressing thoughts trying to overtake him, he reached for the ignition button to start the car, just as the radio squawked.

"Sheriff-1, Dispatch. We've got a citizen's report of a possible body floating in the water near Jenkins Landing, just past the old light tower. 1-Adam-12 is on scene. 3-Baker-21 and 2-Adam-7 are en route for backup."

The radio hissed and crackled through Sheriff Douglas's cruiser as the V8 HEMI engine growled to life in his Dodge Charger 'police package' sedan, the blue strobes glinting off the sides of the diner.

"10-4, Dispatch. What's the 10-20 on Echo-6?"

"Echo-6 is 10-76 from the coroner's office, Sheriff. ETA approximately eight minutes."

"Copy that. I'm 10-76 to the scene, Code-3. Patch me through to 1-Adam-12 for an update."

"10-4, Sheriff-1. You're live with 1-Adam-12."

"Sheriff-1, this is 1-Adam-12. I've got one body in the water, caught on the downstream pilings. Looks male. No signs of movement. I'm holding perimeter until Echo-6 arrives."

"Copy, 1-Adam-12. Keep civilians back. Make sure no one touches that shoreline. 3-Baker-21, set up traffic control on the access road."

"10-4, Sheriff-1. I'll divert all vehicle and foot traffic starting at Coleman's Bridge."

The Charger's tires hummed louder as the Sheriff accelerated down the smooth highway, the car cruising as if gliding on a sheet of air.

"Sheriff-1, this is 1-Adam-12, the currents shifting. That body's about to move. Should I secure it?"

"Negative, 1-Adam-12. Hold position. Wait for Echo-6. We don't want to contaminate the body before the coroner sees it."

A few minutes pass by before the radio crackles again.

"Sheriff-1, this is 1-Adam-12, Echo-6 is 10-97, Coroner Liaison on-scene."

"10-4, 1-Adam-12. My ETA is three minutes."

"Copy that, Sheriff-1. They're securing the body now… hold up — looks like there's another one further down. I can see a body or maybe clothing."

A silence pressed between the static. Douglas's knuckles whitened on the steering wheel.

"Dispatch, this is Sheriff-1. What's the 10-20 on Delta-5?"

"Delta-5's 10-76, Sheriff. ETA ten minutes. The evidence van is loading up now."

"Copy that. Have Echo-6 send photos of the victims to my phone as soon as possible."

"10-4, Sheriff-1. Echo-6 notified."

Sheriff Douglas eased off the gas as the reflection of flashing lights appeared ahead, rolling over the riverbank. He pulled up to the landing and parked next to Deputy Jamison's patrol car.

He stepped out, breathing in the air thick with the scent of river mud and wet pine as his boots sank into the mush. Two deputies stood near the water, using telescopic poles with large body hooks attached, to ease the motionless figure up onto the bank.

Sheriff Douglas thumbed the mic-button clipped to his shoulder.

"Dispatch, Sheriff-1 — 10-97, Jenkins Landing."

"10-4, Sheriff-1."

He slowly glanced around, listening to the wind moving through the reeds and the murmurs of men who'd already seen too much today.

Jamison was talking to two fishermen near the boat ramp — mud-caked boots, heavy jackets, and faces weathered by more than the cold. One gestured wildly as he spoke, his words rolling out faster than his thoughts. The other hung back, pale and silent, eyes fixed on the water as if afraid it might reach out and drag him under.

Sheriff Douglas moved closer, hearing part of the man's story as he stuttered nervously. The younger deputy looked up, relief flickering in his eyes briefly, before turning back to continue taking notes.

"— was just casting my line when I saw somethin' floatin' up by the reeds," the animated fisherman said, voice shaking. "Thought it was driftwood till it didn't drift right. Then I saw the head."

The Sheriff followed the man's gesture and continued down the riverbank, where thick grass had been forced to bow under the weight of the passing storm. The coroner liaison had already placed the first body face up in the open body bag as J.T. approached.

The dead man was dressed in dark jeans, heavy work boots, and a thick canvas jacket that looked out of place for fishing on the river. Sheriff Douglas crouched beside him, looking at the man's face for some sign of recognition as Deputy Tony Bass, the coroner liaison, continued preparations for transporting the body. The ground was chaos — boot prints layered over tire tracks, drag marks dissolving into slick earth — but nothing distinct enough to indicate foul play. The storm had scrubbed it clean.

"Can you give me an approximate time of death, Tony?" he asked while continuing to study the body.

"Not definitively, Sheriff, but I would guess somewhere between 12-24 hours, but we won't know for sure until the autopsy is done,"

He straightened up, eyes focusing downriver. Twenty yards away, the tall grass thickened into a wall of green where the second body was supposed to be.

He moved closer until he saw the second man: half-hidden, water lapping against his back. The body was wedged under a fallen branch, with a baseball cap still clinging to his head like it was bolted on.

The sound of tires crunching gravel caught his attention as a black unmarked sedan rolled to a stop beside the patrol units. The driver's door opened, and Detective Brandy Phillips stepped out — all business, gloves, a digital recorder, and a camera already in hand. She ducked under the crime-scene tape and made her way towards the sheriff, her boots sinking into the same soft earth.

Sheriff Douglas keyed his radio.

"Dispatch, this is Sheriff-1. Confirm two deceased at Jenkins Landing. Delta-5 is 10-97."

"10-4, Sheriff-1."

"Afternoon, Sheriff," greeted Detective Phillips, voice low. "Heard we've got two."

Douglas nodded. "You heard right. First one's bagged. Second one's in the reeds."

Detective Phillips moved closer towards the floating body, scanning the head, the clothing, and then the waterline.

"No wallet, no ID?"

"No one's touched this body yet, and there's nothing on the other one," Douglas said, pointing in the opposite direction. "Tony Bass, not too long ago, pulled him out."

She nodded once, then turned back towards him.

"I'll start down here. Looks like he got caught before the current could take him. Might be some clues left along the grass line."

The Sheriff nodded as the hairs on his skin got that prickly feeling whenever he was at the scene of a questionable death.

"You may want to do it quickly," he called out as she started moving away. "The current's not on our side today."

As Detective Phillips disappeared into the reeds, the wind started to pick up again, carrying the smell of the river along with the presence of something colder — something that didn't belong to the water at all.

Sheriff Douglas continued to scan the surrounding area and waterline when a flash of silver caught his eye. He squinted, stepping closer to the river's edge.

A canoe. Metal, dented, half-buried in the water.

He stepped closer, brushing the grass aside. The boat was empty, its bow lodged against the muddy bank, one oar still inside. The paint was scraped and dull, like it had been dragged or flipped. He couldn't tell yet if it belonged to either man — but he would find out.

"Jamison," he called.

The deputy looked up, nodded once, and made his way over. His boots squelched with each step.

"You get anything from the witnesses?" J.T. asked.

Jamison flipped his notebook open. "Fishermen recognized the one lying face up —Dylan Tyler. Used to do maintenance out at the fairgrounds before he moved up to working as a night guard. The other guy," he gestured towards the man face down in the river, "they think that's Jeb Howser. The two were thick as thieves. Always together. And, they just happen to be two of the witnesses we interviewed."

J.T. felt a knot forming in his gut. "Both guards," he said quietly.

"Yes, sir."

He looked out at the river again. Two guards from Donovan's crew. Two men who'd been on the losing end of a fight just days ago — and now they'd both drowned in a storm, in the same stretch of river, in the same boat.

"Fishing accident?" Jamison said after a moment, as if trying to convince himself. "Storm came up, boat flipped. Happens."

"Yeah," J.T. muttered, though his tone made it sound like a curse. "Happens."

He knelt beside the body bag again, studying the man's appearance. The body hadn't been there long — his jacket still held its color. But there were small details that didn't fit: no life vest, no gloves, no rods or tackle, nothing in or around the canoe but an oar. And both men were fully dressed, jackets zipped. Not how people went fishing — not around here, anyway.

J.T. rose slowly, one hand pressed to the small of his back. He could feel Jamison's eyes on him.

"You all right, Sheriff?"

"Fine," he lied, as his mind began writing an uncomfortable narrative in his head.

A pattern was forming, clear and precise. Two local guards who had failed at their job in dealing with an intruder decided to go fishing at night in a metal boat on the river during an approaching thunderstorm. A ruthless, unforgiving boss who had a hidden agenda yet to be revealed. A storm that covered the sound of anything. A river that washed away evidence.

It was too neat. Too perfect.

The wind picked up a little more, brushing the tall grass so that it whispered like voices just out of reach. Sheriff Douglas turned and stared at Deputy Jamison with an expression that conveyed a sense of urgency.

"Find Jackson," he said finally. His voice had gone cold, authoritative. "He's probably at Del's. Ask him to come down to my office as soon as possible."

Jamison blinked. "Yes, sir."

"Politely," J.T. emphasized, locking eyes with him. "He's not a suspect in this case. I just want to talk to him about another unrelated matter. Make sure he understands that."

Jamison nodded. "Understood, Sheriff."

They heard the distant rumble of another approaching vehicle — tires grinding on gravel as the Mobile Evidence Unit/Crime Scene Investigation van approached. J.T. watched as a CSI technician stepped out and began unpacking tarps and evidence markers. Jamison met him halfway, passing off his notes and filling him in on the fishermen's statements.

As the teams went about their work, J.T. lingered by the bank one last time. He looked down at the canoe glinting dully in the water, then at the motionless forms that had once been men caught up in the wrong place at the wrong time.

He felt a flicker of anger flare up somewhere deep in his chest.

This was Donovan's doing, and he wasn't going to stop here.

Sheriff Douglas exhaled slowly, trying to relieve the pressure growing in his head. "God help us," he murmured.

Jenkins Landing faded in the cruiser's rearview mirror as he drove down the empty highway. Ahead, the road curved back towards town, towards the quiet office where he hoped to find the information he would need for the upcoming battle he had been forced to undertake.

J.T. tightened his grip on the steering wheel, his eyes fixed on the horizon. The wipers smeared the windshield as a sudden rain shower blurred the world into gray streaks.

Two men dead, a girl marked for disappearance, and a madman working in the shadows. He had no plan yet, but the beginning of one was forming in the same place where fear had taken hold of him not long before.

"Not on my watch," he whispered under his breath as the engine growled beneath him.

The Sheriff turned onto a service road towards Bishops Creek as the car's tires hissed over the wet road, sounding like a loose air hose. The rain followed him all the way back to town, then suddenly stopped as if a door had closed at the city limit, prohibiting the bad weather from entering. He drove slowly through the back streets of Bishops Creek, looking for any additional damage or potential problems.

Finally, he turned into the narrow street where the Sheriff's Office stood — a squat brick building with faded letters that read:

BISHOPS CREEK POLICE DEPARTMENT.

The storm had washed the air clean but had left behind the faint smell of ozone and wet earth. J.T. parked the cruiser in his reserved spot, shut off the engine, and sat in the car for a long moment before entering the building.

He wasn't ready for another conversation, but there was no time left to wait. Donovan was closing his circle tighter and tighter each day, and now the river had given him two warnings wrapped in pale, wet skins.

Inside, the building was busier than usual, with much of the electronic documentation being done manually due to the administrative systems operating at only two-thirds power. Deputy Jamison had returned to the station and was at his desk writing a field report as J.T. entered.

"Jackson's here, Sheriff," Jamison said. "Got him waiting outside your office like you asked."

J.T. nodded, unbuttoning his jacket. "Did he ask you why I wanted to talk to him?"

Jamison hesitated, reading the weight in his voice. "Yes, sir. I said that you just wanted a word. He didn't seem worried."

"Good." The Sheriff's tone carried finality. "You can head back down to Jenkins Landing for any follow-up needed, and make sure the investigator has everything she needs before they pull out."

"Yes, sir," Jamison replied as he grabbed his hat and left, the door swinging shut behind him.

For a few seconds, the Sheriff stood still in the silence that followed, breathing through his nose, steadying himself. Then, he proceeded down the hall to his office, and, with any luck, a resolution to a problem that had been too long in coming.

Chapter 14 – Two Men, One Truth

Damion sat in a chair across from the Sheriff's office, his posture relaxed but eyes and ears on full alert. He had changed out of the dirty work clothes he'd worn earlier and was now wearing a clean outfit — blue jeans and a faded gray T-shirt that made the bruises along his cheekbone stand out in dull purple hues. He stood up as the Sheriff approached.

"Afternoon, Sheriff," Damion said.

"Jackson," J.T. returned the greeting with a nod, beckoning for Damion to follow him into the office while walking around behind his desk. He gestured toward the coffee pot in the corner. "Close the door and help yourself. It's fresh — or close enough."

Damion shook his head. "I'm good."

The Sheriff sank into his chair as the old springs protested with a low groan. For a long moment, the room was heavy with silence. J.T.'s eyes lingered on Damion's face, taking in the bruises, but he didn't ask how they got there.

"You hear about the storm damage by the pier at Jenkins Landing?" J.T. asked finally, voice casual, but his eyes never leaving Damion's face.

Damion shook his head. "I don't know where that's located, but I've only heard about downed power lines and flooded roads, mostly from the radio."

The Sheriff nodded slowly. "You might've heard wrong, then. There are no downed power lines out there. Only two men, who were found floating in the river this afternoon. Possibly a boating accident."

Damion's jaw flexed once, but he said nothing.

"They worked at the fairgrounds," J.T. continued. "Went missing sometime last night. It appears that they decided to go fishing in the middle of a thunderstorm."

"That so?" Damion asked, voice steady. "No disrespect to the dead, but that doesn't sound very smart."

"No, it doesn't, but that's what the story'll say." The Sheriff leaned back, folding his hands over his stomach. "But me — I don't like stories that come too neatly packaged."

The silence between them stretched, filled only by the faint whine of the generator outside the building. J.T. studied Damion — the way he kept his shoulders loose, how his fingers stayed still against the armrest. A man who knew not to move unless it was necessary.

"You've been busy since yesterday?" the Sheriff asked.

"Helped Del clean up her yard after the storm," Damion said. "That's about it."

"She's a good woman," J.T. said absently, tapping his fingers once on the desk. "I hear her boy likes you."

"Kids like anybody who doesn't tell them they have to brush their teeth."

The Sheriff gave a small chuckle. It didn't last. "You get any rest last night?"

"Some, but that storm didn't make it easy. I was expecting a tree to come flying through Del's roof at any time."

"That's good," J.T. said, though his voice suggested he wasn't really talking about sleep anymore.

"You see, Jackson, I keep thinking about those two men in the water today. I shouldn't be sharing this, but Tyler and Howser were their names. Worked night security at the fairgrounds. They were alive less than forty-eight hours ago, and had gotten into a scuffle with someone who handed both of them their hats Saturday night. Somebody who, after beating them both unconscious, walked away and left them breathing."

Damion's eyes met his. "You got a point, Sheriff?"

"Maybe."

The Sheriff reached into his pocket, pulled out his phone, and set it on the table. He swiped through a few images, the faint glow of the screen cutting across his weathered face. He turned the phone and slid it across to Damion.

"Pictures came in from the coroner. These are the two we pulled from the water."

Damion hesitated only a second before looking.

The photos were clinical but clear — the two men laid out on a stainless-steel table, water still glistening in their hair, skin pale under the LED light. One had a split lip and bruising around the eye; the other bore a deep gash along his temple. The cap he'd worn was placed neatly beside him. Death had washed away their cruelty, leaving them looking almost human again — but Damion knew those faces. The armed guards. The ones he'd fought on the stage in the dark at the fairgrounds. He felt a jolt in his chest, but maintained his composure with a perfect poker face.

J.T. studied him closely. "The sight of dead bodies doesn't bother you? Not even a little bit?"

Damion looked at him with a smirk, "This is not my first time looking at dead bodies, Sheriff. Comes with the job."

"Oh yeah, I forgot – Chief Master-At-Arms," he replied, nodding. "You ever seen these two before?"

Damion's eyes didn't move from the screen, but the lie formed easily — clean, practiced. "No, Sheriff. Can't say that I have."

The Sheriff's gaze lingered. He'd been doing this too long not to feel the ripple in the air when a man lied — the faint tightening around the mouth, the pause that's half a breath too long. But he didn't call it out. Not yet.

"Strange," J.T. replied casually. "Because they sure had reason to be where you were."

Damion met his eyes again, unflinching. "I'm not sure I understand what you mean, Sheriff, but if they were anywhere in my vicinity, it wasn't because of me."

J.T. exhaled, leaned back in his chair, and reclaimed his phone. The light from the screen disappeared, and with it, the faintest hint of hope that maybe the truth would surface on its own.

"Well," he said after a moment, "I suppose the river's the only one who knows what really happened out there."

He slid the phone back into his pocket, then drummed his fingers against the desk — slow, thoughtful.

"You're not officially under suspicion for anything yet, Jackson," he continued, "but I've been doing this job long enough to know when something stinks. And the air around this town is starting to smell like rot."

"I've noticed," Damion replied.

"Then maybe," the Sheriff said, leaning forward slightly, "you and I should make sure it doesn't spread."

"You and I?" Damion asked guardedly.

For a moment, neither man spoke, with the only sounds now coming from the busy outer office muted in the background, as the staff and emergency workers continued their efforts to return the station to its full operational state. Sheriff Douglas leaned back in his chair, the leather sighing again under his weight. The afternoon sunlight cut through the blinds in pale stripes that fell across the desk, creating a silhouette of prison bars across the folder sitting between them.

"I ran a background check on you," the Sheriff began, his voice steady, but suggestive. "Don't take it personally, but you've been orbiting around some messy business in my town, and just so that we understand one another, I like to know who's standing either by my side, or in my rifle's crosshairs."

Damion sat silent in the chair opposite him, hands resting on his knees, his expression unreadable. He'd been through this before — different offices, same tone. Authority figures liked to measure men like him before deciding which box to put them in. This was no different. Sheriff Douglas flipped the folder open and let out a low breath.

"Baltimore boy. Joined the Navy right outta' high school. Boot camp down in Florida, then off to Master-at-Arms 'A' school. Multiple duty stations - all with outstanding performance evaluations, a Secret security clearance, and no disciplinary marks. Promoted like clockwork every time you became eligible, right up to Chief Petty Officer. That's not easy."

He turned another page, his brow furrowing. "Weapons expert, and you're also highly decorated. Twenty-plus medals and awards; some of these, I'll be honest, I've never even heard of." He glanced up, studying Damion closely. "Whatever they had you doing, it wasn't just paperwork and gate checks."

Damion didn't answer as his eyes shifted towards the window, the faintest twitch in his jaw the only sign of life.

Sheriff Douglas kept going, voice lower now. "You aren't special ops, but it looks like you may have trained with some of them. Kali, Krav Maga, Muay Thai — stuff that's meant for getting up close and personal. That's not Navy standard issue training from what I'm told."

He closed the folder slowly and leaned forward, elbows resting on the desk. "I've heard about your asking around town about the Feather & Fork and the girl, as well as your... let's just call it *research*." When Damion didn't respond, the Sheriff continued.

"Before that thunderstorm blew in Sunday afternoon, Deputy Jamison had already gone back to the fairgrounds to look for clues to help identify the assailant from Saturday night. Can you believe that he actually found blood on the stage where the fight took place? It could have belonged to the guards, or maybe it belonged to the attacker," he said with a smile, eyeing Damion closely. "He was about to send it to the state lab for processing before I stopped him. Do you know why I did that, Jackson?"

"I'm sure you are going to tell me," Damion replied, making no attempt to hide his impatience.

"Because I believe that that blood…is yours, and if it is, then I would have to arrest you on probable cause for trespassing, aggravated assault, and battery against those two men in the morgue. After the fact, of course. But," he paused for a moment, "that wouldn't benefit me at all."

Damion allowed the anxiety that had slowly been building inside of him to turn into a low-simmering anger, not the fighting kind, but the kind that allowed him to focus on a problem and adapt to unexpected situations.

Sheriff Douglas continued.

"You strike me as the type of man who always follows the rules, Jackson. Crossing every 'T' and dotting every 'I' - *until* the rules get someone you care about hurt. I fully understand that the Navy gave you training and discipline, Chief." He paused, eyes narrowing. "But life gave you principles, a moral compass, and a commitment to justice."

For a long moment, neither man moved; each one sizing up the other as if checkmate was only one move away. Damion suspected where this conversation was heading, but he needed more details, and he was not going to be the one to place his cards on the table first. Something had the Sheriff on edge, and Damion had a strong suspicion of what or *who* it was. Before he could finish his thoughts, J.T. spoke again.

"I need your help, Jackson," he said, leaning forward with his forearms on the desk. "I'm taking a huge chance here, but I think you are the only one I can trust to help me with this situation."

"Help you with what, Sheriff? I don't know how long I'm going to be here," Damion replied.

"Bull," J.T. replied flatly.

"Excuse me?" remarked Damion, surprised by the abrupt response.

"I said, *bull*, Jackson. You and I both know that you have no intention of leaving here until you find out what happened with that girl, or you get yourself broken up or killed like those two idiots did."

The air in the office felt thick with the kind of silence that builds between men who know too much. Sheriff Douglas stood up slowly and began to pace around the small room. The soles of his boots, still wet from the mud and damp earth, squeaked faintly on the tile. He moved towards the window and stared out through the narrow blinds into the dimly lit outer office. The desks out there were half full — paperwork stacked in crooked piles, phones ringing, coffee cups half-finished.

J.T. took a long, steady breath and exhaled through his nose.

"My problem," he said quietly, his voice low but taut, "is a man named Sebastian Donovan."

"The white suit," Damion replied, revealing that he wasn't entirely in the dark about who was running things.

The Sheriff turned, caught off guard. For a heartbeat, the surprise, and maybe even a little caution, flickered on his face before he nodded once. "Yeah," he answered. "The white suit."

He leaned back against the edge of his desk, folding his arms, as if bracing for the story he was about to tell.

"When Donovan first came to Bishops Creek, he acted like he was the town's savior. Bought the Feather & Fork plant after it went bankrupt, said he wanted to put locals back to work. He showed up with promises and clean money, the kind that doesn't smell bad until much later."

He began pacing again, one hand rubbing at the back of his neck. His voice carried a weight that felt years old.

"He offered me and my deputies some extra income on the side — security work during renovations. It sounded harmless enough. The pay was good, cash, tax-free, and no questions asked. I figured it'd boost morale. Maybe keep a few families from struggling too much in this economy." He paused, shaking his head. "Should've known better. I learned too late that that man never does anything without an angle."

Damion said nothing. His gaze followed the Sheriff's slow movements, reading the cracks in his voice more than the words themselves.

"At first," J.T. continued, "he was all smiles. Always talking about community, about helping folks. But then he started making little comments — about how grateful he was for the department's 'understanding' when it came to overlooking a few minor infractions by his crew. I didn't see the hook until I was already on the line."

He moved behind his desk, resting both hands on the back of his chair, leaning into the memory. "One day, a truck from his plant got pulled over — migrant workers in the back, no papers. One of my deputies was only doing his job. But Donovan called me that night, said he thought we had an understanding. Told me that he didn't appreciate the unnecessary interference."

The Sheriff's voice went hard. "I told him I'd handle it. And I did. I talked to my men and made sure it didn't happen again. After that, he knew he had me."

"Then came the box," J.T. said quietly.

Damion's eyes narrowed slightly. "Box?"

The Sheriff nodded, his jaw tightening. "Showed up at my office one morning. No note, no return address. Just an expensive black-and-gold coffee mug. On one side, my badge and the town's motto. On the other..." His voice faltered for a moment. "...was a photo of my daughter and grandkids. Smiling. Playing in a park another state over.

Someone took it without her knowing. Under the picture, it said — 'Thank you for protecting us every day, Grandpa.'"

He let the words hang there, the sound of them colder than anything outside.

"I didn't need to call her," he said, his voice barely above a whisper. "She didn't send it. The message was clear — Donovan had eyes everywhere, and I'd crossed a line I couldn't uncross."

He turned then, meeting Damion's gaze squarely. "That's when I stopped being the Sheriff in charge of this town and became a man working for someone else."

For a long moment, neither man spoke. J.T. sat down heavily, rubbing his forehead with both hands.

"I can't move against him, Jackson. Not without putting my family in danger. But you…" He looked up, eyes sharp again. "You don't owe this town anything. Donovan doesn't know what you can do. If you can get me something solid — something the feds can't ignore — I can make a case without him ever knowing where it came from."

Damion leaned back slightly in his chair, his arms resting on the sides. He stared at the floor for a long while before finally speaking.

"This isn't my fight, Sheriff. I didn't come here to play hero. You've got family to think about — I get that. Maybe it's time you pack up, take them, and start over somewhere else."

J.T. gave a bitter laugh. "Start over? A man doesn't get the opportunity to start over when the devil's already sitting at the dinner table and demanding second helpings of your favorite meal."

Damion's tone stayed even, but there was iron underneath.

"Look, all I care about is doing right by the girl. She's the one who's been through hell. That's my only fight."

The Sheriff studied him quietly. There was no false nobility or arrogance in Damion's voice, just a flat conviction. The kind that's rarely seen in public these days, thought J.T.

"Then maybe you'll want to hear what I have to say next," he said. He hesitated, lowered his voice, and stared Damion straight in the eyes.

"Donovan is planning on killing the girl."

The words came out like a confession, heavy and final.

Damion's expression didn't change, but the temperature in the room seemed to drop.

J.T. continued, his voice tightening. "He told me himself, in so many words. He's waiting for Child Protective Services to pick her up. She will be transported out of the county and processed at a state facility. But somewhere between Bishops Creek and the CPS office, his men will intercept the car. They'll probably make it look like an accident. The case worker and the girl — both silenced."

For a moment, the only sound in the room was the ticking of the wall clock.

Damion's jaw set hard. The muscles in his cheek tightened. He didn't move, didn't speak. But his eyes changed — the calm surface giving way to something darker underneath.

The Sheriff felt a chill as he watched it happen, the quiet anger that rolled through Damion like a storm front.

"I'm not dirty, Jackson. I will not have that girl's death on my conscience, but you understand why I can't stop him outright," J.T. said softly. "He's watching everything I do. Every call, every patrol, every car that leaves the station. If I make a move, my family will suffer for it."

Damion finally spoke, his voice low and edged. "You've got yourself tangled up with a man who doesn't believe in the lines, Sheriff. You think he's going to let your family go when he's done with Bishops Creek?"

J.T. didn't answer. He didn't have to. The silence was his reply.

Damion exhaled through his nose, his pulse loud in his ears. He'd seen this before — in ports and deserts, in alleys overseas where men traded lives for leverage. He'd thought he'd left it behind.

Then Douglas asked, quietly but with a weight that filled the space between them.

"So, will you help me or not? Because I need to know who I'm dealing with right now, Jackson — the Navy Chief..." he paused. "...or the man they stopped writing reports about?"

The question hit like a challenge and a plea all at once.

Damion looked up slowly, meeting the Sheriff's gaze head-on. For a second, neither of them blinked.

Finally, Damion said, "Depends on which one you need."

J.T. nodded once, as if he'd been waiting for that answer.

"I need the man they stopped writing about," he said quietly.

The tension between them shifted — no longer adversarial, but forged into something else: a mutual understanding, mutual necessity, and a single focus towards a common goal.

Damion leaned forward, elbows on his knees. "What exactly is it you want me to do?"

The Sheriff drew in a long breath, unlocked the bottom drawer of his desk, and pulled out a folder. He placed it between them, flipping it open to reveal photographs of Donovan's plant.

"I need proof, something irrefutable," J.T. said. "Donovan keeps his hands clean, but everything runs through that facility. I believe he's using it as a cover — counterfeit goods, maybe drugs, maybe worse. The plant is just outside the city limit, so I can't report anything based on a rumor. I need something that will get the state police or the feds' attention. You find it, I'll make sure it lands on the right desk without ever touching mine."

Damion studied the papers in silence, his mind already tracing angles and entry points.

"Security?" he asked.

"I would assume that they have rotating patrols like at the fairgrounds," J.T. said. "Donovan brought some of the ones in the plant with him, so they may have better training than Tyler and Howser.

Damion closed the folder. "Then that's where I'll start."

The Sheriff nodded, though his expression stayed grim. "Be careful, Jackson. Donovan's not just dangerous, he's smart and tactical. The kind of man who makes people vanish without any noise."

Damion stood, slipping the folder under his arm. "Noise isn't my problem," he said.

J.T. rose too, much more slowly, the years and the current situation weighing heavily on his movements.

"You really think you can take him down?"

Damion looked toward the window, where his reflection blurred, ghostlike. "I don't need to take him down," he said. "I just need to make him bleed. Let the DOJ sharks do the rest."

The Sheriff didn't respond. He only nodded once — not in approval, but in understanding. The kind shared between two men who both knew they were past the point of turning back.

As Damion reached the door, J.T. added quietly, "Jackson — if you find something, and if it goes the way I think it might, you make sure that the girl walks away from this. No matter what happens to the rest of us."

Damion paused with his hand on the knob.

"She will," he said. "I'll make sure of it."

After Damion left, Sheriff Douglas stood alone for a long time, staring at the closed door. He knew that another storm was coming, one that would change the lives of everyone involved for better or for worse.

He finally sat back down, folded his hands together, and whispered a quiet prayer — not for forgiveness or personal salvation, but for time.

Chapter 15 – The Unsworn

The unusually high humidity in the night air hung thick and heavy over Bishops Creek. Every surface glistened faintly, and every movement left behind a thin sheen of sweat. Even the insects were quiet, with their usual nighttime chorus muffled beneath the damp stillness that clung to everything.

Damion crouched by the tree line, his breath shallow and steady. He was clad once again in his black MIO uniform, boots, balaclava, and full-fingered gloves. But tonight, there was no firearm and no knife. Just the Canon PowerShot G7 X III compact camera in a zippered pocket, and the twin improvised batons strapped to his back, which he could quickly discard if necessary. Each baton was crafted from the handle of a broken broomstick he'd bought earlier that day. Beneath the black electrical tape that wrapped them tightly were five lightweight metal rods for self-defense blocks and striking. Improvised, but lethal enough if used correctly.

When he'd told Del about his conversation with Sheriff Douglas and his plan earlier that evening, she hadn't questioned him or attempted to dissuade him from going to the plant. She'd sat on the couch in silence, watching her son play with his toy cars in the center of the small living room. Her fingers twisted the edge of a dish towel in her lap. "Just be careful," was all she'd said. He had nodded once, because anything more would have been a promise he couldn't keep.

Now, he had parked Del's car a mile from the Feather &
Fork plant and moved in on foot through the night's
drifting haze.

The humidity was unnatural, thick as soup, and sticky like
oil on his skin. It coated everything around him, giving the
world a fantasy-like shimmer. Soon, the poultry plant
loomed in the darkness. A monolith of steel and concrete,
its presence too industrial for the wild, overgrown field that
surrounded it. The perimeter fence caught the floodlamps'
light, turning it into a silver grid that shimmered faintly in
the mist.

Spotlights hummed overhead, carving pale cones through
the humid air, their beams refracting into faint halos. The
parking lot gleamed with a mirror-like sheen, as rows of
yellow-lined parking spaces stretched in perfect order.
There were only two vehicles on the front side of the
building: a black van parked crooked near the loading bay
and a white sedan stationed near the front entrance.
However, there was no guard at the main entrance.

Damion crouched behind several company vehicles near
the outer fence, their roofs damp and reflecting distorted
glimmers of light. He scanned the scene methodically,
tracing the fence line, the dips in the terrain where drainage
had failed, and the fixed ladder bolted near the west corner
of the building. His eyes caught the faint glint of an open
storm drain, a possible exit route if things got out of hand
and went south.

He'd mapped the surveillance zones previously during his
daylight visit. The stationary cameras hadn't changed

positions and there were no indications of any hidden security systems. Donovan wasn't running a government lab — just a disguised operation in an old poultry facility. Hidden cameras cost a lot of money. And Donovan, as careful as he was, most likely preferred to rely on intimidation instead of technology.

Through the slits of the reinforced windows, the facility seemed to pulse faintly with life. One office light glowed steadily on the upper floor — a thin gold rectangle suspended above the dark shell of the building. The blinds shifted in the artificial draft, creating shadows that moved across the wall like gestures made by unseen hands.

The production floor below was intermittently illuminated by timed sensors, flaring in white bursts before fading again. Each flash exposed something sterile and cold: the arc of a conveyor belt, the glint of a stainless-steel blade, the ribbed underside of an assembly platform. Between the flashes, the building seemed to hold its breath.

Steam rose periodically from the external storage vents in slow, ghostlike tendrils. The humidity made the vapor linger longer than usual, hanging in sheets that rippled like smoke in the night air.

Down at the loading docks, a hydraulic lift sat half-lowered, dripping condensation that spattered against the pavement with rhythmic patience. The metallic plink echoed faintly against the corrugated walls.

Then, movement — a faint silhouette inside the dock, bending over a pallet, pausing, then disappearing into the shadows.

Damion checked his watch. It was just past midnight. No legitimate poultry operations ran this late. And no cleaning crews.

He stayed low, watching the entire building and listening to the night sounds around him. Then came the sound of a metallic click near the dock, followed by the brief scrape of steel against concrete. Damion held his breath while observing the loading bay. A moment later, the light in the upper office dimmed, as if someone had decided that they had worked enough for the night and was about to leave.

As he waited for the unknown person to exit the building, the sound of an approaching engine drew his attention. He shifted into a crouch and pivoted as headlights washed over the far gate. A white cargo truck rolled in slowly, its tires crunching against the gravel. The air around it distorted in the heavy humidity, like a mirage on the move.

The truck backed up to the dock, brake lights glowing red against the wet pavement. Two men got out. Both wore dark clothing, their movements sharp and deliberate. They checked the perimeter before reaching into the truck's cab and removing several assault rifles.

Damion adjusted his camera manually. ISO set to high, aperture wide, shutter speed slow — and began snapping multiple photographs. Click. Adjust. Click. The faint whir of the autofocus sounded overly loud in his ears, but he knew that it would be impossible for the men at the dock to hear the camera from this distance, and above the sound of the steam vents.

The men moved to the rear of the truck and opened the door. What followed was a silent procession of human shadows — twenty, maybe more. Migrants. Dirty, thin, moving in tight clusters under menacing orders. A third armed man appeared at the door and waved them inside. Damion kept shooting. Frames of desperation and control — rifles, gloved hands, and the slumped shoulders of men and women lead like cattle without resistance.

Then, silence as the door closed behind them. He waited a full minute before moving. The air clung to him like wet fabric, his breath leaving faint ghosts in the humid haze. He advanced slowly toward the chain-link fence, each step measured. The rhythmic cycle of the security lights pulsed across the yard — sixty seconds bright, sixty seconds dark. He waited for the blackout, then moved quickly while still silently counting in his head.

The fence was weathered, and the lower bolts rusted. He pried one loose with the edge of his baton, lifted the corner just high enough, and slid under as the damp gravel pressed cold against his forearms. On the other side, the air felt denser still, thick with the faint hum of machinery behind the processing plant. The service door was thirty feet away, its keypad light steady, like a single red eye watching whomever would dare to enter. Damion wiped condensation off the panel, studied the worn digits — 3, 5, 9 — and entered them in sequence. The LED flickered green, and the lock disengaged with a faint metallic sigh. He eased the door open slightly, then slipped inside.

The air changed instantly — cooler, with the smell of bleach and ammonia. Fluorescent lights hummed overhead while their sterile white glow stretched long shadows down the corridor.

The walls were scrubbed white up to the ceiling, then gray above. A crooked sign by the elevator read:

Production Level – Authorized Personnel Only.

He ignored it and climbed the steel staircase instead, his boots making soft, hollow clangs that echoed upward into the mesh of ductwork and pipes.

On the second floor, the door marked **ENGINEERING & PROCESSING** opened into a cavernous chamber. Stainless-steel surfaces gleamed under the emergency lights as conveyor belts snaked throughout the space. A light sound caused Damion to freeze. Movement below — faint, but definite. Two figures by the coolant tanks.

He crouched behind a support beam and listened. Their voices floated up, muffled but distinct.

"...border shipments... twenty new ones coming through this week..."

"Boss said to keep them quiet — they don't speak English anyway."

A laugh. Low, harsh.

"They don't need to. Half of 'em can't tell the difference between feed powder and the real stuff. As long as they fill the bags, who cares?"

Damion's stomach turned cold.

The second voice chimed in. "You hear what they're doing down south? When they catch a bunch of migrants, they don't turn 'em in to ICE anymore. Half of 'em get fed the product in baggies and sent back across the border as mules. The other half stay here as insurance, they call it, to make sure the mules don't talk to the cops on the other side."

A pause. Then laughter again, like the kind men share when they've stopped seeing people as people.

"My brother works the border for Donovan. Got me this gig here. He said that one of the migrants, a guy named Miguel, has been 'caught' twenty-four times. Check out these pics he sent me."

Their laughter echoed off the walls as they disappeared down the corridor, scrolling through the photos on his cell phone.

Damion exhaled slowly, steadying the tremor in his hands. He eased behind a pallet stack, crouching low, camera ready. Somewhere below, more movement — a different rhythm now. Chains. Machinery. Then the coughs and whispers of men, women, *and* children.

He knew that sound. Fear breathing through exhaustion.

He crept along the wall until the floor opened up beneath him — a wide overlook. The production floor stretched out below, lit in half-shadow by the flicker of overhead fluorescents.

Migrants lined both sides of a long stainless-steel table, their movements mechanical. Some sorted pills; others packed them into plastic bags; others loaded the bags into boxes marked with frozen-food labels. The stench of chemicals rode beneath the cool air, a synthetic ghost rising through the vents.

Damion began photographing everything. Frame after frame. Then video recording. The whine of the lens motor blended with the droning of the ventilation system. Each photo was evidence. Each second of footage was a lifeline.

Then he saw it — a man looking up.

A migrant near the center of the line, his hands trembling, face slick with sweat. His eyes had caught the faint gleam of the lens above and locked onto Damion's position.

Before Damion could signal for silence, a guard barked at him in Spanish. The migrant froze as the guard strode over with his rifle slung low. He grabbed the smaller man by the collar and drove a fist into his stomach.

"Stop looking up for help," the guard growled. "No one's coming to save you."

The man fell to his knees, gasping. The guard laughed — a cruel, hollow sound that echoed throughout the chamber — then he turned, scanning the catwalk above.

Damion pressed flat to the grated floor, motionless. Sweat soaked the tactical mask as the guard's flashlight swept across the catwalk once, twice, then lowered.

After a long minute, the guard moved on.

Damion backed away, inch by inch, his body low and controlled. He reached the stairwell, pocketed the camera, and slipped back down, retracing his steps through the silent corridors.

When he emerged from the service door, the outside air hit him like a wall — wet and suffocating. The humidity wrapped him tighter now, even more sticky and oppressive than before. He made it to the fence and crouched down just as the service door opened again. Another group of migrants being escorted out by men armed with assault rifles. He snapped more photos. The captives climbed into the same truck, their faces blank and their eyes downcast. The truck doors slammed, and the vehicle rolled out into the night. Damion stayed still, waiting to see if anything else would happen next.

Minutes later, a dark pickup arrived. Two men stepped out, exchanging words with someone inside the plant. The roll-up door opened, and they began loading boxes marked *Frozen Wings* and *Premium Fillets* into the truck bed. When they left, the night went quiet again.

After several more minutes, Damion slipped back through the hole in the fence and vanished into the dark field beyond, every instinct alive and screaming.

Behind him, the processing plant stood still and silent, its floodlights cutting clean through the wet haze — a monument to something far uglier than raw poultry.

The road heading back to Bishops Creek was empty, as the highway shimmered faintly under the Chevelle's bright headlights. Damion drove with the windows down, trying to coax in air that didn't exist. The humidity sat in the car like a living thing—dense, unmoving, and heavy enough to taste. He had changed into a T-shirt and jeans after returning to the car, but the fabric still clung to his back, every movement pulling at the damp cotton.

The rhythmic hum of the tires on the wet road was the only sound that kept him tethered, the only thing preventing his mind from looping back to what he had just seen.

Every time he blinked, the image came back of the plant's production floor bathed in sterile white light, the rows of migrants working in silence, their faces blank, their stiff movements mechanical; how the guard had laughed as his fist connected with the man's stomach. The echo of that hollow sound beneath the hum of the machinery. And that look—brief, wordless, unforgettable—when the migrant had lifted his head and locked eyes with Damion through the haze above. It wasn't fear he'd seen there. It was a beacon of hope. A desperate plea from the powerless to the powerful: *Please, do something.*

He gripped the steering wheel tighter until his knuckles ached.

The clock on the dashboard read 3:17 a.m. as he turned off the main road, onto the narrow gravel path leading to Del's trailer. The tires crunched softly over the damp stones as the car cut a path through the low fog that hovered in the early morning air. Her place appeared in the distance, quiet and dark, except for the single porch light that welcomed him back.

Damion slowed the car to a crawl and rolled to a stop along the edge of the yard. The trailer's windows glowed faintly with the soft amber of a night lamp. Through the thin lace curtains, he could see the slow sway of fabric stirred by the oscillating fan. He turned off the ignition and listened to the ticking of the cooling engine, while the humidity pressed through the open windows, thick and sticky, clinging to his skin like sweat that refused to dry.

For a long moment, he just sat there, staring at the trailer. He pictured Del asleep on the couch, listening for him to come in so that she would know that he was okay. The idea of going inside pulled at him—the comfort of being around another human being that didn't include despair and violence. But he couldn't do it. Not tonight. Not with the weight of what he carried.

He reached for the camera on the passenger seat. The casing was cool, its black metal body slick with condensation. He flipped it on and scrolled through the images.

Faces of prisoners captured mid-motion with hollowed eyes and the men who believed themselves untouchable. He stopped on one photo—the man who had looked up at him from below. The image was slightly blurred, but his expression wasn't. The pleading in his eyes reached through the lens, through the pixels, through time itself.

Damion leaned back in the seat, his head resting against the headrest, eyes closing slowly. Now he had proof of Donovan's operation and maybe enough, at least, to shut down this part of his criminal enterprise. But evidence didn't equal protection for the girl, who had unknowingly drawn the first clues that had led him here.

He set the camera down on the seat and exhaled, slow and measured. The fog outside swirled faintly through the open window, ghosting across the dashboard as the digital clock changed again—3:41 a.m.

Certain that he would not be going inside the trailer, Damion locked the doors and rolled up the windows, leaving just enough space for the outside air to flow in. He picked up the camera again, ejected the small memory card, slid it into its plastic case, and then tucked it deep between the car seat cushions. The camera itself he placed in the glove compartment, as an intentional misdirection in case someone came looking who suspected him of taking photos of Donovan's operation. Damion and the Sheriff were temporary allies, but that didn't mean that he trusted him.

He climbed into the back seat, grabbed his backpack, and used it as a makeshift pillow as he changed position, trying to get comfortable. His muscles throbbed with fatigue—the strain from crawling under fences, holding still on steel catwalks, and moving in silence for hours. But it wasn't the physical ache that kept him awake. It was the graphic echo of what he'd seen and heard. The first-hand knowledge that these men were operating their drug and human trafficking empire, using fear and desperation as weapons on U.S. soil, and sleeping soundly at night. He had seen it many times before around the world, but it still didn't make accepting it any easier.

He shifted slightly, watching the fireflies drifting near the tree line. Their slow, lazy pulses of light moved in rhythm with the faint hum of the crickets returning. The whole scene felt surreal, suspended in some dreamlike balance between night and dawn.

He glanced once more at the trailer and the steady glow of the porch light, finally letting the weight of exhaustion pull him under. He didn't know exactly when sleep found him, but when it did, one image played over and over in his head: a destitute man staring up into the dark, hoping someone out there was coming to rescue him.

Chapter 16 – Where Justice Sleeps

Damion was back on board the *Daniel Shaw*. A young deck seaman stood near the ship's bow, chipping paint with a hammer that didn't sound quite right. *Tap-tap-tap.* The rhythm was soft, too soft, as if the hammer was wrapped in cotton. Damion frowned. This wasn't right. He'd already left the ship. He wasn't supposed to be here.

Tap-tap-tap.

He turned, scanning the deck, but the sound no longer came from the seaman. It was coming from somewhere else; someplace further away. Suddenly, the world around him began to fade away as the ship dissolved into a blur of white fog, with only the tapping sound remaining. Damion slowly blinked, straining his eyes to open in the glaring, early morning sun.

For a moment, he didn't know where he was. The fog of sleep clung to him like a warm blanket until a shape outside the window came into focus. Del. She stood there in a faded sweatshirt loose around her shoulders, her hair tousled, and her eyes full of concern. Sunlight caught the edges of her face as she smiled and tapped lightly on the glass in a cautious way someone might do when waking a sleeping stray dog.

Tap-tap-tap.

Damion sat up slowly, rubbing his face. The air inside the car was musty and heavy, making his shirt stick to his skin.

He cracked open the door, and a wave of humid morning air rolled in — warmer now, carrying the usual faint scent of damp earth.

"Morning," Del said softly. "You planning on staying out here all day, or do you want to come in and grab a shower and something hot to eat?"

"Good morning," Damion replied, glancing past her towards the trailer. He exhaled slowly, the sound more of a sigh than a breath. "I didn't want to wake you when I came back," he said, pushing the door open fully.

Del stepped back, crossing her arms. "You didn't," she said. "But the sound of that car engine clicking at three-something in the morning did. When you didn't come in, I figured you'd gone off again to do something else stupid. Glad you proved me wrong."

He looked at the digital clock — 7:05.

He gave her a faint smile as he climbed out. Del watched him quietly for a moment, then nodded toward the trailer. "C'mon. Shower's cold, but at least it's running. I got coffee and breakfast going. I don't start work until 10, but I'm gonna need your sleeping quarters here to get me there," she said with a smirk.

He hesitated, glancing at the trailer again. The thought of normalcy — breakfast, conversation, maybe even laughter — felt unfair after what he'd seen hours earlier. But the smell of cooked food hit him, and his body reminded him that it had been almost twelve hours since he'd consumed anything that wasn't adrenaline.

He shut the car door and followed her up the steps.

The air inside the trailer was cooler, a small blessing after the weight of the outside humidity. The oscillating fan in the corner hummed quietly, stirring the smell of breakfast through the narrow space — grits, eggs, bacon, coffee, and toast.

Her son sat at the table wearing his pajamas, tapping a spoon against a bowl of cereal and humming to himself. He looked up at Damion with a sleepy grin, then went right back to whatever imaginary song was playing in his head.

"You look like you crawled through hell last night," she said, after he had closed the door behind them.

He almost laughed. "You're not too far off."

"Did you find what you were looking for?" she asked quietly.

Damion locked eyes with her for a moment — long enough to see the worry sitting there, quiet and unspoken. "Yeah," he answered in a low tone. "I did."

Del turned back towards the table, nodding slowly. "You know where the bathroom is," she said. "Clean towels are already on the rack. Go get yourself cleaned up and join me for breakfast."

He started down the short hallway, his boots making faint thuds on the linoleum. Inside the small bathroom, the mirror was streaked from humidity, and the showerhead dripped in a slow, steady rhythm. He turned on the faucet. The water came out in a thin, wavering stream, lukewarm at best, but it was enough. As he stripped off his damp clothes, he caught his reflection in the mirror — eyes bloodshot, jaw tight, and a faint streak of dirt smeared across his cheek. He stood there for a moment, staring, then stepped into the shower.

The bathroom mirror was still fogged when Damion stepped out, the air dense with steam and the slow trail of condensation down the glass. He wiped his face with a towel, feeling cleaner but not lighter. The shower had washed away the dirt, but not the images. He pulled on a pair of clean jeans and a white T-shirt he had taken from his duffel bag, then slung the towel over his shoulder. The faint hum of the oscillating fan and the private laughter of Del and her son carried down the hallway. It should have felt like peace, but instead, it felt like a moment stolen from someone else's life.

He opened the door halfway, listened a second longer, then slipped into the small bedroom where his bag was. He crouched beside the bed, unzipped the bag, and pulled out his laptop. He then reached into a hidden side pocket and removed the SD card — the same one he'd wedged deep into the seat cushions a few hours ago. It felt lighter than it should have, considering the weight of the information it contained.

He slid it into the laptop's port and accessed the card. Images appeared one after another: grainy but clear, each frame a piece of evidence. The truck. The rifles. The guards. The line of migrants working in silence in the production room. Their bodies washed in white light; their faces distorted by malnourishment, exhaustion, and fear.

Damion leaned closer, scanning each frame, checking focus, exposure, details, and timestamps. Evidence — not conjecture, not hearsay. This was solid. Enough to draw attention from outside authorities, if it got that far.

He inserted a small USB drive next — old, dented, disguised as a car diagnostic stick. He plugged it in, then began the transfer.

The progress bar crawled slowly, a thin blue line inching across the screen. 6%... 11%... 17%.

Outside the window, a bird sang — cheerful and quick. The kind of morning sound that didn't belong in the heaviness of the air. He wiped the back of his neck. Even after the shower, he still felt dirty while looking at the photos.

Footsteps moved down the hall — light, deliberate. Del's voice followed, gentle but focused. "Coffee's almost ready."

"Okay," Damion answered, not looking away from the screen. "Be there in a minute."

The footsteps faded again.

He kept his eyes on the bar. 62%. 83%. 94%.

When the transfer finished, he created a second copy, this one tucked into a hidden folder labeled *System Diagnostics*, encrypted beneath layers of meaningless file extensions.

He ejected the SD card and held it between his fingers. Small. Harmless. But it could kill careers, or get people killed.

He slipped it into his pocket then removed the USB drive next. He turned it over, attached a small strip of duct tape to it, then reached under the bed frame and pressed it against the steel rail, where it stuck perfectly out of sight.

He then opened his email application and typed a short, detailed message to four recipients, and uploaded twenty of the photos. The email was saved and given an automatic transmit date of four days from today. A small, invisible insurance policy.

Damion shut down the laptop and slid it back into the bag, pulling the zipper shut. He took one last look around the room — the bag, the bed, the faint trail of moisture on the floor from his shower — then exhaled slowly. Time to play normal again.

Del had two plates waiting at the table when he came in — grits, scrambled eggs, bacon, toast, and two steaming mugs of coffee. Her son had already finished with his cereal and was sitting cross-legged on the couch watching cartoons.

"Morning again," she said without looking up. "Hope the shower helped."

"It did, thanks," Damion replied, eyeing the food hungrily.

Damion sat down as Del took the seat across from him, elbows on the table, and her chin resting on her hands. She watched him eat without saying a word. When he finally looked up, she said quietly, "Whatever you found last night... I can see it on your face."

He set down his fork, the sound of metal against ceramic, small but sharp.

"Yeah," he replied softly. "I guess you probably can." He took a sip of the strong black coffee before continuing. "I took some photos and video inside the processing plant that I can show you if you want, but I think it's better if I don't."

Del nodded slowly, and they continued to eat in silence. She did not ask him what he was going to do next, but both of them knew that whatever peace this morning offered, it wouldn't last long.

As they finished breakfast, the soft clatter of dishes filled the kitchen. Sunlight pressed through the window blinds in thin, hazy bands, cutting across the small table. Damion set his coffee mug down and leaned back in his chair.

"I'm heading over to see Sheriff Douglas this morning," he said. "We need to talk about what I saw at the plant." Then, glancing toward the counter where Del was wiping her hands, he added, "I'll be making a stop at the supermarket to restock your pantry. I've been eating you out of house and home."

Del turned, a faint smile tugging at the corner of her mouth. "You don't have to do that," she said.

"Maybe not," he replied, standing and moving towards her. "But I want to. So, make me a full list — real things, not just coffee and paper towels. And make sure to write down what kind of ice cream your son likes."

At the words *ice cream*, Del's son shot upright from the couch like a spring uncoiled. "Chocolate!" he shouted, his small voice bursting through the room.

They both froze and stared for a second before laughing out loud, breaking all of the tension that had been hanging loosely in the air.

Del shook her head, still smiling. "I guess that answers your question."

———

Damion figured he'd visit the Sheriff first to drop off the SD card, then go to the supermarket before heading straight back to Del's. When he entered the police station, it didn't seem as busy as it had been the previous day, and things looked like they were back to normal operations. Damion informed the front desk officer that Sheriff Douglas was expecting him, and after checking the visitor's list, the officer buzzed him through to the back offices.

The door to the Sheriff's office stood half open as Damion paused outside, with one hand resting on the worn brass handle. He could hear voices inside — low, steady, and formal. Not the tone of small-town lawmen. It was the tone of business.

He knocked three times, then stepped in.

Sheriff Douglas looked up from his desk — startled — and quickly sat up straight in his chair. Across from him stood a man Damion didn't expect to see. Sebastian Donovan. White suit, polished shoes, calm posture. The kind of man who could control a room without saying a word.

The silence that followed his entrance wasn't casual. It was measured — a pause that belonged to men already mid-conversation in a topic not meant to be heard by everyone.

Donovan turned at the sound of the door. The smile that formed on his face reminded Damion of a crooked politician, the kind that came from habit, not sincerity.

"Mr. Jackson," Donovan said, his tone smooth, as though they'd already met before. "We were just talking about you."

Damion didn't answer right away. His eyes flicked from Donovan to the Sheriff, then to the folder on the desk. The office felt smaller than before, as if someone had placed a vice grip tight around the three men who suddenly had too much history between them.

"And, you are?" Damion asked, feigning ignorance of the man in the white suit's identity.

"Sebastian Donovan, but I'm sure you already know that," he said, observing Damion.

The Sheriff cleared his throat. "Jackson, come in. Close the door, would you?"

Damion pushed the door shut, but didn't move closer. His stance stayed firm near the door, arms relaxed but ready.

"Sorry, Sheriff. I didn't mean to interrupt your meeting."

"You didn't," Donovan interjected. "Actually, your timing's perfect."

J.T. rubbed at the side of his badge with his thumb, eyes cast down at the desk.

"Mr. Donovan's been helping us coordinate with some agencies outside the county," he said, his voice careful, as though each word were being weighed before leaving his mouth. "Homeland Security mainly."

Damion nodded once, slowly. "Is that right?"

Donovan's smile widened, just slightly. "We all do our part, Mr. Jackson. Small towns affect the big picture — it's all connected these days. Information flows in all directions."

Sheriff Douglas gave a quick nod, but it looked forced. He adjusted the papers on his desk even though they didn't need adjusting.

"Mr. Donovan's been helping us manage some... ongoing issues that could negatively impact Bishops Creek," he added.

Damion's eyes moved between the two men. The air in the room was thick with something unspoken — not tension exactly, but choreography. Every movement between them was off by half a beat, the way it gets when one man's afraid and the other one knows it.

Donovan turned back toward the window, pulling down the edge of the blind with one finger to peer outside.

"You've made quite an impression in town," he said, conversationally. "Playing the Good Samaritan and rescuing people. That's a rare thing these days."

Damion didn't reply.

"People notice and appreciate good intentions," Donovan continued. "They also notice when a man starts asking too many questions about things that don't concern him."

The Sheriff's chair creaked as he shifted. "Sebastian—"

Donovan lifted a hand and smiled, just enough to silence him.

"What was it that the young people used to say? *My bad*," he said smoothly before continuing. "No harm done, J.T. Curiosity isn't a crime. But it can be... misunderstood."

"That really depends on who's doing the misunderstanding," Damion replied, his voice just sharp enough to make his point.

Donovan met his gaze from across the room, a smile still fixed, but no longer warm.

"Exactly," he replied, with his index finger pointing towards the ceiling.

For a few seconds, no one spoke. The clock ticked on the Sheriff's desk, and somewhere in the outer office, a phone rang twice, then stopped.

Sheriff Douglas exhaled through his nose and finally broke the silence.

"Jackson, maybe you and I could talk later. One-on-one."

Donovan stepped away from the window and smoothed the front of his jacket.

"Oh, I don't think Mr. Jackson is in any hurry, J.T. I'm sure that he can spare a few more minutes of conversation."

Damion glanced towards Sheriff Douglas, whose gaze was downturned, and couldn't even hold eye contact anymore.

He knew, right then, that the walls in this office didn't just close in around the Sheriff. They closed around everyone who walked in. This man owned the Sheriff, through and through.

Donovan's polished shoes made no sound as he crossed the office floor.
He stopped at the edge of the Sheriff's desk, resting one hand lightly on the surface as if to claim it.

"Sheriff Douglas tells me that you've been keeping busy and helping out," he said, his voice easy but deliberate. "It appears that you seem to find yourself in interesting places at interesting times. Day…and night."

Damion stayed quiet.

Donovan tilted his head. "I think you're a man who notices things that others don't. I am too. That can be a strength or a liability depending on how the information observed is used."

The Sheriff shifted in his seat, his voice a low murmur. "Sebastian—"

"I'm only stating facts, J.T. There's no harm in clarity."

He turned back to Damion, eyes sharp behind his smooth exterior and smile like a jackal.

"I like to think of Bishops Creek as an orderly town. Not the kind of place where people go wandering into private property after hours."

The words landed softly, but they carried a lot of weight.

Damion didn't flinch. "I wouldn't know what people in Bishops Creek do with their time after hours. I haven't been here that long."

The Sheriff's pen rolled off his desk and clattered onto the floor. He didn't pick it up.

Donovan stepped closer to him but maintained a proper distance outside of Damion's personal space.

"You were inside my processing plant last night," he said bluntly, voice low and steady. "Don't bother denying it. You moved well, but not well enough. We have footage. Slightly blurred and no facial identification, but sufficient enough to know that the local idiots in this town don't move the way our visitor did last night. I also believe that it was you who attacked my guards at the fairgrounds last Saturday evening."

Damion remained quiet, offering neither a confirmation nor a denial of Donovan's accusations as he continued speculating.

"You see, Mr. Jackson, in a small town like Bishops Creek, it's almost entirely possible to account for everyone's location at any time during the day or night. Everyone, except for you. So, when odd things start to happen, an unknown visitor can quickly become a suspect in all kinds of *unsolicited* behavior."

The Sheriff's face drained of color. "Sebastian—"

Donovan finally turned his full gaze on him. "Relax, J.T. If I wanted him arrested, he'd already be in cuffs. I'm giving him the courtesy of a conversation."

Donovan's mouth curved back into something that wasn't quite a smile.

"I know this because it's part of my business to know. You see, security is a delicate thing. And men like you —very professional and highly-trained men like you —sometimes make a mistake, however small."

He walked to the window again, then looked back at Damion.

"You saw something you weren't meant to see, and I expect that you haven't yet made a mess of it. That shows a certain degree of discipline and restraint. I have much respect for a man who values control."

Damion's reply came accented with a tone that was quiet but harsh. "Even if I had visited your plant, like you said, you have no proof. Also, you tend to talk a lot about control for a man who hides behind it."

Donovan's eyes hardened, just for an instant. Then the sharp smile returned. "We all hide behind something, Mr. Jackson. Uniforms. Titles. Causes."

He adjusted his cufflinks, staring thoughtfully into the air.

"I will put this plainly, for everyone's sake. Let's not even pretend that this is a fight you can win, Mr. Jackson. I know you were there. I know why. And I know who you've been talking to."

The Sheriff's hand trembled slightly as he reached for his coffee mug. The sound of porcelain against the desk was louder than it should've been.

Damion didn't take his eyes off Donovan. "Then say what you came to say; otherwise, this conversation is over."

Donovan folded his hands behind him. "I came to extend to you an olive branch, so to speak, and a warning. Leave it alone. Whatever you think you saw doesn't exist outside of your imagination. There's no story here. No conspiracy. No victims. If you walk away now, you'll never hear my name again."

"And if I don't?"

Donovan smiled again, like a man signing a contract only he can read. "Then I suppose I'll have to make sure you do."

The Sheriff spoke quietly, his voice brittle. "Jackson... just go."

Donovan turned towards the window again, pulling at the blinds with the casualness of a man checking the weather.

"Be careful who you trust, Mr. Jackson. Bishops Creek has a way of burying men who dig too deep."

Damion glanced at the Sheriff, who only looked away.

"By the way, what did you want to talk to Sheriff Douglas about?" Donovan asked, smiling like the predator he was.

"It's a personal matter," Damion answered back, turning towards the door.

"Well then, I guess we will have to talk again later. You have yourself a good day, Mr. Jackson. And say hello to that pretty waitress and her son. What is her name, again? Oh yes, Del."

Damion opened the door and stepped out into the corridor. Donovan's veiled threats, along with the sound of the door closing behind him, felt like the sealing of a steel vault. He didn't have to look back as he headed down the narrow hallway to know that Sebastian Donovan, white suit and all, was still watching. But he didn't care. There was no turning back now. Boundaries were drawn, and lines were crossed.

The only thing left now was taking action.

Chapter 17 – The Shadow That Watches

The low hum of the supermarket's refrigeration units filled the aisle like a steady mechanical heartbeat. Damion stood before the frosted glass doors while his reflection ghosted against rows of colorful cartons and tubs. The cold bled into his palms through the glass as he lingered there, staring into the coffin-shaped freezer. Chocolate. Vanilla. Cookie dough. Butter pecan. So many choices for something that didn't matter—and yet it did. He needed this distraction — a moment to think and regroup after the conversation with Donovan. The mission had gone sideways, and he was burnt.

"I'm more partial to the Rocky Road myself," came a familiar voice behind him.

Damion turned fast, his instincts firing before recognition set in. Pastor Jeremiah Coburn stood behind a cart, smiling with a calm that only came from years of watching storms break over other people's lives.

"Del's son says he likes chocolate ice cream," Damion said, matching the smile as best he could. "Figured I'd grab something else too. I didn't know that shopping for ice cream had become such a complicated process."

"They sure don't make it easy on the parents," Pastor Coburn replied, eyes glinting from the fluorescent lights.

Damion caught the implication, but kept a neutral tone. "Well, regardless of what some people might think, I don't plan on being here long enough for the kid to think I'm anything more than his mother's houseguest."

He pulled a gallon of vanilla from the freezer, the cold mist clinging to his forearm like smoke, then tossed in a box of popsicles for good measure. The two men walked down the aisle together, carts rattling over the polished linoleum.

"Oh, so you've got what you wanted regarding the migrant girl?" Pastor Coburn asked. "That was fast."

Damion stopped mid-step, the wheels of his cart squeaking.

"No. Not even close. But I did have a short meeting at the Sheriff's office—with Sebastian Donovan. He didn't have to say much, and yet, he said a mouthful. The message was clear enough. If I keep digging, people around me are going to get hurt. People like Del and her son. Maybe even you."

The pastor's face sobered. "I understand. Was the Sheriff also present during this meeting?"

Damion nodded slowly.

"Okay, then. So, what's next? You don't strike me as the kind of man to turn tail and run. You got a plan?"

"I'll talk to Del first," Damion said, voice low. "Then I'll figure out the rest. I've got photos and video—proof of what Donovan's doing after hours at that plant. The real evidence is hidden away. After I leave town and things cool down, I'll make sure the right people get them. But for right now," he looked down at the half-full cart, "I'm going to finish filling this thing up, and restock Del's food supply."

"That's a mighty nice thing to do for someone," Pastor Coburn replied softly.

"She's been letting me stay at her place while I try to figure things out. Free of charge. No strings attached. It's the least I can do."

The pastor nodded. "Well, if I don't hear from you or see you in church on Sunday, I'll know that you're gone. You take care of yourself, son, and may the Lord watch over you."

Damion extended his hand. "It was good meeting you, Pastor Jeremiah Coburn—*no relation to the actor, James Coburn.*"

The pastor gave a jubilant laugh before shaking his hand warmly and disappearing down another aisle.

Damion finished filling the cart and checked out, ignoring the cashier's practiced smile and the flirty lingering of her eyes. He loaded the groceries into the trunk and passenger seats of his car, rolled down the window, and pulled onto the two-lane road that cut through the heart of the small town.

The sun rode high in the clear blue sky, painting rooftops and sidewalks with an easy warmth. On Main Street, shop doors were propped open, flags waved lazily from poles, and someone's radio bled faint country music from a garage. To anyone else, the world looked normal again.

But Damion knew better. Donovan's calm wasn't peace—it was a pause before a storm. He was smug, dangerous, and in Bishops Creek—protected. The kind of man who smiled

while sharpening the knife behind his back or loading the next bullet.

Damion turned off the main road and took the familiar gravel curve leading to Del's trailer. Her car wasn't there, as expected, which meant that she was at work and her son was at daycare. Good.

He backed up close to the trailer, then started carrying the first couple of bags up the stairs when he noticed that the front door was slightly ajar.

He froze for an instant before placing the bags down and moving silently up the remaining steps.

Damion gently pushed the door open just enough for a sliver of light to cut through the dim interior. The air was still. He listened carefully, but only heard silence. There were no voices, no footsteps, and no creaking of old, loose floorboards indicative of someone sneaking around inside. Moving in slow, methodical sweeps, he checked each room. Living room. Kitchen. Bedroom. Bathroom. Empty.

Everything looked undisturbed—until he reached the small spare room where he'd placed his travel bags.

His gut tightened.

The place had been torn apart.

The blanket and sheet had been removed from the bed and thrown on the floor. Clothes were scattered around like discarded evidence from the empty travel bags tossed into corners. His laptop sat on the nightstand with the screen punched in, the spiderweb cracks reflecting a thin line of afternoon light. He stepped closer, jaw tightening as he took it all in.

"Message received," he muttered sharply.

His focus then shifted back to the bed. He slowly crouched down to check along the metal frame—the hidden railing where he'd duct taped the encrypted USB—his pulse quickened. The drive was gone.

That's why Donovan had been so overly confident. He thought he'd already won.

Damion straightened up, the corner of his mouth curving into a quiet grin. Always back up the backup. The originals were safe, duplicated, and ready to be emailed. Donovan had stolen a second backup copy, since Damion still had the SD card.

Now, he had to clean up this mess. He gathered his clothes into the bags again, then paused when he spotted the tiny toy cars lined up in the middle of the living room floor—frozen mid-race, waiting for Del's son to come home and start up again.

The anger subsided into something colder. The intruders were very careful, targeting only his belongings. They actually went out of their way not to damage anything belonging to Del or her son. An idea clicked into place as he thought about an old nineties ninja movie where the black-clad assassins had hidden in plain sight.

He called Del, and she answered on the second ring.

"Del, it's me," he said calmly. "Someone broke into your place. Don't panic. Nothing of yours was touched. Just my stuff thrown around. A little warning from Donovan."

Her voice came fast and worried.

"I'll explain everything later," he said. "But right now, it's handled. You and your son are not in any danger. It was just a subtle push for me to back off. We can talk more after you get off work." He hung up before she could argue, exhaled slowly, and set the phone down.

Next task—the food. The groceries went into the refrigerator, freezer, and the cabinets before he sat down at the small table, phone in hand, and pulled up his encrypted email. The time-delayed message he'd queued earlier was still there. He edited it, adjusted the schedule, then hit save again. Damion sat there, thinking about the mess Donovan's men had made. He'd been ready to leave Bishops Creek; to reluctantly cut ties before anyone else got caught up in the crossfire. But then, Donovan had changed the rules while they were having their conversation. He'd made it personal by including Del and her son in his threat.

"Well, I guess I'm staying after all," Damion said to the empty room.

A dog barked excitedly somewhere down the road at a dump truck driving by its fenced-in yard, and the same bird continued singing its song outside the trailer's window. To most people, it was just another beautiful day in Bishops Creek, North Carolina. But to some others, it was a perfect scene whose time had run out. A firestorm was forming on the horizon, and this time, Damion would be the one lighting the match.

The trailer walls felt like they were closing in, the faint hum of the refrigerator throbbing against the silence. Damion stood still for a moment, then exhaled. His chest felt tight. He needed some fresh air.

Stepping out onto the small wooden porch, he closed the door behind him with a hollow thud. The warm, afternoon sun met him full in the face, spreading across his skin like a passing wave. For a moment, he closed his eyes and took a deep breath, filling his lungs with the sweet scent of honeysuckle drifting in the air. He listened as a robin sang from somewhere near the tree line. For the first time all day, he felt a flicker of peace, something fragile and unexplainable, as though nature itself was whispering to him that everything was going to be all right.

Then, he opened his eyes.

At the end of the gravel drive, half-shrouded in dust and shadows, sat a Ford Bronco in full camouflage paint, its dark-tinted windows reflecting the glare. The engine idled with a slow, rumbling growl that vibrated through the still air. The stance of the vehicle—slanted, angled slightly toward him—made it look like a predator crouched before the strike.

Damion's body stiffened, his instincts already mapping distances, cover, and angles.

He crossed his arms and stared at the windshield. Whoever sat behind that glass didn't flinch. The Bronco's engine revved, deep and guttural, like an animal baring its teeth.

Damion took a single step forward.

The Bronco began to roll back—slow, deliberate.

He stopped.

It stopped. The engine growled again, steady now, taunting him.

The two stood locked in silent combat—man and machine, hunter and hunted—until Damion broke the standoff. He turned, locked the trailer door behind him, and walked down the porch steps to his car, deliberate and unhurried.

The Bronco didn't move.

He climbed into the Mustang, started the ignition, and stared at the truck blocking the driveway. He stepped on the accelerator, causing the deep snarl of the 430-horsepower V8 to fill the air. Ahead, the Bronco reversed slowly, backing into the street where it paused there, waiting.

"What are you playing at, Donovan?" Damion muttered to himself.

He gripped the steering wheel, weighing his options. If this was Donovan's idea of intimidation, it was a seriously theatrical one. The smarter move would've been to ambush him inside the trailer, not stage a roadside staring contest; unless this wasn't Donovan's doing at all. Maybe another player is involved? Another motive? Well, there was only one way to find out.

He eased forward until he was almost at the end of the driveway before the Bronco pulled away, heading towards the center of town. Damion followed, maintaining the speed limit and keeping a steady two-car distance between them.

The drive through Bishops Creek carried the illusion of a postcard-peaceful town. Late afternoon light spilling across brick storefronts, with the rhythm of small-town life continuing as if untouched by the outside world. He passed the familiar landmarks: the old bank with its clock tower showing 2:36 pm, the corner barbershop with its rotating red-and-white pole, and the hardware store with tools stacked in the window like trophies.

They slowed through Main Street—thirty-five miles an hour dropping to twenty as they rolled through the heart of town. Locals crossed at faded crosswalks with grocery bags in hand. The sunlight reflected off car windshields and the windows of the small stores lining both sides of the street. A woman swept the sidewalk in front of a bakery, and a small boy attempted to do wheelies down the street on a bicycle.

The Bronco cruised by it all in no rush, its rumbling engine turning heads as it passed by. Damion stayed back, watching for any sign that he was driving into a trap. Past 9th Street. Then, 10th. Then, 11th. At 12th Street, the Bronco's right turn signal blinked once, twice—bright against its mottled paint.

Up ahead, the white steeple of Pastor Coburn's church rose above the trees as sunlight glinted off the cross at its peak. Damion's eyes narrowed, eyeing the front yard to see if the pastor had returned and was out working as usual.

The Bronco slowed, then made a right turn onto 13th Street. It rolled forward fifty feet, then took an immediate left into the church parking lot.

"What the…?"

Damion followed, turning off Main Street, then driving the same route leading into the church parking lot as gravel crunched beneath his tires. The Bronco came to a complete stop near the side entrance to the church. The driver's door swung open, and a man stepped out—ballcap, scraggly beard, denim jacket, heavy build. Damion recognized him instantly. The same guy from the diner booth, the one who'd offered him advice to mind his own business. The man didn't look back as he walked toward the church doors and disappeared inside.

Damion parked at the opposite end of the parking lot, engine idling low before shutting it off. The silence felt heavy. He stepped out, closed the car door quietly, and walked towards the entrance, glancing around for any unwanted surprises.

Inside, the church was as he remembered - bright, modern, and clean. The faint scent of lavender still lingered in the air, fresh and calming, carried by the building's silent ventilation system.

A few people were scattered throughout the sanctuary. Two elderly women sat together near the front; their heads bowed in prayer. Across the aisle, an older man read silently from a worn Bible. And in the far back corner—the ballcap.

The man sat alone, hands clasped, and his gaze fixed forward.

Damion walked slowly down the center aisle, alert and eyes scanning. He turned into the row behind the man and slid into a chair one seat over, close enough for his words to be heard, but not carried around the quiet room.

The man didn't turn. Didn't flinch.

Damion leaned forward slightly, his voice low.

"So, who are you and what do you want?" he asked.

The silence between them stretched long enough to make time feel like an eternity. The man sat motionless, his eyes distant, his breathing uneven. The faint sounds of life beyond their corner faded — leaving only calm, like the air itself had agreed to keep their words private. After a long pause, the man exhaled, the sound breaking the silence like a groan from somewhere deep in his being.

"I come here every day to pray for an answer or a sign," he said quietly, his voice sounding coarse and worn thin by more than just exhaustion. "My name is Jacob. Her name is Marisol."

Damion cocked his head, leaning closer. "*Whose* name is Marisol?"

Jacob's hands twisted together as he spoke. "She's a missing woman. My… friend." His voice caught on the word 'friend', and for a moment, he looked as if he were attempting to swallow it back.

He told Damion that he had been searching for her for weeks — ever since she vanished after coming into town one night.

"Did you file a missing persons report?" Damion asked.

Jacob shook his head. "No. I can't."

"Why not?"

"She doesn't have papers." The words stood heavily between them.

Damion's expression shifted slightly, confusion giving way to realization as Jacob related his story. He described how he had been out hunting and found her hiding in the woods — starved, filthy, terrified — almost a mirror image of the migrant girl Damion had rescued. She spoke English and had begged him not to call the police. She said that she was tricked with the promise of a green card and work in the U.S., and would be put in detention or worse if they came and took her. She promised to work for him instead, if he would only keep her safe.

"She told me she escaped from men who were taking migrants and forcing them to make drugs in some kind of factory," Jacob said. "She didn't know where. One evening, when no one was watching, she took the chance to escape and ran in the dark away from the building. She just kept running until she couldn't run anymore." He stopped, swallowing hard.

"She said others tried to escape, too. She thought they were caught. Maybe killed."

The room felt quieter than before. Whatever weight had been in Jacob's voice was now in Damion's chest as the realizations struck home.

"She stayed," Jacob said. "I didn't intend on it at first, but she stayed. And over time... we got close. Closer than I expected."

Damion sat back slightly, measuring the man, his voice, and trembling hands. When he'd first seen Jacob, everything about him looked wrong: the clothes, the agitation, the impression of someone violent who carried only dark secrets. Damion had assumed that he was the type of person who made people disappear in places like cold, dark cellars, not the one trying to help them or provide them comfort.

Jacob went on. "I thought I was getting close to finding her — until you showed up. You with that migrant girl, asking questions." He shook his head. "After that, the trail went cold. That's why I tried to warn you off. I thought maybe you were part of it, or that they were watching you."

After a brief silence, Damion leaned forward. "Why are you so sure that she was taken? Maybe she decided to leave on her own."

Jacob's eyes lifted, sharp and confident. "Because she was happy with me. She had nothing to go back to, and we were working on getting her legal papers. A real life. She wanted that more than anything." His voice lowered as the quiet between them returned. After a few moments of silence, he continued.

"We got careless. One night, when we were in town, she saw a man sitting in a truck, the same kind used when she was taken the first time. She froze. Another man came up behind us. Big guy, missing a bunch of teeth. When Marisol saw him, she started shaking and whispered, *'It's them.'*"

Jacob drew a shaky breath, rubbing the back of his head. "Next thing I know, I'm on the ground. Someone hit me from behind. When I came to, she was gone. So was the truck. No one saw anything."

He looked at Damion with bloodshot eyes, not from tears, but from sleeplessness and regret. "I didn't recognize the men, but I did see that truck again."

"Where?" Damion asked.

"At the Feather & Fork plant where I work. I'm on the loading docks in the evenings. Saw it pull in a few times — same model, same markings. When I asked the foreman about it, he told me to mind my own business."

Damion's mind raced quickly, connecting dots that seemed to be fitting together more clearly.

"How often do you see it?"

"Every day," Jacob said. "Never the same time, but it's always coming there, and not picking up or delivering chicken."

Damion sat back, his eyes fixed on the man in front of him. The sanctuary felt even more sacred now — the only place left untouched by the corruption and depravity outside its doors. It felt safe to think, to breathe, to plan.

"Maybe," Damion said slowly, "if we work together, we can find out where they're transporting to, and hopefully find your friend. But you need to understand something, Jacob; these people are drug dealers, human traffickers, and most likely murderers. They are not going to take kindly to us messing with their business."

Jacob met his gaze. There was fear in his eyes, but there was something else also - the spark of determination that comes from either having everything to lose, or nothing at all.

He nodded once. "Then, let's do it."

Damion gave a slight nod in return, a plan already taking shape in his head.

Chapter 18 – Whispers Beneath the Skin

Jacob leaned back in his chair, rubbing his palms together as Damion laid out the plan in a calm, measured tone.

"I need you to put an AirTag on the truck," Damion said. "You know what those are?"

Jacob let out a short chuckle. "Course I do," he said. "I use 'em on my dogs."

That caught Damion off guard. He leaned forward slightly, a faint smirk written on his face. *"Your dogs?"*

Jacob nodded, suddenly more animated. "Yeah. They tend to get hurt when we're out huntin' wild animals — hogs, mostly. Sometimes they run off. Easier to find 'em that way. And the AirTags don't charge a subscription like those overpriced GPS collars do."

Damion couldn't help the amused grin that formed. "That's actually… pretty smart," he admitted.

Jacob shrugged. "Practical," he said. "And cheap. But isn't the Bluetooth range limited? How are you gonna' track them?"

"With the global tracking network," Damion replied. "You are correct: the range outdoors is approximately 100 feet, but as long as another cell phone or device in the vicinity of the tag is connected to the network, then we have unlimited tracking capability. And, the beauty of it is that the signal is relayed anonymously, so they won't even know that their phones are helping us track them. When I was at the plant,

I saw guards taking selfies and using the types of mobile phones we need for this to work. Hopefully, the transport drivers will also have the same types. If they do, then we can track them."

"I may be able to help make that less of a hope and more of a certainty," Jacob replied, rubbing the stubble on his face.

They continued discussing the plan in detail. Jacob would go to work early and hang around outside the loading bay until his shift began. If the transporters arrived before then, and he had a clear shot at planting the device on the cargo truck, he would take it. Once that was done, he would immediately contact Damion with a single-worded text.

Damion would then follow the signal to see where it stopped. Hopefully, it would lead them to several other locations in Donovan's operation outside of Bishops Creek that they could either disrupt themselves or make a report anonymously to outside authorities. If other facilities were found, Jacob and Damion would each take a location to hit simultaneously, giving Donovan something else to worry about, such as a rival moving in on his territory.

"Hybrid warfare," remarked Jacob, nodding approvingly.

"Simple, but effective," Damion said. "Maybe there's a chance that we could even find your friend, Marisol, or at least some idea of her location."

Jacob's eyes watered at the sound of her name, a brief spark of light tempered by caution. "That's a really long shot," he said quietly. Damion could see his hope slowly fading away.

"Yes, it is," Damion agreed, his voice steady. "But it's a shot, nonetheless."

Jacob straightened in his chair, resolve forming in his eyes. "Then I'm coming with you."

Damion shook his head. "No. You tag the truck and go back to work like nothing happened. I'll tail it. If something turns up, I'll call you in. Until then, stay clear. The less you're seen, the better."

Jacob looked like he wanted to argue, but stopped himself. "Fine," he muttered. "But if things start to go bad, you'll need backup."

"I promise I'll contact you if I think I will need help," Damion assured him.

They went over the finer details: weapons, supplies, and communications, as well as what actions to take if the tag was discovered. When they finished, Jacob stood, gave a nod of understanding, and said, "I'll head to the plant now. I'll text when it's done."

Damion nodded back. "Be careful," he said.

"I always am," Jacob answered, though his tone carried the weight of a man who'd seen too much enemy action to believe his own words.

After he left, Damion remained seated, staring at the back of the chair in front of him. Jacob was a wild card. Ex-Army Sergeant — he revealed during their conversation. Two tours in the 'Stan. That explained the composure under pressure — and the fatigue behind his eyes. He'd be a good man to have if things turned ugly, but Damion knew better than to trust too quickly. Combat operations made people unpredictable. It carved things out of them that never really healed. Plus, Jacob had a deep, personal connection, which could make his actions even more biased and impulsive.

Damion exhaled slowly, pushing his doubts aside, and decided to head back to Del's trailer.

When he stepped outside, the parking lot was almost empty. Jacob's Bronco was gone, and a black pickup was parked next to his car.

The moment he spotted it, his situational awareness kicked in — not out of fear, but out of instinct.

As he neared his vehicle, both pickup doors opened at once. Two men got out, tall, bearded, and heavyset — built like men who did their talking with their hands, not words. Each one stood a half-foot taller than Damion and twice as broad across the shoulders. Their boots hit the ground with the dull weight accumulated from far too many large meals.

Damion slowed, scanning them without turning his head. He nodded once, planning to walk past them, but the larger of the two men stepped directly in his path.

"Can I help you, gentlemen?" Damion asked, stopping in place. His voice was calm with a tone casual enough to be mistaken for friendly.

The man to his right smirked. "Mr. Donovan wanted to make sure you got his message."

The other one — thicker in the neck, with a face like a slab of meat — let out a laugh that sounded more like a snorting pig than a chuckle.

Damion glanced at him briefly, then looked back at the first man. "Yeah, I got it," he replied flatly. "I'm just not sure what I'm supposed to do with it."

The smirk vanished. The man stepped closer until Damion could smell his breath.

"Then I guess you didn't get it," he said. "But don't worry — we'll make sure you do."

Damion's feet shifted subtly, lowering his stance by inches.

"You mean right now?" he asked, eyes flicking between them with raised eyebrows. "Right here, in the church parking lot?"

The man's grin returned. "That's right. Bubba here is gonna' make sure you… understand. He's the local power slapping champion, so you had better brace yourself, fella."

Damion turned toward the bigger one — Bubba — who was nodding enthusiastically, with a wide, gap-toothed smile plastered across his face.

"Okay then, Bubba," Damion said quietly. "Let's get this over with."

Bubba immediately stopped smiling. He drew his fist back and swung with everything he had — big, clumsy, and slow.

Damion shifted smoothly to his left, dropping to one knee as Bubba's punch cut through empty air. He drove his open palm up hard between the big man's legs.

Bubba made a sound halfway between a grunt and a whine, as his whole body folded inward. He fell to both knees, clutching himself, gasping like a wounded ox.

The second man froze, eyes wide in disbelief. Damion rose in one controlled motion and faced him squarely.

There was a moment's hesitation — just long enough for the man to question whether this was worth it. Then pride got the better of him. He lunged, swinging wild and slow.

Damion stepped inside the arc, his left arm brushing past the man's elbow, and snapped a solid backhand across the side of his head, turning his ear blood red.

The slap echoed like a gunshot. The man spun halfway around, dazed, stumbled into the front of the truck, and dropped to one knee.

Before he could recover, Damion closed the distance. His right hand shot out, thumb driving hard into the side of the man's neck — deep into the carotid artery.

The man gagged, clawing at Damion's arm, eyes wide in panic.

Damion leaned in close — his voice a menacing whisper in the man's ear.

"You tell Donovan I got his message," he said, his tone calm and cold. "And if he sends any more of his delivery boys after me, they won't be walking back home."

He gave one final squeeze, enough to make the man's eyes glaze, then released him. The incapacitated man slumped sideways, gasping, with his hands pressed against his neck. Bubba groaned nearby, still cradling his groin and rocking gently in pain.

Damion felt no sympathy for the two and didn't spare them another look. He straightened his jacket, walked to his car, and got in. He glanced at the church and saw Pastor Coburn watching from one of the clear glass windows. Damion nodded to him once, started the engine, and eased out of the parking lot.

In the mirror, the two men were still down — one on his knees, one on his side. Whatever message they planned on delivering, Damion had intercepted it and sent a message of his own. They would probably tell Donovan a different story about what had happened, but it didn't matter. He would find out Damion's response soon enough.

———

The cargo van rolled down the highway at a steady fifty miles per hour. The windows were down, and the fresh, country air flowed in, carrying with it the hum of asphalt under the fast plucking on a banjo. A fiddle joined in somewhere mid-song, and the two men in the cab bobbed their heads in time to the Kentucky Blue Grass melody, arms hanging out the windows as the open air washed over them.

They'd been driving for hours — six, maybe a little more. Three stops behind them, one to go. At each stop, another piece of the puzzle was loaded up and sealed tight in barrels marked Cooking Oil, in bold white letters. Ten barrels in total — precious cargo, though not for the reasons their labels claimed. The liquids in the barrels sloshed faintly when the road curved, the sound light, deceptively harmless. But the two men knew better. Inside those drums were volatile chemicals, the kind that turned into financial gold on the street if handled correctly… or fire and death if they weren't.

Both men knew the stakes. One small, unintentional spark or puncture in the wrong place, the wrong seal, or even the wrong temperature — and they'd be nothing but smoke and a headline. But even that kind of threat of death didn't scare them as much as the thought of what would happen if they showed up without the right materials, or with several damaged goods. Everyone in the organization knew the stories. Everyone had heard them. And everyone knew that Sebastian "The Butcher" Donovan was not a man to be trifled with.

The name alone carried its own weight. He didn't smile, didn't yell, and never had to lift a finger himself. He didn't have to. That's what his "Four Horsemen" were for — the quiet men who handled things when someone needed a lesson. These were the ones who caused people to suddenly disappear and made murders look like accidents.

The men in the van had seen it firsthand at the fairgrounds. They'd been close enough to see a man murdered, and watch the crowd walk away, thinking it was just a freak accident. The horsemen had made it look so clean, so believable, that it was almost beautiful in its precision. It also made one thing clear: when Donovan said *move something*, you moved it. You didn't question what, where, or why.

Now, nearing their final stop, both men let out small, almost synchronized sighs of relief. The home stretch. The job was nearly done. Just one more delivery, and the danger, the frayed nerves, the heavy shadow of Donovan's name would fade away — at least until tomorrow.

The van slowed as they approached the gate. The armed guard recognized them, giving a lazy nod and a wave before opening it. No questions asked. No clipboard, no paperwork. They drove around to the rear of the building and backed up to the loading bay, the van's brakes squealing softly as it came to a stop beside the hydraulic lift. Both men climbed out, stretching stiff limbs. The driver spotted a familiar face near the bay — a worker leaning against the wall, smoking like he was trying to exhale twenty years of regret.

"Hey! How about giving us a hand unloading these barrels?" the driver barked, the tone a little too sharp for casual talk.

Jacob turned his head slowly, like he was waking from a long nap he didn't want to end. He looked at them with a tired, unimpressed stare that said everything he needed to without speaking. Then, with an exaggerated sigh, he flicked ash to the ground, pushed off the wall, and started toward them.

"What's your problem, dude?" the driver snapped. "Pick up the pace, will ya? And lose the cigarette — you tryin' to get us all killed?"

Jacob stopped mid-step, cigarette still between his fingers, and his voice a low, bored drawl. "My shift hasn't started yet, and I'm not as motivated if I ain't gettin' paid extra for this."

The driver took a step forward, face tightening into something between irritation and a threat. "I'll tell you what — if you want to keep your useless job, you'd better get a move on. How's that for motivation?"

Jacob stared at him for a second, unreadable, then exhaled through his nose. "I'm comin', ain't I?"

He flicked the cigarette away from the building, the ember flaring in a small arc before it hit the concrete, and walked to the back of the van.

The driver glared at him but said nothing else. They popped the latch and started unloading the barrels, each one landing with a deep metallic thud on the lift. Jacob worked beside them. His pace was deliberate — not slow enough to warrant a complaint, but steady enough to allow him time to size them up. He noted the tattoos on one man's arm — mostly black widow spiders, the cut across the other's eyebrow, the way they moved together like a team that didn't need words. He filed it all away — faces, height, weight, mannerisms — the small details a man needed to remember when he was fighting for his life, or trying to save someone else's.

When the last barrel was offloaded, the passenger stretched his back and slapped the driver on the shoulder. "Hey, I gotta use the john before we head out."

"Yeah, me too," the driver replied, then turned back toward Jacob with a smirk. "If it's not too much trouble, you think you can find it within yourself to keep an eye on the van till we get back?" The words dripped with sarcasm.

Jacob pulled another cigarette from his shirt pocket, lighting it with a flick from his Zippo lighter. "You're the boss," he said.

The driver's grin grew, cold and unfriendly. "Stupid locals," he muttered under his breath as he walked away with his partner, both men disappearing through the doorway.

Jacob took a slow drag, exhaled, and waited until the sound of their voices faded. Then he began to move — casual, unhurried. He circled the van once, scanning for cameras or stray eyes. No one was watching. No one ever really watched, not here.

He slipped his hand into his pocket and pulled out a small AirTag — white, smooth, unremarkable, except for what it could do. He leaned into the driver's seat, pressing the tag deep into the crease between the cushion and the backrest. He circled around the van and repeated the same action on the passenger side, careful not to leave a trace. After another quick glance around, Jacob removed a third item from his pocket and dropped it on the floor under the passenger seat.

When he straightened up, he was still smoking, still wearing the face of a man killing time. To anyone watching, he was just another worker too lazy to care. But inside, his pulse had quickened.

He maintained the ruse for the remaining minutes — pacing back and forth, taking slow drags from the cigarette, and blowing smoke into the air. He didn't need to look at the van again; his mind was already inside, imagining the route it would take, picturing every mile it would cover, and seeing the moment when the tag's signal would light up and tell them exactly where Donovan's people were operating.

An obnoxious voice broke through his thoughts.

"We're finished with you, dude. You can crawl back into your hole now!" The driver's laughter was harsh and ugly.

Jacob turned away slowly, eyes cold, and said nothing. He stepped aside as they climbed in, started the van, and pulled away towards the gate.

Once they were gone, he pulled out his phone, opened the message app, and typed one word:

Done.

He sent it, slipped the phone back into his pocket, and watched the van roll down the service road until it disappeared. A faint smile crept across his face — the kind of smile that didn't reflect joy, but quiet satisfaction.

For the first time in a long while, Jacob felt the weight of his quest shift ever so slightly. He'd finally done something that mattered. Something that might bring them closer to stopping the evil that had infested their town, and maybe, just maybe, closer to finding Marisol.

Chapter 19 – Hunting the Hunters

When Damion pulled up to the trailer, he didn't expect to see another car in the driveway. He sat there for a moment, engine still running, watching the faint silhouette moving behind the curtains. Del had come home early. She looked up quickly as he came inside, relief washing across her face before it hardened into quiet worry. Inside, the air carried the scent of freshly brewed coffee as her hand gripped the steaming cup in front of her.

She stood up, walked over to him, and, without a word, hugged him tightly around his neck.

After a moment of silence, she whispered, "Are you okay? I was worried and decided to come and check on you. I thought you would still be here when I came home."

"I'm good," Damion replied, closing the door behind him. "I had intended to wait here, but my plans got changed."

Del crossed her arms. "Because of the break-in?"

He shook his head. "No, because of another unexpected visitor — the guy you didn't see at the diner with the ballcap and the scratchy voice. His name is Jacob."

Del gave a faint sigh, then sat down again. Damion sat across from her, with his elbows resting on the table. He told her about following the Bronco to the church and about the confrontation with the two men who were waiting for him in the parking lot, bearing a message from Donovan.

"So, what now?" she asked, while shaking her head slowly. "You've got that look again — like you're about to do something questionable or dangerous."

He smiled faintly at that. "Maybe," he said. "Jacob and I came up with something."

A bewildered expression formed on her face as her head shot forward. "Jacob? The man you followed to the church — who's been following you — and threatened you to stay away? *That Jacob?*"

"Yeah. Turns out he's not quite the threat I thought he was," Damion said, leaning back with an amused smile. "He's been trying to find a woman who disappeared. Her name's Marisol. From what he told me, it sounds like she was part of the same migrant network as the girl. And, check this out — he works at the processing plant and saw one of the trucks that matched Marisol's description of the one that took her. We think it's tied to Donovan's operation."

Del frowned. "And your plan is… what? To walk up to them and ask if they're kidnapping people and using them illegally for forced labor?"

"Something like that," he said dryly. "Jacob's going in early to work. He will tag the truck with a small tracking device. Once it moves, I'll follow it. If we're lucky, it will lead us to wherever they're keeping those kidnapped people."

Del looked at him like she wasn't sure whether to admire him or slap him. "You know how dangerous that sounds, right?"

"I do."

"You could get yourself killed."

He didn't reply, just looked down for a moment, then back up. "Del, if that's where they're holding them — if Marisol's still alive, if others are — then we can't just sit here pretending that we don't know what's going on."

Her voice softened. "And if you're wrong?"

"Then I'll know for sure. But, if we're right, we may save some lives."

They sat there for a long moment, the silence between them full of things neither of them wanted to say out loud. Then Del leaned forward slightly.

"So, this man — Jacob — do you trust him?"

"I trust his pain," Damion said. "He's got the look of someone who's lost everything and still hasn't given up yet."

Del gave a faint nod, like she understood. "And what happens after you find this place?"

"Then, I call the Sheriff," he said, though his tone betrayed doubt even as he said it.

Del picked up the hesitation immediately. "You don't sound very convinced about that."

Damion let out a sigh, "Because I'm not. The Sheriff's stuck between doing what's right and surviving Donovan. I don't know which side of that line he's standing on anymore."

Del looked away, biting her lip. "Then, be careful which side you decide to land on."

Damion was about to reply when his phone buzzed on the table beside him. Both of them looked at it. Only one word glowed on the screen:

Done.

Del's gaze met his. "Jacob?"

He nodded. "Yeah."

"So, it's starting," she said quietly.

He pocketed the phone and stood, grabbing his jacket from the back of the chair. "It's already started."

Del rose as well, stepping closer. "Promise me something," she said, her voice barely above a whisper. "If this goes bad… you walk away. You've done enough already."

Damion's jaw tightened. He wanted to make her a promise, but the words wouldn't come. Instead, he brushed aside a lock of red hair that had fallen between her eyes and gave her a long kiss. Without another word, he turned towards the door as Del silently watched him leave. Her reflection in the dark window caught his shape passing by — shoulders squared, and his stride steady. She closed her eyes briefly and whispered a prayer she didn't expect anyone to hear.

Outside, the world was quiet. In Damion's pocket, the phone buzzed again — the AirTag signal was functioning perfectly. The van was moving and getting closer. He headed quickly to his car and connected his phone to the Mustang's installed navigation system. When he was sure that the only road the van could take was the one that passed by Del's, he eased onto the street and drove two miles ahead of the oncoming vehicle before pulling off into the driveway of a darkened trailer.

Damion shut off his engine and waited, watching the GPS display as the symbol on the map drew closer. He was so focused on watching the digital screen that he was slightly startled when his phone suddenly buzzed again. The text message scrolled across the top of the car's multi-function display — three question marks. Jacob. Damion picked up his phone and sent a response. 'Out hunting wild hogs. Will call later.' Two seconds later, a small 'thumbs-up' symbol appeared on the display.

Several pairs of headlights appeared in his rearview mirror, coming around the curve. Damion looked at the GPS closely, but the tracking symbol was further back than the vehicles approaching. As they drew closer, he could see that the first one was a large pickup, followed by a small sedan. The second group of lights drew closer as he glanced at the map display again. The tracking symbol for the tag appeared to stop as the two vehicles passed by — the first was another smaller pickup truck driven by a middle-aged woman, and the second was a van with two tired-looking men inside.

Damion closed his eyes, rested his head back, and let out a small sigh before glancing at the screen again. His eyes narrowed, and he cursed under his breath while starting the Mustang's powerful engine. The tracking signal had jumped from approaching his position to past his position, further down the road. That van with the two men and the country music blaring was the one he had been waiting for. After quickly checking for traffic, he eased back onto the two-lane street and accelerated up to the speed limit. The hunt was on.

Over the next several hours, the van made three stops before getting onto the highway heading towards the State Line. At each stop, Damion had saved the location on his phone and sent a location pin to Jacob. After each transmission, Jacob quickly sent a thumbs-up icon. Since the stops appeared to be in wooded areas, Damion had parked a safe distance away and did not risk driving onto any single access roads leading into or out of the locations. After the last stop, he texted Jacob that he was 'heading back home after a good hunt,' then turned on some jazz music. As he headed back to Bishops Creek, he called Del to let her know he was okay and, on a side note, that he hadn't done anything stupid or dangerous. He could hear the relief in her voice as she laughed over the car's speakers. She said she had returned to the diner to work the evening shift for Peaches, in case he wanted to stop by for a bite to eat. He admitted that he could use some food after the drive and would be there in thirty minutes.

The diner was mostly empty of customers as Damion sat in a corner booth devouring his meal. The grilled corned-beef sandwich, sausage potato hash, and candied yams were quickly pushing away the hunger that had built up inside him. This was not a food combination he had ever tried, but with Del's recommendation, he had given in. And he was happy that he had. The meal, along with the cold and perfectly sweetened iced tea, checked all the right boxes.

Damion was washing down a forkful of food with the iced tea when Sheriff Douglas entered the diner. He glanced over at Damion, gave a curt nod, then proceeded to the counter and sat down. Del went over to him and they exchanged some friendly small talk before she left to get his order. Damion ate with his gaze down, not wanting to make eye contact with the Sheriff, who, it appeared, felt likewise. Del came over to him, and they talked and laughed for a bit about nothing in particular, when Damion saw the Sheriff annoyingly reaching for his cell phone. Damion could see from the Sheriff's expression that whoever it was, he was not happy to answer it.

Sheriff Douglas got up from his meal, nodding, grabbed his hat, and started heading towards the door. When he passed Damion's booth, he stopped and turned back to look at him with a confused expression on his face. Damion glanced up with a mouth full of food as the Sheriff held the cell phone to his ear. Damion could clearly hear someone yelling on the other end before the Sheriff attempted to get a word in.

"No, I can't do that. Why not? Because it's not possible." He paused, still looking at Damion. "Sebastian, *Sebastian,* listen to me. It couldn't have been Jackson because *he's here at the diner eating dinner.* He can't have been there and here at the same time." The Sheriff eased over to a corner of the diner as the yelling through the earpiece continued. When the call ended, he looked at the cell phone nervously, then returned it to his pocket before approaching Damion's booth. He stood there looking at the plate of food before Damion broke the silence.

"I take it that was Donovan. What's he blaming me for this time?" Damion asked.

Sheriff Douglas glanced up at him with an expression that looked as if someone had sucked all of the oxygen out of his body.

"Someone torched two of his businesses," he replied, softly. "Not in Bishops Creek; outside the county."

"And he thinks that I did it?" Damion answered back.

"Not anymore. It happened about twenty minutes ago in places miles apart. You have a rock-solid alibi with witnesses who can confirm that you are here. Nothing for you to worry about."

Damion noticed that he had said *'places'* instead of *'towns'*. "That's a relief," he replied, then added, smiling, "Maybe it was someone moving in on his operation, or maybe - just a disgruntled employee."

Sheriff Douglas looked at him sharply before responding. "Just make sure you aren't anywhere near *any* of his properties before you leave town." He then walked back to the counter to finish his meal, leaving Damion with some troubling thoughts. Del came over and leaned on the side of the booth, her voice low.

"What was that all about?" she asked.

"Sheriff got a call from Donovan. Someone torched two of his businesses, and he tried to blame it on me. Fortunately, I was here, and the Sheriff could verify it."

The jingle of the bell sounded as the door opened. A man wearing a ball cap, denim jacket, and rough stubble on his chin looked around the diner, made brief eye contact with Damion, then headed to a booth on the other side of the room. After the man was seated, Del went over to take his order. She stood there briefly, then left, returning about a minute later with a coffee pot and mug. The man thanked her, looked at the menu, then placed his order. Damion glanced at him, then the Sheriff, who was eating his meal as if it were the last one he would ever have. When he finished, Sheriff Douglas placed a tip on the counter, then left the diner without a word.

Del came over and opened her mouth to say something, but was interrupted by the buzzing from Damion's phone. He glanced at the message, then turned the phone so Del could see it too.

"Thanks for the tip on those huntin' spots. Got a couple of big hogs today."

Damion quickly texted back. "Thought you were working today."

"Decided to take the day off. Didn't wanna' miss a chance at gettin' them big pigs. They don't stay in the same area for too long," came the reply.

Damion thought for a moment, then started typing. "What are you going to do next?"

"Right now, I'm 'bout to get a stack of hot cakes at that diner you like so much."

Del's eyes went wide as she read the last line, then stared at Damion. He nodded slightly while quickly cutting his eyes towards Jacob. Del took a deep breath, put on her perfect smile, and went back to work as a couple of new customers came in.

Damion finished eating, waved to Del, and left a twenty-dollar bill on the table before leaving. Once he was in the privacy of his car, he texted Jacob to meet him at the gas station in thirty minutes. After receiving the thumbs-up, Damion started the engine and drove away.

The thirty minutes dragged by as if time were stuck in molasses, but he was finally standing in the gas station staring at the candy rack, desperately trying to decide on which kind of processed sugar treat to buy. At least that's what he hoped the teenage girl behind the counter, staring at her cell phone, would think if she bothered to look up from it. On the opposite side of the rack, several spaces down, stood Jacob, also apparently trying to decide on what to buy.

"I thought the plan was for both of us to hit the locations together," Damion said, his voice low and tight with something between anger and accusation.

Jacob didn't flinch. He set his jaw and continued staring at the rack, calm in a way that had nothing to do with comfort. "It was," he admitted. "But I figured that my way would be better — and give you deniability."

Damion thought about his response, then realized that he actually had needed that deniability when the time had come. "How'd you pull it off?" he asked.

Jacob scratched the back of his head and spoke with a lazy, southern drawl. "I planted a burner phone in the van," he said. "The GPS on it fed a location I could follow. The phone connected to the global tracking network so you could get the tag signals, while allowing me to shadow the van to within visual range of each site by its GPS." He shrugged as if the technical aspects of his expertise were almost trivial.

"If anyone had seen me nearby, I had a story. Huntin' wild boar. That's a lot easier to sell than a man sneakin' 'round a building in the middle of nowhere driving an exotic orange Mustang. Besides, I'm sure all of Donovan's men know what you look like by now, or at least have a description."

Damion listened as his brow furrowed. He nodded once.

"All right. You followed it. Then what?"

Jacob's eyes hardened at the memory. "At each place, the men you saw in the van did their pick-ups. Migrants locked up inside buildings — no guards posted, and no sign of Marisol. After they left, I went in. There were labs in both of them: flammable chemicals, equipment, packaging, printers, the whole ugly assembly. I placed improvised explosive devices on one chemical barrel at each location." He didn't elaborate; the sentence stopped raw in the air.

Damion's throat tightened as a lump formed in his chest.

"You placed IEDs in the buildings?"

"Listen," Jacob said quickly, cutting off the rising edge of Damion's anger before it could become a shout. "I used my Army Combat Engineer training with explosives. I didn't go to make a show; they taught us how to contain what we wanted to destroy to avoid collateral damage. I put measures in place to destroy the production, not to hurt people. I was careful about that. Then I left the area, waited until we were both clear and back near Bishops Creek, and remotely detonated them by cell phone."

Damion could see the picture forming in his head — fire and ruined vats, evidence turned to ash. He'd wanted the operation exposed, not erased. "You destroyed the buildings?" he asked, voice low and stunned. "You burned the labs and everything in them?"

Jacob nodded. "Yes. They won't be using those again."

For a long moment, Damion said nothing. He ran through the likely outcomes as if testing specimens under a microscope, before finally speaking again. "There could have been innocent people returned to those buildings," he said finally. "You could've killed those migrants — or at least removed the chance to find survivors. You could've wiped out evidence that would have told us where else they keep people."

Jacob's face was flushed with confidence. "I made sure they weren't there, and there were no indications that those were anything other than labs. No documents left out anywhere. Also, I left trail cameras on the access roads at each entrance. If anyone had come back in the time between when I left and when I detonated, I'd have seen them."

Damion stared at him, impressed by the meticulousness, short-term planning, and execution of the move — the way someone with combat-engineer training thinks three steps ahead — was undeniable. Still, part of him bristled at the finality of it. Evidence gone. Structures wrecked. A dent in Donovan's machine for sure, but at what cost?

"He called the Sheriff afterwards," Damion added, as if that were the missing conclusion to Jacob's story. "Donovan screamed over the phone concerning the attack against his business. He even tried to blame me for doing it. It's a good thing I had that deniability," he said with a smirk. "The Sheriff was standing right in front of me at the diner during the conversation, and I could hear Donovan's meltdown."

Damion let the thought settle. Jacob's shadow work, the tracking, the destruction — all of it made another player's presence believable. It meant Donovan's suspicion could be steered; it meant they'd given the butcher something else to think about.

"I'm not happy that you pulled a lone wolf on this," Damion started, the words blunt and honest. "But I'd be lying if I said I wasn't impressed by the big dent you put in his operation today. Good job, partner."

Jacob gave a small, tired half-smile. "That's all I wanted," he said, "to distract him and take away his edge until we can take him down. If he doesn't know we are the ones hitting him, he's got to look elsewhere for blame. We bought some time."

Damion's mind was already calculating his next steps — how to use the chaos, where to nudge the Sheriff, and which walls might crack under pressure. Jacob's gamble had changed their plan; whether it made their goal easier or tougher was a question Damion couldn't answer yet.

He grabbed three chocolate bars and slowly headed past Jacob. "That really was some fine work," he said finally. "But next time, give me a heads-up before you torch a place."

Jacob's jaw tightened, then relaxed into a nod. "Next time," he agreed.

For now, they had what they needed: a dent in Donovan's empire, a solid alibi for Damion, and the knowledge that something in the fight had shifted. It wouldn't end the battle, but it would certainly change how they fought it.

Chapter 20 – Shadows and Silhouettes

The sun rose bright and early, ushering in another beautiful day over the enormous, waterside mansion sitting along the banks of Lake Townsend, just north of Greensboro, North Carolina. The immaculately maintained property, situated on six acres of prime real estate, reflected a picture of elegance, sophistication, and wealth.

The first crash came without warning. A crystal decanter exploding against the far wall, with aged whiskey dripping down the custom wood paneling in golden streaks. Sebastian Donovan stood behind his desk — the once personification of power, fractured into something feral. His jaw was tense, his white suit jacket somehow torn at the shoulder, and his gold tie loosened like a noose waiting for a body to drop. Another crash followed — a chair, then a bookshelf. Antique books rained down from the toppled shelf, leather-bound spines slapping on the floor like broken ribs. The men in the room didn't move. Not one of them. They'd seen Donovan angry before, but not like this. This was different. This was the kind of rage that came from caged or cornered wild animals — the unbridled rage laced with fear.

"Two facilities," Donovan hissed, his voice sharp as broken glass. "Two!" He slammed his fist against the desk, rattling the drawer handles. "Do you know what that cost me? Do you have any idea what I have just lost?"

The men exchanged uneasy glances but said nothing. The silence stretched on until one of them — the driver from the van — finally spoke.

"Sir, we're—"

Donovan turned and pointed at him, his dark eyes cutting through the man like a razor-sharp blade.

"Don't speak unless you have something to say that you are willing to gamble your life on," he replied, the words slowly dripping off his tongue like burning acid.

The man's throat bobbed once before he quickly lowered his gaze, as Donovan paced around the room, running his hands through his hair.

"Chemicals gone. Equipment destroyed. Distribution routes compromised. You tell me—how does someone find two hidden sites in separate locations and destroy them at the same time? You think that's a coincidence?" He stopped, staring out the tinted window as though the answer were written in the reflection of his own fury.

"No. Someone is trying to disrupt my operation — someone using well-coordinated attacks." He turned back towards the group, his eyes wild with accusation. "And I know who it is." The name hung in the air before he even said it.

"Damion Jackson."

The men shifted uncomfortably. One of them spoke up, hesitant.

"Sir, we've been watching him ever since you ordered us to. He hasn't been near any of our people. Only the waitress and that preacher at the church."

Donovan smiled — the kind of smile that carried no warmth. "Then maybe the preacher found religion in something other than God."

He reached behind his desk, grabbing the machete that sat in a custom wooden frame on the wall — an old relic from a time when his lessons were more hands-on. The metal blade caught the light as he swung it slowly, slicing back and forth through the air like the conductor of a symphony orchestra.

"You see this?" he said, eyes locking on his men. "This is the last thing one can expect to see at the end of their usefulness — when they forget who they work for." He lowered the blade and pressed its flat edge against the desk, the sound of metal tapping against wood. "Find out how Jackson knew about my facilities. Find out who talked, intentionally or by accident, while drunk, I don't care. And if one of you even thinks of covering for a friend or try lying to me—"

He didn't get to finish the sentence. At that moment, the door opened and another man entered, clutching something in his hands.

"Boss," he said nervously, "we found these in the van."

He held up a cell phone and two round, white keychain-looking devices. Donovan's eyes narrowed. He snatched the phone, stared at it for a long second, then hurled it across the room. The phone shattered against the wall, sending small, splintered pieces skidding over the floor. He then threw the tags down and stomped on them.

"Trackers," Donovan muttered. "He used them to find us, but how did he get them in the van?" The room remained silent except for his heavy breathing.

"Who had access to that van?" he barked finally.

No one answered.

His voice dropped an octave, low and dangerous. "I said — who had access?"

The driver stammered. "Everyone on the loading crew, sir. We rotate the vehicles sometimes, depending on shift changes—"

Donovan's glare could've cut through bone. "Then you'd better start remembering which one of your friends is a traitor before I start *cutting* through the list myself."

Before anyone could answer, two more men burst in — carrying something bulky. They set them down on the floor. Trail cameras.

Donovan stared, his eyes blazing with anger. "Where did you find those?"

"Perimeter access roads, Boss," one of the men said. "It looks like someone set them before the explosions. Motion-sensor activated. We think they may have been watching the roads and approach routes in case we returned early."

For a heartbeat, Donovan said nothing. Then the sound came — a low growl deep in his throat before he suddenly spun around and drove his fist into the man nearest him.

The blow landed with a dull thud as the man crumpled to the floor. The others didn't move. Didn't even dare to breathe hard. Donovan stood over the gasping man, flexing his hand.

"I molded my empire with an iron fist and my friend here," he said, his voice trembling with anger as he waved the sharp machete again. "And now someone's out there tearing it apart piece by piece, and they think I'm just going to stand here and watch?"

He turned to the other men; his fury now transformed into something even colder.

"Damion Jackson," he said again, the name tasting like poison in his mouth. "He has something to do with this, and someone is giving him information. Maybe the church, maybe that woman at the diner — I don't know who, but I'm going to find out."

He leaned on his desk, breathing through his teeth, then smiled. "He wants to keep sticking his nose where it doesn't belong? Fine. We'll give him something to stick his nose in."

One of the men looked up, puzzled. "Sir?"

Donovan straightened, the plan already forming behind his eyes. "We'll feed him something — a whisper, a note. Something that looks real. He's been asking questions. Let's give him an answer."

He walked around the desk, stopping at the fallen bookcase. From the floor, he picked up a torn sheet of paper — the corner of an old ledger — and stared at it, as if testing the idea's weight.

"Have one of the boys leave him a message," he said finally. "Something he can't ignore. Make it look like it came from a scared worker — someone who's seen too much. Say that they have important information about the people he's been asking about, and leave it on his car. He will come running like their knight in shining armor, and when he does—we'll be waiting."

———

Damion stared at the small screen on his cell phone. The blinking dots marking the van's location suddenly vanished. For nearly a minute, he watched, waiting for the feed to refresh. It didn't. He called Jacob, who answered on the second ring.

"You seeing what I'm seeing?" asked Damion.

"Nothing," Jacob exhaled sharply, the sound heavy with understanding. "They're gone. They must've torn the van apart and found the phone and the tags."

Jacob went quiet. In the background, a muffled hum — maybe his truck idling, or perhaps just the sound of him thinking out loud.

"We knew it wouldn't last long," he said finally. "But I didn't think they would find them this fast."

"Donovan must have had his men check everything for bugs after the labs were destroyed," Damion replied. "Hopefully, he thinks that one of his own crew turned on him and placed the trackers. Either way, he's too vindictive to let this attack go unanswered."

Jacob's tone hardened. "So, what's next?"

"We lay low and wait. Let him make the next move," Damion replied casually.

Another silence, this one longer. "You think they'll come after you?" Jacob asked.

Damion's jaw clenched. "They did once, so there's no reason to believe that they won't try again."

Jacob's voice filled with caution. "They'll probably try and snatch you when no one's around, so watch your back, brother."

The line went dead a moment later, and Damion sat there staring at the blank screen. The absence of the blinking dots had left him more unsettled than their movements had done.

Damion spent the morning making minor repairs to Del's trailer and waiting to see if he would get any additional uninvited visitors. By noon, he was becoming hungry and decided to go to the diner. The place was crowded, as usual. He sat in a corner booth, actively listening to the conversations around him while half pretending to read the newspaper.

Del was working the counter, smiling in that practiced way she did when her mind was focused on work. She caught his eye once, and he gave a smile and a slight nod, enough to let her know that everything was fine.

When he finally stepped outside, the air felt different — cooler. He glanced around the parking lot out of habit. His Mustang sat in the gravel spot where he'd left it, as sunlight glinted off the hood and windows.

Then, he saw it—a folded piece of paper tucked beneath the wiper blade. Damion looked around again, but saw no one. No eyes watching. No unusual movement in the windows. He pulled the note free and unfolded it. The handwriting was rough, slanted, and most likely written in haste.

I heard you've been asking questions.
If you want answers about the Shadows, I can help.
They're moving them again tonight and will be switching vehicles. I can show you where.
Come alone.

A location – Jenkins Landing – and the time followed. No name. No number.

Damion stared at it for a long moment. A forensic analysis would probably have shown that the person was trembling when it was written — not out of fear, but out of urgency. It looked authentic enough to pass for truth, but was more likely bait, thought Damion. He folded the paper once and slipped it into his pocket.

The sound of the diner door opening behind him made him glance back — just a couple of customers stepping out, laughing about something trivial. He turned away, his face blank, but his pulse had already started to rise. Whoever had left the note knew precisely what to say to entice him.

He stood by the car for another minute, then got in and sat there after starting the engine. This was Donovan's next move, and he had to play along, but he wasn't going to do it alone.

"Looks like we're in business," Damion began, his eyes switching between the road and the folded paper in his hand, as he talked to Jacob using the hands-free connection. "I found an anonymous note under my wipers. The writer says that they know where the migrants are being moved tonight."

Jacob didn't hesitate. "You're not going alone." A statement — not a question.

"I don't plan on making it a social call," Damion said. "The timing of the message after your attack, plus whoever left it volunteering information, smells like Donovan."

"Good," Jacob said. "We can talk more about it when I see you. I'm already on my way."

Damion blinked. "Already?"

Jacob's chuckle came through the speaker like gravel rolling in a tin cup. "Let's just say I've been keeping tabs on you."

"Tabs?" Damion asked, suspiciously.

There was a pause — a deliberate one. Then Jacob responded as if he'd been waiting for Damion to ask. "You're heading south on Road 258. Two miles from the split near Jenkins Landing."

Damion frowned. "You tracking *me* now?"

Jacob laughed. "Don't get your pride hurt. I taped a burner phone under your rear bumper."

Damion shook his head but couldn't help the half-smile that crept across his face. "So, you bugged my car?"

"Consider it an insurance policy," Jacob said. "I can't have my partner disappearing on me without warning."

"I didn't know you cared, Army," replied Damion with a chuckle.

"Don't go getting all sentimental — just be ready. If this is what I think it is, you're walking into a setup. And we're not playing by Donovan's rules tonight."

Damion's tone softened. "You've got a plan."

"Yeah," Jacob said assertively. "I have a plan, and I think you'll like it."

———

Four of Donovan's men crouched in the shadows near the water's edge, waiting. The air was thick with their breath and impatience. Each man had his role — the cutter, the bruisers, and the driver — but as the minutes dragged on, discipline had thinned to irritation.

Finally, they saw headlights approaching in the distance and stiffened like coiled wire. Then the beams widened across the gravel road, and their confusion began.

It wasn't a car that appeared in the dark, but a large SUV, rumbling slowly with lights flashing across the reeds. It rolled to a stop about twenty yards from the dock.

All of the doors opened, and four men climbed out, their laughter loud and careless. One popped open the tailgate and hauled out a cooler. Another unfolded a set of camping chairs, the metallic snap of aluminum cutting through the night. In minutes, they were sitting around drinking beer, boots propped on the bumper, talking over the soft hiss of an old country radio.

Donovan's men exchanged uncertain looks. The ambush point was now a picnic.

"What the heck is this?" one muttered.

"They're hunters," another of the men said. "Locals. We can't just run them off without drawing attention and explaining why we're out here."

The first man swore under his breath. "Great. Jackson's gonna' show up any minute, and we've got a tailgate party at ground zero."

They argued quietly in the dark until one of them groaned and voiced the inevitable: "We'd better call Mr. Donovan."

No one moved.

Finally, they decided to flip a coin. The loser cursed and fished out his phone, holding it away like it might bite him. Donovan answered on the first ring.

"Is it done?"

The man swallowed. "Uh, not yet, sir. We, uh... we've got a situation." He described the scene — the beer-drinking men, the cooler, and the folding chairs. Donovan's silence was worse than shouting.

"Stay put and get it done," Donovan hissed finally. "If Jackson shows up and leaves, you follow him. Don't miss. Don't fail. If you do...don't come back."

The line went dead.

Moments later, the low, steady growl of an engine echoed across the clearing. An orange Mustang appeared, its bright headlights sweeping the hunters' makeshift camp.

Donovan's men froze in their hiding places as nervous sweat began to run down their faces.

The car stopped, and Damion stepped out, took in the scene, and gave a cautious nod to one of the men drinking beer. Whatever he said made them laugh, and they offered him a cold beer, too, surprising the hidden men.

He sat with them for a while, the glow of cigarette tips and glass bottles flickering in the dark. No tension. No fear. Just men laughing at nothing, pretending the world outside didn't exist.

Then, as quickly as it had started, the gathering abruptly ended. Damion stood up, finished his beer, and walked back to his car. The hunters packed up their cooler, folded the chairs, and soon, their truck rumbled back towards the woods, its taillights vanishing in the dark.

Donovan's men took their cue. They sprinted for their own vehicle, hopped in, and gunned the engine.

"Get moving!" one ordered. "We'll take him before he hits the main road."

The race was short but challenging, as the dirt road turned into a twisting corridor of gravel and mud. The car's tires dug into the soft edges as the driver fought the wheel, nearly clipping a tree at the bend, but maintained control of the car. They pulled over at a choke point where the road curved and slowed — the perfect place for an ambush.

The driver turned on the hazard lights and popped open the hood. He got out and leaned over the engine while the others crouched low in the car. Everything was picture-perfect — a harmless situation involving a fellow motorist in need of help, whose vehicle had mechanical trouble and broke down in the woods. Now, there was just the short wait.

They heard the Mustang's engine first, low and powerful. Damion rolled to a stop behind the disabled car. He stepped out, glancing at the vehicle, then focused on the driver.

"Hey, is everything okay? Do you need a hand?" he asked.

The man slowly looked up from under the hood, a smile twisting across his face.

"No, mister, I don't need help." His grin turned sharp. "But you do."

Damion's posture shifted, small, almost imperceptible — the preparation of a man ready for anything.

"You should've listened to Mr. Donovan, Jackson," one of the other three men said, as they all stepped out from the car.

Damion's voice remained calm. "No, he should've listened to me."

They all laughed — a snorting, guttural sound — and that's when it came.

A faint whisper of air. Then, *thunk — thunk — thunk.*

Three men cried out, dropping instantly to the ground. Fiberglass arrows jutted from the backs of their legs, each one buried deep in their quadriceps muscles. The man at the hood froze, eyes wide, confusion turning to terror as the dark underbrush erupted.

Four masked figures stepped out from the tree line, moving with silent precision, compound bows drawn. They spread out in a half-circle around the fourth man, black silhouettes against the headlights.

"On your knees," Damion said quietly.

The standing man obeyed without hesitation, dropping so fast his knees scraped the gravel.

Damion slowly approached him, shaking his head. "Four men this time. I guess Donovan wanted to make sure that I went away…permanently."

The kneeling man stared at the ground, saying nothing.

Damion squatted to meet his eyes. "You're going to tell us everything — where the kidnapped people are, where Donovan's storing his drugs, if there are any other labs, all of it."

The man's lip quivered. "Donovan will kill me—"

"Then you've got a decision to make," Damion said softly. "Because right now, *I'm* the one standing in front of you, which makes Donovan the least of your problems."

One of the masked figures stepped closer, his voice low and ragged. "You want us to move them off the road — dump 'em in a ditch?"

Damion let the question hang in the air, as the four men on the ground looked at him wide-eyed with terror.

After a moment, Damion shook his head. "Not yet. Just tag 'em and bag 'em."

The four masked figures moved in unison — tasers crackled, bodies twitched, and five seconds later, Donovan's men lay unconscious on the ground. Plastic zip ties clicked tight around their wrists and ankles.

Damion watched as the incapacitated hitmen were dragged into their car. Then, one by one, the masked figures pulled off their hoods.

Jacob stood there, barely breathing, with a big grin on his face. Beside him were three men built like him — the same stiff shoulders, the same quiet focus, the same comical smile.

"Good timing," Damion said, exhaling. "How did you know where they would try to ambush me?"

Jacob shrugged. "It was the only place they could do it without potential witnesses. My brothers and I hunt these woods. We know all the vantage points." He gestured towards the car. "They never saw us, but we had eyes on them the entire time. Carl here, tagged their vehicle while they were settin' up. We've been tracking them since sunset."

Carl nodded with a crooked grin. "Figured we'd join in on the party when things got interesting."

Damion nodded, then took one last look at the car with the bound men. "You got somewhere to question them?"

"Yeah," one of the other brothers said. "Quiet. Nobody'll hear 'em scream."

Damion's eyes hardened. "Remember, guys — they talk, but they don't die. We need information, not bodies."

Jacob gave a firm nod. "Understood."

They exchanged a final look — one built on trust and mutual respect — before Damion turned back to his Mustang. As the car roared to life, he caught sight of Jacob's Bronco and the hitmen's car pulling away. The captured men would be dealt with quietly somewhere deep in the woods, far away from anywhere anyone would ever think to look for them. If they cooperated quickly, Jacob promised Damion that he'd release them in some remote place where they couldn't become an immediate problem. If they didn't cooperate quickly, he'd let them go in a location not even remotely close to civilization, wearing nothing but their birthday suits. Basically – naked.

And Damion knew then that tonight, the momentum of the battle had shifted. Sebastian Donovan had drawn first blood, but now, Damion and his makeshift team of combat warriors were striking back.

Chapter 21 – Under No Authority

The sound of a chainsaw idling low and steady echoed through the wooden walls like the growl of some wild animal grinding its teeth. It was the first thing Donovan's men heard when they awoke — that, and the click of a drill penetrating a resistant piece of wood somewhere nearby.

The air was heavy with the smell of pine and damp timber. The hunting cabin sat deep in the woods, a hundred miles from any main road, the kind of place no one ever stumbled across by accident. A single lantern hung from a beam above, its light pushing hard shadows against the walls.

Four of Donovan's men sat tied to rough wooden chairs, blindfolded, and their wrists bound tight behind them with plastic zip-ties cutting into their skin. One of them started breathing fast, jerky, and uneven as the chainsaw sputtered louder, then died abruptly. The sudden silence that filled the emptiness was worse than the angry noise.

"Alright, alright! We'll talk! We'll tell you everything!" one of them blurted out, voice cracking.

A few seconds passed, then the sound of boots on creaking floorboards slowly approached. Someone stepped close to the man who yelled out and tore the blindfold from his face. He flinched under the burst of white light that filled his eyes. The lamp had been repositioned to aim directly at him, making everything beyond its glow unreadable in the shadows. All he could make out were shapes — broad shoulders, masks, the faint gleam of steel.

A voice as deep as a grave spoke from the dark.

"You work for Sebastian Donovan?"

The man swallowed. "Y-Yes."

"How many operations does he have in North Carolina?"

The man blinked rapidly against the light.

"A lot— I mean— I don't know how many exactly—"

A new sound interrupted his reply—a second chainsaw spinning continuously, sharp and hungry. The man found his voice again as he nearly jumped out of the seat.

"Okay, okay! I'll tell you! He's got stash houses — twelve of them that I know of for sure — in three different counties. Small towns mostly. Empty lots with trucks coming in and out at night. I can give you locations."

A large hand grabbed his shoulder roughly and hauled him up. Someone guided him — or shoved him — across the room until he felt a table press against his thighs. On the table, a paper map was spread out under a small light. A gloved hand held his wrist down, and another pressed a pen into it.

"Show us."

He pointed to one spot, then another, his hand shaking so badly the pen scraped more than it wrote. "Here, near the old mill. And here — south of the bridge in Barlow County. There's a warehouse near the river that gets deliveries by boat. They store— they store the big shipments there."

When he was done, the hand released him, and someone dragged him back to his chair and zip-tied him again. The light snapped off for a moment, the darkness swallowing him whole.

The voice returned. "Next."

One by one, the other three were questioned. None of them resisted. One even started crying before anyone said a word. The threats didn't need to be spoken; the sound of the chainsaw being revved again every few minutes said enough.

When the last man was returned to his seat, the light was turned off completely. The faint creak of a door opened and closed. Then a voice — deeper this time, weary but calm.

"Guess Donovan's men ain't as loyal as he thinks."

A pair of boots moved toward the door, then out onto the porch. The night air was thick and cool as Jacob pulled off his mask and placed a call on his phone.

The call connected after one ring.

"Jacob?" Damion's voice sounded alert, cautious. "That was fast. I thought it'd take all night."

Jacob smiled faintly into the dark. "Those guys were no fun. . They broke before we even asked. Must've thought we were about to cut them up."

Damion exhaled. "What'd you get?"

"Everything," Jacob said. "Twelve locations. Stash houses, storage sites, drop points. They even gave up two of his production sites outside the county, and a place they called the 'party house'. Donovan's men weren't sure what kind of operation was taking place there because they were not allowed inside; they were only allowed outside the front gate, but they had a good guess. They said they had seen several important-looking people go into the place, and there was always a party with lots of good-looking women — they were sure that the women were female escorts. All of that info without any force or blood. I think you are starting to rub off on us, Navy."

"Good work," Damion replied, laughing. "We can use this. If we feed those stash house locations to the right people, the authorities will raid them without him ever knowing we were involved. It'll hit Donovan where it hurts most."

Jacob leaned against a post, the phone pressed to his ear, the glow of the cabin light painting faint lines across his jaw.

"That's what I was thinking. But I'm not stopping there. Me and my brothers — we're going to torch the two production sites. Put those labs out of business, permanently."

Damion thought for a moment. "You're sure?"

"Positive. You'll have an alibi, anyway. We'll handle it."

"Alright," Damion said finally. "Then I'll make myself useful and do some recon on one of the other locations they mentioned. The one they said hosts parties. I need to see what's going on there before we decide how to hit it."

Jacob grunted in approval. "Be careful. Those men said that place's got heavy traffic — big money people, women, music. Could be a front. Could be worse."

"It's Donovan," Damion said flatly. "It's definitely worse."

After a short pause, Jacob changed the subject. "We got what we needed from these guys. Cecil's heading west tomorrow. He'll drop them off somewhere between Tennessee and Oregon since they talked fast, and didn't give us a hard time."

Damion chuckled, "You're too kind. What if they decide to call their boss?"

Jacob smirked. "Don't worry. I told them I'd make sure Donovan knew exactly who spilled everything, and I was going to send him photos we took of them while they were out. Let's just say they'll be looking for new jobs when we let them go."

"Good. Keep me posted," Damion said.

Jacob nodded, even though Damion couldn't see it. "Copy that, boss."

The call ended, and Jacob slid the phone into his pocket, glancing back through the window. His brothers were already packing up the gear, securing the cabin for the trip out. The four men they'd interrogated sat motionless, still blindfolded. It would be dawn before they woke up again from the tasers.

———

It was almost two in the morning when Damion eased the car down the narrow country road toward the location Donovan's men had described. He expected darkness — an abandoned farmhouse, maybe a warehouse with a few cars parked outside. What he found instead was light, and a lot of it over the entire outdoor space.

Soft yellow light spilled through open windows. Hundreds of candles flickered along the porch railings, the front walk, the garden, and the driveway. Laughter carried faintly across the open air, and the low pulse of salsa music rolled across the fields like distant thunder.

Damion killed the engine and stepped out quietly, his black MIO gear blending into the night. From where he crouched near a tree line, he could see people drifting around the yard — old men in expensive shoes and clothes, younger women in tight, glittering dresses that caught the light every time they moved. The age gap between them was impossible to ignore, along with the forced smiles, excessive makeup, and uneasy stances.

Damion's jaw tightened. This wasn't just a party. This was human commerce at its worst: trafficking and prostitution.

He scanned the surroundings for Donovan — no sign at first. Then a flash of movement upstairs caught his eye. Through a window, he saw him — Sebastian Donovan, face flushed with fury, pacing the room, phone pressed to his ear. Even from a distance, Damion could tell the man was yelling. He slammed the phone down, sending it skidding across a table before storming out of sight.

Moments later, the front door opened. A black SUV rolled up the drive, headlights slicing across the grass. Donovan emerged with several men, climbed in, and the vehicle roared off down the road, tires spitting gravel.

Damion's phone vibrated once in his pocket. He glanced down—a message from Jacob.

We've got two bonfires lit. You should see them.

A smiley face emoji followed the message.

Damion smiled faintly. "That explains the tantrum," he muttered under his breath as he turned his focus back to the house. Now was the time to move.

He slipped from shadow to shadow, the dark fabric of his clothing absorbing what little light remained. The laughter and music made it easy to blend in — the drunks too far gone to notice the quiet ghost moving along the perimeter, and the guards too focused on making sure the drunks behaved...properly.

Behind the house, he spotted a propane tank — large, white, gleaming faintly in the candlelight. Someone, careless or ignorant, had set two large candles right beside it. Damion exhaled slowly through his nose. Perfect distraction.

He dropped low, crawling through the grass until a faint cough prompted him to freeze in place. The smell of cigarette smoke drifted on a thin breeze. Four feet to his right, a man leaned against a tree, the red glow of his cigarette flaring as he inhaled.

Damion waited until the man turned away, exhaling smoke toward the open field. Then he moved — silent like the nocturnal hunter he was. His arm wrapped tightly around the man's neck in a sleeper hold, cutting off the blood circulation in his arteries before a sound could escape. The man struggled, feet scraping the dirt, but Damion's grip didn't waver. In seconds, his body went limp.

Damion laid him down gently behind the tree, zip-tied his wrists, unloaded and tossed his rifle into the dark. Then he crawled the rest of the way to the propane tank and twisted the main valve open until it hissed. The heavy scent of gas began to bleed into the air.

He moved again, circling toward the back of the house until he found an old double-door cellar entrance. The latch gave easily beneath his fingers. He slipped inside, shutting it softly behind him.

The cool air below smelled of oak and aged stone. He flicked on his penlight and descended the stairs. What greeted him wasn't the dirt-floored cellar he expected, but a finished lounge — polished wood, leather, the faint glint of glass bottles behind a marble bar. A large-screen television sat dark, a pool table untouched in the center.

Donovan's private den. His personal man cave.

Damion began searching, scanning along the walls for false panels, safes, anything out of place. His steps were quiet and careful, then— the creak of a door opening at the top of the stairs.

A man's drunken voice drifted down, laughing and slurring, followed by the sound of heels scuffing against the steps. Damion killed the light and stepped back into the shadows.

The man stumbled down the stairs, with a wine bottle in one hand, and dragging a girl with the other. Her sequined dress shimmered under the dim lights, her face pale and blank. The man threw himself onto a sofa, took a heavy gulp, and laughed.

"You should be grateful," he slurred. "You could be back where you came from. Mr. Donovan saved you, sweetheart. You owe him, which means you owe me."

The girl didn't move or respond. Damion couldn't tell if she understood what the obnoxious drunk said, but she did understand what he wanted. He reached for her, and she flinched. He laughed harder, reaching for her again and grabbing her roughly by the arm. That was enough.

Damion silently moved from the darkness. His arm looped around the man's throat before he even registered the shadow behind him. The wine bottle hit the floor and rolled under the table. The girl gasped, her eyes wide with fear, but didn't scream.

The man struggled, clawing weakly at Damion's arm until his body gave way. Damion tightened, feeling the man's esophagus just short of being crushed, when he looked at the young woman standing there, terrified. He snapped out of his rage and released the man, letting him drop to the rug, gasping. When the man looked up again, the heel of Damion's boot met his face.

Silence.

Damion turned to the young woman, raising a finger to his lips. Her eyes widened, trembling with understanding. She nodded once, her breath uneven but silent. He glanced down at the unconscious man sprawled on the rug — the same man who had dragged her down here, now face-down in a puddle of spilled wine and shame. Damion pulled the man's suit jacket from his limp body and gently placed it around her shoulders. The fabric hung loose on her, sleeves covering her small hands.

Up close, she looked even younger than he'd thought — maybe fourteen, fifteen at most. Too young to be here. Too young to have already seen this much of the world's rot. Damion's gaze drifted back to the man on the floor. His jaw tightened. For a moment, the temptation was there — to leave this dirtbag with a different kind of reminder of tonight – one that he would never forget.

Just as he started moving towards the man, a small, gentle hand tugged at his arm. He looked down. The girl shook her head, barely perceptible, but firm. He held her stare for a few seconds, then gave a single nod.

"Alright," he whispered.

He guided her towards the cellar doors leading outside the house. The hinges groaned softly as he eased one open. They slipped out into the cool night air and crouched low, staying close to the ground as they crossed the yard. The sound of laughter and music behind them had dulled to a murmur — the party now seemed somewhere distant and muffled. At the edge of the trees, the girl stopped suddenly. She turned to him with a faint smile, her eyes glistening in the low light.

"*Gracias, señor*," she whispered.

 Before he could say anything, she stepped forward and hugged him tightly. Then, without hesitation, she disappeared into the darkness between the trees.

Damion stayed crouched, watching the forest swallow her whole. Then he looked back towards the house. His face hardened. Whatever pity or restraint he had left turned into cold, steady purpose. This place, and these people, needed to be dealt with.

He crept back towards the glow of the house. The laughter had changed tone — sharper now, broken by shouts. Men were moving quickly through the crowd, waving their hands in front of their faces. Some of the guests covered their noses, others stumbled away from the source of the odor.

Propane.

The heavy, invisible gas rolled low across the yard. It wasn't enough to ignite, but it was enough to make people panic. Damion watched two guards shout to each other, then sprint toward the large candles flickering near the propane tank. Others followed, racing to snuff out every open flame.

Good. The little distraction worked after all.

He moved swiftly, cutting behind the distracted guests. He'd already counted four guards outside — five, if he included the one he'd left zip-tied behind the tree — and now all of them were outside running in circles. Perfect.

Damion slipped into the house through a side entrance, hugging the walls as he moved deeper inside. The smell of perfume, alcohol, and smoke mixed in the air — a stale sweetness that clung to everything. His boots made no sound on the carpet as he worked his way through the hallways, opening doors one by one. The first room — occupied. A couple tangled together, oblivious. He closed the door quietly. Second room — same. He shut it faster this time. Third — a small office, empty, but not the one he'd seen Donovan in. He kept going.

At last, he reached the door he recognized from the outside. The same one where he'd seen Donovan pacing through the glass, shouting into the phone. Damion crouched low, took a breath, and eased the door open. The hinges gave a faint creak, barely audible over the music below. He slipped inside. The room was empty.

Damion crouched low, keeping beneath the sightline of the tall windows. Outside, the muffled chaos of the party carried faintly through the glass — shouts, hurried footsteps, the thump of music trying to outplay the panic. He moved along the edge of the room, staying in the soft shadow that pooled against the walls.

He began his search methodically. The desk first — drawers opened one by one, each emptied of anything meaningful. A few scattered papers, a gold pen, nothing useful. Behind the desk hung several framed photos — black-and-white prints of industrial buildings, construction sites, and one of Donovan shaking hands with a local official. Damion lifted each frame from the wall and checked behind them: nothing but clean drywall.

He crossed the room to a cabinet and opened it. Bottles of whiskey and scotch lined the shelves in precise order. He closed it again. The sofa cushions, the chairs, the side tables — all came up empty. He straightened up slightly, exhaling through his nose, then leaned back against the wall and sank into a crouch. His mind jumbled several possibilities — a false panel, an adjoining room, a code hidden in plain sight—none of it could be located. The place was too sterile. Donovan's ego didn't leave room for loose ends.

Then something caught his eye — a faint discoloration near the corner of the carpet. At first glance, it looked like nothing more than a shadow, but the longer he stared, the more it bothered him. The rest of the carpet was flawless, untouched. This patch, though, was slightly off, like something had been pulled and pressed back into place.

Damion shifted silently onto his knees and crawled across the floor. The carpet was thick, expensive, the kind that resisted creasing. He slipped his fingers under the edge and felt a slight give. It wasn't tacked down.

He lifted the corner carefully. Beneath it, the wood was uneven — one of the floorboards was set differently than the rest. He pried at it with his fingertips until it came loose, revealing a small recessed cavity with a safe embedded deep into the floor. It contained a digital lock with a keypad illuminating the light blue digits.

Damion stared at it, thinking fast. There was no way he could break into it now — not without time, tools, and silence. He took out his phone, snapped several photos of the safe, the keypad, and the faintly stamped model number along the side. Then he sent them to Jacob with a brief message:

Found something. Hidden safe in Donovan's office at the party house. Embedded under carpet. Anyone with lockpicking skills? If not, include photos with the info we send to the feds.

He waited two seconds — no reply yet. That was fine. Jacob would know what to do.

Damion replaced the board, pressed the carpet back into place, and smoothed it with his palm until it looked almost untouched. He gave the room one final glance, then slipped out the door.

The hallway was empty, but the voices downstairs had changed. Louder now. Urgent. He made his way towards the stairs, his body low, his steps quiet. As he reached the bottom, he heard the distinct rasp of a man's angry tone.

"Somebody opened that valve on purpose. It wasn't an accident."

Another voice responded, "We found a guest passed out in Donovan's den. A girl's missing too. Donovan's gonna really lose his mind when he finds out. Good thing he's heading down south right now. I don't want to be here when he returns in a couple of days."

Damion froze halfway down the hall. His pulse kicked once, hard. The girl. They must've found the man he'd left in the basement — and realized she was gone. He moved quickly, ducking into a side room and closing the door just enough to leave a thin crack open. The voices passed by — murmurs fading towards the main foyer.

He waited five long seconds, then slipped out again, keeping close to the wall. The air in the hallway was thick with perfume and the faint tang of spilled alcohol. His every step felt louder than it actually was. He reached the side door — the same one he'd entered through earlier. He grasped the handle, eased it open, and looked up—straight into the face of a guard.

"Leaving so soon?" the man asked, smiling. His breath smelled of cheap whiskey and arrogance.

Damion's muscles tensed. He felt it before he saw it — a shift in the air behind him, the presence closing in. He started to turn, but something heavy cracked against the back of his skull. White exploded behind his eyes. The floor tilted as the world narrowed to a ringing hum and fading light.

Then, Damion's world went black.

Chapter 22 – Nothing Buries Quietly

Damion awoke in darkness. A scratchy potato sack clung to his face, damp with his own breath, the stench of mildew and sweat pressed into the fibers. His wrists burned from the coarse rope biting into them, pulled tight behind his back. The floor beneath him was steel, shuddering and rattling from the rumble of a diesel engine, every bump driving pain deeper into the knot at the base of his skull.

The air in the back of the truck was a stew of human misery. Unwashed bodies. Sour sweat. The smell of urine and human feces baked into the metal. Someone coughed hard beside him—wet, rattling, like lungs drowning in their own filth. Another voice whimpered, while the copper smell of blood from fresh wounds hung heavy in the mix.

Damion flexed his shoulders against the ropes, his muscles stiff as if they'd been locked for hours. His head pulsed with a savage throb, a reminder of the blow that had dropped him. He couldn't tell how long he'd been out, but the aching in his back told him that time had dragged on for longer than he would be able to guess.

From the cab up front came muffled voices, two men laughing, their words tumbling through the static of a cheap radio.

"…what the eel's gonna do with this batch…"
"…heck, don't matter. Ain't our problem…"

A burst of sudden hollering cut through the air, startling the unfortunate riders.
"Yee haa! Welcome back to the wild and wonderful!"

Then only the twang of a country tune remained, its cheerful strumming and depressing lyrics mocking the misery in the truck's belly.

Time passed slowly. It could have been an hour, or it could've been three. Finally, the truck jolted to a stop. Hinges shrieked. Boots thudded. The back doors banged open and fresh air poured in—flowing through the sack. Voices barked orders, rough and angry. Prisoners stumbled, shoved into the open, their groans drowned out by shouting.

Damion stayed still. Lying there, listening. Until heavy hands clamped down, dragging him to the threshold of the truck. The sack ripped off, the world exploding into light. Two men, one obesely large and the other anorexic slim, dragged him under his arms across a dirt lot towards a silhouetted building.

He blinked hard, vision swimming into focus. A barn— weathered planks, rusted hinges, dirt for a floor. Inside, they dumped him like a sack of grain. The two men left the space, slamming the door behind them.

Damion sucked in a breath, testing the ropes. No give. He scanned the dim interior: a graveyard of farm relics. An old tractor eaten by rust. An anvil squatting in the shadows. A plow tangled in weeds. Everything smelled of decay and neglect.

But the roof… that was different. Steel beams crossed high overhead, welded in thick X's, bracing the structure against a weight it was never meant to hold. Something unnatural hung over this place. Something seriously wrong.

The side door creaked.

They came in—the two from before, flanking a third. He wasn't big, but he moved like a man who thought he owned the ground he walked on. Wiry, slicked back hair, and sharp edges under a hunter's vest and flannel short-sleeved shirt. Tattoos climbed his neck like barbed vines. His boots crunched the dirt as he circled in wide arcs, chewing a piece of straw like some backwoods predator sizing up his catch.

His eyes were shallow, restless. Damion had seen that look before—in addicts, in killers. Dangerous either way.

Damion studied him, and the man studied back. The silence was heavy, broken only when the stranger slowly turned to face the other two men. On his vest, colored strips caught Damion's attention in the light. Not fashion or a brand logo. Ribbons. *Military award ribbons.* And right above the ribbons – two silver bars. The man had turned fully and was now focused on something in his hand when Damion saw a tattoo that made his blood run cold. The little girl's bird with the long beak and the giant fork. No wonder she was so silent and afraid. She had met this man before, or at least, had seen him committing atrocities that she could only communicate through her notebook. Somehow, she had either been here or he had been near Bishops Creek, where he found the girl. Regardless, Damion now knew that this man was dangerous. Extremely dangerous.

In his haste to help the girl, he had probably broken two of the first rules of investigation when he'd targeted the poultry plant during his search. First, he assumed that the plant was the source of the disappearances and was the center of this illegal operation. And second, he didn't objectively consider the source – the notebook – and that the girl's drawings may have gotten some crucial details incorrect.

The images stabbed through his brain like a hot knife. The bird that she drew had been fat with wide, round eyes and a crooked orange beak that stretched too far across its face. One wing had jutted upward like it was waving hello, while the other drooped low, its feathers scribbled in uneven sticks. In its hand, the bird had clutched what looked more like a giant dinner fork than a weapon, its zigzagging teeth bent and crooked. An upside-down letter "T" leaned to the side as if it were about to topple, and a wiggly line floated above it, looping in the air without touching anything. To finish it off, the girl had sketched a tiny water gun poking out from under the bird's wing, while oversized stars tumbled around its head.

Looking down at the dirt-covered floor, Damion shook his head slowly as the gravity of his situation sank in—the reality of what the girl had seen and tried to draw.

The *real* bird wasn't a fat, happy cartoon—it was an eagle with outstretched wings, every feather sharp and deliberate. Its beak was hooked and cruel, not playful. The bird didn't wave; it clutched, holding tight to a trident, anchor, and flintlock pistol, symbols of sea, air, and land. Each piece meant precision, power, and discipline—the mark of warriors forged through trials that most men would never survive. Where the child's picture looked like something out of a school art project, the real insignia radiated authority, danger, and a legacy that was anything but child's play. The emblem of a U.S. Navy SEAL.

Damion listened intently, trying to hear what they were discussing, when the man slowly turned around, his voice sounding like a steel grate dragging across gravel.

"Jackson. Damion. CPO. United States Navy," the man spat out the words as if they were something sour in his mouth. "You a long way from home, boy. Why you been snoopin' 'round my operation?"

Damion steadied his breathing, forcing down the headache pounding behind his eyes. The wiry man's stare cut into him, shallow pupils gleaming under the dim light like a predator testing how much fight was left in its prey.

So, this was the eel. Not a creature. Not a code word. A man.

The decorations on his vest told one story - honor, service, sacrifice - but the discolored ink on his flesh and the dead look in his eyes told another.

Damion lifted his chin, meeting the man's gaze. This guy could probably kill him without breaking a sweat, but if he wanted to see fear, he'd be disappointed.

"You're the eel," Damion said, his voice low, measured. Not a question. A fact.

The man smiled, thin and sharp. The straw shifted between his teeth as he tilted his head, studying Damion the way a snake tastes the air.

"That's what they call me," he drawled. "Slipperier than water off a duck's back. Hard to catch. Harder to kill." He spread his arms slightly, as if inviting Damion to take a shot.

"But you already figured that out, didn't you, sailor boy?"

Damion didn't move, didn't blink. "You were also Navy."

A flash of something passed over the man's face - pride, resentment, a memory. It was gone before it settled.

"Was," the eel echoed, spitting the word out onto the dirt. "Now I run things my way. No orders. No uniforms. No flag to salute. Just power. And money. And people who have to do whatever I say."

He stepped closer, boots crunching in the dirt, until the stale heat of his whiskey-tainted breath burned against Damion's face. The straw brushed his lip as he leaned down.

"And you?" he hissed. "You came pokin' 'round where you don't belong. For what? Some little girl with a notebook full of doodles? That's right, I know about you finding the filthy runt that slipped away when these two boneheads weren't watching. You really got under the boss's skin. Mr. Donovan wanted to be here to skin you himself after he heard that we had you. Lucky for you, he had someplace else to be, but he gave me some instructions on what to do. I guess you aren't so lucky after all." The eel paused, eyeing Damion closely. "You really thought you'd just sniff out the truth, huh? Thought you could play hero? Save the day?"

Damion kept his eyes steady, his voice like steel wrapped in calm. "I don't play."

The eel chuckled, a dry rasp that carried zero humor. "Good to know, 'cause neither do I."

He straightened up, circling again, as his hand brushed the hilt of the hunting knife riding his hip. Suddenly, he drew the knife from its scabbard, closed the distance between them, and placed the tip of the shiny blade on the bridge of Damion's nose, right between his eyes.

"You're in my house now, *Chief*. My rules. My game. Question is…" He slowly rocked on his heels from side to side like a cobra, eyes narrowing into slits, "…how long do you think you can last in it?"

Just when Damion was sure the eel was about to finish him off, the door opened and another similarly clad bearded man entered.

"It's time, *Cap*," he said while sneering at Damion.

The eel nodded, then slowly turned to Damion.

"Well, *Chief*, duty calls. I'm sure you understand. I would rather stay here and finish our conversation, but we got a delivery to make." Then, turning to the two men standing further back in the barn, "Badger, Gopher, take him out to the pit. Bring me back a souvenir when you're done."

Whatever the 'pit' was, Damion was sure that it wasn't good based on the child-like glee emanating from the two men's faces. The big man snatched him to his feet and forced him out a back door of the barn and into a forest of thick grass and trees, followed closely by the walking bag of bones. Damion couldn't tell which direction they were headed in, and the only saving grace was that they were going in a straight line. If he were able to escape, at least he might be able to backtrack to the barn and then follow the road out that they came in on, however far that went, *and* if he didn't get caught first.

He needed to do something before they reached what would probably be his final destination. He thought about the old stumbling and falling down routine, but most likely that wouldn't work. They could just knock him out again and carry him the rest of the way. And, he didn't have much of a chance against both of them with his hands tied behind his back anyway. No, he needed to think of something else, and fast.

"So, how did you guys end up working for the LT? Did you serve with him somewhere?" Damion asked, slowing his steps as he tried to buy some time to come up with a plan.

"LT? What's an LT?" asked the larger of the two men.

"The Lieutenant. In the barn? *Your boss*?" Damion added.

"You sho' is dumb for a military man; don't even know your ranks," replied the man while shaking his head.

Damion continued, "He was wearing the silver bars of a Navy Lieutenant above his ribbons, that's why I'm asking. No offense."

"He's a *Captain*, not a Lieutenant," replied the other man behind him.

Damion went silent for a second, thinking, but he was starting to sense a flicker in the darkness. He had to be very careful with how he proceeded next.

"But two silver bars..."

"Is a Navy Captain, idiot!" snarled the large man, moving in front of Damion and poking him in the chest. "Don't disrespect his rank!" he snarled, his face less than a foot from Damion's, as his hot, putrid breath flowed over him like a volcano spewing molten lava. Damion nodded in feigned submission, and when the big man was satisfied that he was back in control, he took two steps back and twisted his foot on what appeared to be a fallen tree branch with hourglass carvings on it. Looking down, the man's face quickly turned ashen in terror as his mouth opened into a silent scream.

Damion thought that his eyes were playing tricks on him as the thick, three-foot-long tree branch suddenly changed shape from straight to curvy and, in the blink of an eye, attached itself to the man's calf. The man yelled as he stumbled to Damion's left, swinging the butt of his rifle down in the grass. The stick-man pushed past Damion, pulling out his hunting knife and grumbling, *"Copperhead!"* Damion watched as the man hacked apart the venomous snake attached to his friend's leg as the big man fell to the ground. After chopping the snake into several pieces, *stick-man* stooped down to check the other man's wound.

With the big man down and stick-man temporarily distracted, Damion saw his chance. He sprang forward towards the two men just as the skinny, little man, squatting near his friend, pivoted around towards him. Damion, carried by his momentum, hopped forward and caught the man in the side of his head with the heel of his boot. The impact snapped the man's head viciously to the right and sent his body flailing across his friend into an unconscious heap. The big man, already feeling the effects of the snake venom, shakily reached for his rifle as Damion hopped in the air again and landed square on the man's forehead. The blow didn't knock him out, but he was incapacitated enough not to be of any further threat. As for the venom, well, there was nothing he could do about that.

Damion squatted next to the big man's side, removed his hunting knife, and cut his ropes free. After carefully looking around for any more strange-looking *tree branches,* he tied up the stick-man and retrieved both men's AR-15 assault rifles. *'Better not to have to look over your shoulder,'* he thought to himself after getting his bearings.

Crouching low, he started slowly back through the trees in the direction of the barn. Although he was now well-armed, he had no delusions about his situation. He did not know where he was, but he was way out of his element – walking through what could easily pass for an enemy jungle, filled with venomous snakes and equally venomous men. He had two AR-15 assault rifles with two standard magazines; a total of maybe sixty rounds if they were fully loaded – plus the 'Rambo' sized hunting knife; against what? Possibly a small army headed by a former Navy SEAL with crazy eyes.

And then, it hit him. Again. *Cap. Captain.* The man in the barn had addressed him as *'Cap,'* and those other two referred to him as a *Captain.* A smile crept across Damion's face. The 'eel' was wearing silver bars and calling himself a *Captain,* while sporting Navy SEAL ink. That was a mistake; possibly a game-changer. Maybe he had made some other mistakes too that he could take advantage of, thought Damion as he moved more confidently towards his goal. A quick flash went through his mind as he thought about recently working with another person who had fooled everyone into thinking she was someone that she wasn't, but that had worked out in his favor. Maybe this will too. If his suspicion about the 'eel' was correct, then he might have a fighting chance of taking him down, and him getting out of this mess in one piece.

Chapter 23 – Rust and Iron

Damion could see the trees thinning up ahead as the barn came into view. He made it. Now, all he had to do was stay hidden long enough to find a way out of here before they missed the two men he left in the woods. Just as he reached the ragged edge of the tree line behind the barn, the air filled with a furious, mechanical buzzing — the sound of something large and angry. He looked up and froze in disbelief. Above the barn's corrugated roof, an unmanned aerial vehicle (UAV) hung in the sky like a giant vulture: the size of a small car, matte black, with four helicopter-style rotors whipping up leaves and dust. A camera pod tracked slowly beneath it, whirring in a mechanical sweep. Luckily, it was pointed down at the gravel lot, not towards the tree line, where Damion's shocked face was sticking out. Even more bizarre was the round object mounted under the belly of the UAV — the size of a beach ball, also matte black but trimmed with thin, deliberate gold stripes. The large camera rotated through its range —a diagnostic sweep —then the whole machine pivoted and drifted away. Voices barked orders. Truck engines rumbled to life.

Damion stayed low, listening to the commotion and quickly capturing glimpses of several trucks as they rapidly headed towards the guarded gate. A creaking sound captured his attention, so he faded back into the cover of the trees just as the barn door opened and the 'eel' stepped out, scanning the dark border of trees like a man who expected predators to be waiting for him. Damion flattened himself against a trunk and brought his AR-15 up, sighting on the man ten yards ahead. A second deeper voice — the one that'd called him "*Cap*" earlier — materialized in the doorway. The eel barked orders: load up the workers, move them out; he'd wait for Badger and Gopher to bring his souvenir *of* the Chief, then they'd join him. Leave two extra guards, take the rest to the plant.

After the man left, the eel nervously checked his watch. He lit a cigarette, sucked it down faster than Damion thought was humanly possible, then another, chain-smoking as if the smoke itself could speed up time. Gone was the tough demeanor of a hardcore, stone-cold killer of America's enemies far and wide. The edges of Damion's mouth curled up as a small, savage thrill slid through him. The suspicion that had been circling his skull like a bird of prey now looked less like a wild guess and more like a confirmation. He felt the old, familiar rush he would experience during law enforcement operations when his quarry was in sight. Locking eyes on the eel, a crazy thought suddenly popped into his head: *I wonder if that copperhead felt the same way as I do now — waiting for prey to wander within reach?*

The eel fumbled with his pants zipper, causing Damion's stomach to tighten. He really didn't want to have to watch this, but thankfully, the man pivoted toward the barn and relieved himself on the splintered boards like some mangy, overgrown mutt marking its territory. That's when Damion moved.

Heel-to-toe in a low, cat-like crouch, he quietly slid behind his unsuspecting target. Clutching the hunting knife he'd taken from the big man, Damion, in one fluid motion, grabbed his collar while pressing the sharp, stainless-steel against the soft spot at the base of the eel's neck – cold metal against hot flesh. He pushed the man forward into the wall and spoke in a low, menacing tone, letting extra bass resonate in his voice.

"Make one sound and you're dead."

He felt the eel's skin give as the blade bit a whisper into flesh. The eel whimpered, breath stuttering, as warm urine soaked his pants.

"You, being a SEAL and all," Damion said, savoring the panic in the man's face, "you know exactly where my knife is, right? So, I suggest you don't move an inch."

The eel's lungs worked like two fire pumps on steroids. He didn't say anything, only made that ragged noise that might have been a prayer or a curse, as a puddle formed in the dirt between his feet. Damion, feeling even more certain of his suspicions than before, began to interrogate the quivering man in his grasp.

"Now, tell me - what's gonna' happen if I continue to push in another two inches?"

Silence. Only the sound of his ragged breathing and the increasingly foul odor of whatever bile and fluids were escaping from the man's body. Damion's voice dropped lower.

"Nothing? Well, then…let me tell you. If I jerk my hand or you try to get all touchy-feely, this blade will slip between your vertebrae and sever your spinal cord from your brain stem. You'll be dead before your body hits the dirt."

The man's shuddering worsened until he lost all control and started convulsing. A sour note of pity ticked through Damion for half a second — gone the moment he saw the child's face in his mind, and the truck full of bodies riding to some pit. The sharp point of the knife helped the man find his voice again.

"*Please*, mister. I got a wife and three boys."

Damion almost laughed. "Seriously, dude? And you call yourself a SEAL?" He twisted the knife a fraction, watching the man claw at the plank wall.

"*N-no*," the man gasped. "I went to basic…but got kicked out after two weeks. I got ratted out—had a stash of reefer I was gonna' sell inside."

Confirmation received.

"So where did you get the silver bars and the ribbons?" Damion pressed.

"The old Army surplus…flea market. Lots of good stuff." The man's smirk wilted under the knife's pressure. Damion pushed a little more, just enough for the man to understand that he was not impressed.

He needed facts, and he needed to move. "Where are we? How do I get out of here?"

"You in the *wild and wonderful* Chief," the man croaked. "Long walk back to Bishops Creek from West Virginia."

The words hit like hot lead. *West Virginia?* They'd brought these people from a plant across state lines - migrants kidnapped and shoved into the backs of trucks - then dumped them here to disappear. Damion's grip on the knife tightened.

"Where are they taking them? To this *pit?*"

"Naw, they only go to the pit after they dead. We ship 'em to and from the chicken plant every couple of days – *cheap labor.*"

Damion thought for a moment, then continued. "What's with the drone and that large ball it was carrying?" When the man didn't immediately answer, Damion dug the knife in a little deeper.

"Okay, okay!" hissed the eel. "They use it to carry the *product* over the river, where it drops it in the water. The ball floats down across the state line and is picked up on the other side before it reaches one of the stop-gaps. If it gets to a dam, we got folks who pluck it out of the water for us before the *do-gooders* get hold of it."

Damion thought about the nuances of the operation – full of complications, but also profitable and straightforward if it worked. It was easier to drop the ball in the water and eliminate the risk of being stopped on the highway by a curious State Trooper; if it were intercepted in the water, then there would be no launch point to trace it back to, and they could change the water entry point for their next drop.

"Why is the ball black with gold stripes?" Damion asked, shaking his head at the boldness of the operation.

"They pick it up at night. The gold stripes make it easier to see with the night glasses. They made it round so that it didn't get tangled up easily along the banks," he replied, whimpering pitifully.

Drones and night vision goggles? Damion thought. This did not sound like a bunch of hillbillies running a small-time drug and human trafficking operation. Someone with a lot of money and resources was involved, and he may have once again stumbled into something much bigger than what they imagined.

Two men - incapacitated in the woods. Two guards - near the gate. And, this imposter wannabe with his fake SEAL tattoo and flea-market medals. Time to move.

Damion let the blade slide out and, with a hard, elbow strike, smashed upward into the back of the eel's head, driving his face against the barn. The motion was violent and brutal as the man's nose crunched into the wall, blood spattering across the flaking wooden boards. The eel went down like a sack of rotten potatoes.

Quick and methodical, Damion checked his pockets for any form of identification and was relieved to find his own wallet instead. He then crept into the barn, where he found a coil of rope and an old rag. He tied the eel's wrists and feet, shoved the rag into his mouth, and gagged him. He then dragged the man to a far corner on the backside of the barn and propped him in the shadows where he wouldn't be seen from the lot.

Then, Damion called out in a heavily drawled voice.

"Cap! The Chief's gone!" he called, mimicking the rough intonations he'd heard earlier. *"He broke loose - we gotta' circle! We gotta' get more men over here to help!"*

After several moments, a man's boots thudded. One of the men came running into the barn, calling back for someone else. Damion waited until the figure ran through the doorway, then struck hard with a length of scrap metal - a piece of hardened steel that landed with a sickening thunk. The man crashed hard to the dirt floor, out cold. Damion didn't waste a second. He stepped out the other side of the barn, circled, and came up behind the second guard who'd crept closer to peer into the gloom. One knock to the left temple, and he also dropped in a heap.

Damion hauled the two bodies completely inside and secured them in the same manner as the eel. He worked quickly so that he could get far away from there before anyone decided to come back and check on why the eel hadn't caught up with them yet. As the unconscious men lay in separate spots in the barn, Damion felt that he needed to do more to even the odds if they came after him. He thought about Maya Torres and managed a cold, hard chuckle; if he had her psychotic personality, he would just kill them and be done with it. However, that was not an option, so he did what he could. He quickly gathered the unconscious men's rifles and removed all of the firing pins. He then took the three magazines and shoved them in his pockets. Satisfied for the moment, he was just finishing up when he heard the sound of a truck engine approaching the barn.

Damion peeked through a crack in the wooden wall and saw two figures exit a pickup. The two men glanced around and called out to the eel. When they didn't hear a response, one of the men walked towards a small trailer while the other one approached the barn.

"Hey, Cap, you in there?" came the drawling voice.

Damion thought for a moment, but didn't dare try to imitate the eel's sickening voice. At a distance, he could probably get away with it, but with the man this close, he would most likely know that it wasn't him. He needed another way to draw the man in without alarming him. As the man called out again with a little more caution in his voice, Damion decided to take a huge chance. He put on a ballcap that had been knocked off one of the unconscious men's heads when he hit him, along with the man's hunting vest, and eased over to approximately six feet from the door so that he would be visible as soon as the newcomer stepped inside the barn. He then took a deep breath and knelt down on one knee with his back towards the door as if tying his boots, and laid his rifle on the floor. As the shadow of the new arrival passed into the barn near Damion, he spoke up in his worst southern accent ever.

"*Caps out back,*" he drawled while pointing to the back door of the barn.

The man came closer with his head tilted to the side, as he attempted to see who the down-turned face belonged to.

"*Who are you?*" he asked, while pulling up the rim of the ball cap. He froze with eyes wide, staring at the menacing face looking up at him.

Before the man could call out, Damion punched him square between his legs, causing the air to fly out of the man's mouth in a high-pitched squeal as he doubled over. As the man tumbled forward, Damion hit him with a solid uppercut under his chin that sent the man sprawling onto the floor. Damion slid over to check the unconscious man when suddenly, the world around him erupted. Dirt, splintered wood, and shards of rusted farm equipment exploded into the air as the man's partner opened fire, advancing toward the barn with his rifle blazing.

Damion dove out of sight, rolling hard against the faded doorframe, his hand finding his own weapon. Bullets chewed through the rotted boards above his head, causing splinters and paint chips to rain down on him. He knew that he couldn't stay pinned down; the others who had left might already be circling back at the sound of gunfire.

Then the shooting stopped. A metallic clatter followed — the distinct sound of an empty magazine hitting the ground.

Reloading.

Damion leaned out just far enough, brought the AR-15 to his shoulder, and squeezed the trigger in three quick, controlled double-bursts. The man staggered, stumbling back several steps before collapsing, clutching at his chest.

Keeping the rifle trained on him, Damion advanced carefully. The man groaned on the ground, rolling weakly from side to side. Four hits in the chest and one in the shoulder. Odd — hardly any blood. Damion nudged the man's shirt with the rifle's muzzle and felt the rigid outline beneath - body armor.

"You'll live," he muttered to the semi-conscious man.

He removed several zip ties from the man's belt and bound his wrists and ankles tightly before dragging him into the barn. A quick search of the nearby pickup turned up exactly what he needed — keys still dangling in the ignition, and a mobile phone lying on the seat. He tapped the side button. The screen lit up, unprotected. No password.

A vehicle. A phone. Hope.

Sliding behind the wheel, Damion couldn't help but think about Pastor Coburn as the engine rumbled to life. *Someone may actually be watching over him today.*

Chapter 24 – Crossing the Thin Line

The pickup burst through the break in the tree line, tires spitting gravel before gaining traction on the narrow strip of asphalt. Damion yanked the wheel hard right, the GPS voice flatly insisting he was now on Big Draft Road. The place looked less like a road and more like a scar carved into the wilderness—two fading yellow lines stretched out beneath a canopy of towering hardwoods. The trees closed in tight on both sides, their early-spring leaves restless in the wind, whispering secrets as the truck tore past.

Light fractured through the branches, slashing across the pavement in jagged bands, strobing the windshield like a warning. The shoulders were little more than raw earth and creeping undergrowth, vines and brush clawing for the edge of the blacktop as though eager to swallow it whole. A line of weary power poles marked the way forward, their wires sagging overhead like the last fragile thread tying this stretch of country back to civilization.

The road climbed toward a blind crest, steep, shadowed, and unforgiving, its peak hiding whatever waited on the other side—an open stretch of freedom or something far worse? Damion pressed the accelerator, engine growling too loud for comfort, every sharp curve daring him to push faster, every shadow hinting at the possibility that some animal, or maybe someone, might erupt from the trees. This was no country backroad drive; this was a gauntlet and a race against time.

Damion's grip tightened on the wheel as the pickup ate up the narrow road ahead, but his thoughts drifted back to the call he'd managed to make before tearing out of the hidden compound. He could still hear the static buzz of the line, Del's voice cracking sharply when she saw the location pin he'd sent.

"How are you in West Virginia?!?" she'd almost shouted, her panic bleeding through the phone.

He'd forced his voice steady, giving her the clipped version: how he'd been captured and transported in a truck with a group of kidnapped migrants; how he'd gotten loose, and the 'slight' confrontation with men he'd left incapacitated at the compound and in the woods behind him. He made sure that she understood he was still breathing and still moving, even if that was about all he could promise.

"Listen," he'd told her, his tone dropping low, urgent. "You need to call it in. The police, the feds—whoever picks up. Tell them about the compound, about the trucks hauling illegal migrants out of there. I don't know their exact route, but I'm sure they're heading east towards the Virginia state line, and then into North Carolina. They mentioned the *plant*, so from my position, that's the only direction that makes sense."

He remembered the silence on the other end, the sound of her quick breaths. Then her voice, softer, but edged with fear: "Damion..."

He cut her off before she could spiral into an emotional frenzy, before the worry in her voice could break his focus.

"I'm okay. Just do this. And they will ask you how you got this information. Give them my name and say that I am a Navy Chief who got caught up in this mess. Get the word out. I'll contact you again as soon as I can."

The memory dissolved as the truck crested over the rise, the road unfolding into shadows and blind corners as far as the eye could see. Damion had one more call to make.

Jacob answered on the first ring, his voice already sharp, bracing for bad news.

"Where the heck have you been?"

Damion tightened his grip on the steering wheel as his knuckles caught the faint glow reflecting from the backlit dashboard. His head still throbbed from the bashing, and the muscles in his back were stiff from the trip spent in the back of the truck. Added to that were whatever number of hours he had been tied up and unconscious before they decided to transport him to their remote compound.

"I got tagged," he said. "Caught while searching the party house."

There was a pause on the other end of the line, heavy breathing filling the silence.

"Tagged," Jacob repeated. "As in—"

"As in knocked unconscious, a bag over my head, thrown into a van, and delivered to a compound in West Virginia," Damion said. "But I got out. Heading back to Bishops Creek now."

He could practically hear Jacob sit upright.

"How did you—"

"Long story," Damion cut in. "I took down a couple of Donovan's people while there, and I helped a young girl escape. A kid. Fourteen, maybe fifteen. She was about to be forced to play *hostess* for one of Donovan's guests – predators dressed up as important people."

Jacob cursed loud enough that the phone crackled.

Damion kept talking, because if he stopped, the images of the house would crawl back in—the candlelit chaos, the sad escorts painted up like merchandise, and smug, drunken men pawing at them as if it were their birthright to do so.

"I overheard some things at that house," Damion continued, "a conversation about Donovan leaving town in a hurry. It wasn't a rumor—one of his men confirmed it while I was detained. A slimy little piece of crap they called the eel."

"Okay, that tracks," Jacob muttered.

"And, there was a UAV – a drone," Damion continued. "Carrying a ball of drugs under it for night drops in the river. I'm not sure which one they meant. There was also a pit somewhere in the woods outside the compound, most likely for bodies. They were going to let me see it up close and personal, but that didn't work out so well for them."

Jacob exhaled hard. "Jesus, Damion."

"You were right," Damion said quietly. "This thing's bigger than we thought."

Jacob was silent for a moment, then said, "While you were out partying, we kept moving. My brothers and I took out the production sites, just like we planned, but we didn't stop there. We hit three more places. Found around thirty locked up migrants, scared, hungry, and barely clothed."

Damion felt the muscles in his jaw tighten again.

"Any trouble from Donovan's men?" he asked.

"Two of my brothers came under fire," Jacob admitted. "They returned it with a bit more accuracy and dropped two of his men, permanently. No injuries on their side."

Damion swore under his breath. "Okay. I knew this would eventually happen."

"It almost happened *to you*," Jacob reminded him. "You barely made it out of West Virginia alive."

Damion grunted in agreement. He let the silence sit for a moment before asking the question that had been lingering in the background ever since he met Jacob.

"Any news about Marisol?" he asked quietly.

Jacob's exhale seemed even heavier this time. "No, there was no sign of her. None of the migrants knew her either. If she's alive, she wasn't at any of those sites."

Damion didn't respond. The truck hummed along the asphalt, the road curving before him in a long, unbroken ribbon of black and yellow.

Jacob continued. "I sent an anonymous tip to the FBI's Hotline. Told them about Donovan, the migrants, and the chemical labs."

"And?" Damion asked.

"The Duty Agent didn't believe a word of it… until I mentioned the shootout, the burned-down labs, and then sent my photos plus the ones that you shared with me. After that, his tone changed real fast."

A thin smile tugged at Damion's mouth. "Good."

Jacob's voice softened. "What about Del? You talk to her yet?"

"Yeah," Damion admitted. "But Donovan knows his men grabbed me at the party house. And the way he was acting, I don't know what he'll do or who he'll go after. Can you check on her and the kid? Keep them safe until I get back?"

"I'll send Caleb and one more," Jacob said immediately. "They'll keep an eye on her but not make contact. No need to spook her."

"Thanks," Damion said.

"What's your plan when you get back in town?" Jacob asked.

Damion sighed. "I'm not sure yet. But I'm going to start with Sheriff Douglas. With all this chaos coming down on his pal Donovan, maybe the Sheriff will finally be scared enough to pick the right side."

Suddenly, Damion hissed in pain, and the phone rustled.

"Damion?" Jacob snapped. "What was that?"

A squeal of tires echoed faintly through the connection.

"I'm good," Damion said after a breath. "GPS lagged on the dude's crappy phone. The intersection came unexpectedly out of nowhere, and I had to make a sharp turn. I'm back on track—heading east on I-64."

"Watch out for those State Troopers," Jacob warned. "They take their jobs seriously, and you don't want to end up on the evening news."

"Let them come," Damion muttered—but he eased off the accelerator anyway, slowing to seventy miles per hour.

Just as the needle split the number, a line of flashing blue lights exploded behind him in the rearview mirror. Damion signaled and started slowing, preparing for a traffic stop that would complicate everything. However, the police SUV didn't stop; it blasted past him, its siren silent, pushing well over 100 mph.

Damion shook his head, returned his speed to seventy, and kept driving.

Fifteen minutes later, a blue sign appeared:

VIRGINIA STATE LINE — 1 MILE.

Damion rounded the curve and immediately tensed up. Flashing blue lights from several police vehicles lit up the early evening ahead, blocking the highway.

Damion slowed the truck to a crawl.

Two Virginia State Police cruisers and a West Virginia State Trooper SUV formed a triangle - or felony stop - around a cargo truck. The police officers stood near the cargo truck with their weapons drawn, pointing at two men lying face down on the pavement. The men's wrists were handcuffed behind their backs while a cluster of migrants sat off to the side—hands on their heads and shoulders trembling.

One of the trucks from the convoy. Damion felt something warm bloom in his chest.

Thank you, Del.

A county deputy arrived to direct traffic, and soon waved him through. Damion passed by slowly, observing the scene, then grabbed the phone and called Del and Jacob to tell them what he'd seen.

Satisfied, he cruised further into Virginia, maintaining just five miles above the speed limit. When he reached Clifton Forge, the GPS offered three possible routes back to Bishops Creek. Any one of them could hold another truck of illegal migrants.

He chose US-220 South — minimal traffic, quieter, less of a police presence, and perfect for human traffickers looking to move a group of kidnapped people.

The road wound through flat farmland and bare-limbed trees, crossing small bridges over the James River. His mind drifted to the drone, to its path, to the possibility of a drop-off somewhere in a river to the east.

He didn't get far in his thoughts before the phone erupted with an upbeat country ringtone he vaguely recognized.

He tensed up, wondering if it was one of the men's pals, before checking the number on the screen — Jacob.

"Del and her boy are fine," Jacob said, directly. "Caleb's watching from a distance."

"Good," Damion replied. "I didn't tell her about Donovan possibly coming after her. She's worried enough already."

Jacob chuckled. "I get the feeling you always have women worrying too much about you."

"Only the ones not trying to kill me," Damion replied, flatly.

Jacob's laugh came longer this time.

"Anything else on Donovan?" Damion asked.

"Not really. Only his men at the plant are still visible; the others have basically disappeared. The fairground's empty, and they haven't been seen in town. Maybe Donovan pulled them to protect his remaining assets."

"I hope so," Damion said. "More warm bodies for the Feds to scoop up when they raid."

"How far out are you?" Jacob asked.

"Four hours give or take. But I need gas. The guys I *borrowed* this truck from just weren't polite enough to fill up the tank."

Jacob laughed again.

"Call me when you're close," he said.

"I will."

Damion ended the call and let the silence settle in again. The road curved ahead, long and empty, and he drove toward it with one thought echoing in his mind:

Sebastian Donovan isn't ready for what's coming.

Damion stayed on the accelerator until the road straightened into a long, dark ribbon beneath him, the asphalt carrying him south on Route 220 as if the truck itself were urging him back faster than he could think. He shifted onto Gravel Hill Road, then Lee Highway, weaving through the quiet back routes that cut across the state like forgotten veins. When he reached Troutville, Virginia, the adrenaline finally began to slip from his bloodstream, leaving behind the raw ache of everything his body had endured.

He pulled into a gas station that looked like it was built at the same time as the town. The lights hummed overhead as he filled the tank, the pump clicking rhythmically like a steel metronome trying to hold him together. His head still throbbed faintly from where Donovan's men had clocked him, but the sharpest edge of the pain had softened, dulled now into something he could push aside. When he climbed back into the truck and merged onto Mountain Pass Road, he felt the first real wave of exhaustion begin to settle into his muscles.

The phone's GPS glowed beside him, displaying a painful truth: he had many hours left to drive before he reached Bishops Creek again. He realized only then that he had been speeding—pushing well above the posted speed limit without noticing. His foot had been locked tensely on the accelerator, the way a man angrily grips someone's collar in an argument without realizing it. He set the cruise control, letting the truck carry some of the burden for him. The sudden ease in his leg felt strangely foreign, as though he'd finally admitted that he couldn't keep sprinting through the chaos forever. Jacob's earlier question whispered in the back of his mind as he glanced at the blurred, passing tree line.

What are you going to do when you get back?

Del was safe—for now. Jacob's brothers were more than capable of watching her from the shadows and ensuring no one got too close. That lifted one weight off his conscience, but not by much. Sheriff Douglas, however, remained a knot that he couldn't untangle.

The man said he wanted to fight back against Donovan, and Damion believed that much. But when the moment came to stand, he'd folded under the heavy weight of Donovan's threat like a man whose spine had been made of wet paper. In all honesty, Damion couldn't really blame him, though - not with a daughter and grandkids hanging in Donovan's crosshairs. No parent could withstand that kind of leverage with a clear conscience.

But the tide had shifted. Jacob and his brothers had already carved deep wounds into Donovan's empire, and Damion had done his own share of damage. With federal agencies now preparing to swarm the region—thanks to Jacob's call and the evidence Damion provided—the pressure would soon crush anything Donovan couldn't hide.

Maybe now, Sheriff Douglas would find enough courage under that badge to fight. Or at least enough fear of the truth coming out to stop helping Donovan. Either way, Damion knew one thing: they were seeing this through. All of it. Until there was nothing left of Donovan's operation but ash and memory.

The hours crawled by as he neared Bishops Creek, the sun dipping slowly behind the horizon until the last fragments of daylight clung to the road like dying embers. His body began to relax too much; the lingering shock of adrenaline loss was making his eyelids heavy. When he saw a sign announcing the town of Farmville, he decided not to push his luck. He took the exit onto West 3rd Street and soon spotted a small Country Store just before the main entrance to the town. Two pickup trucks stood by the entrance, their silhouettes familiar in the way all rural vehicles looked familiar after miles of empty highway. Damion parked next to them, stepped out, and stretched his legs, feeling the tight pull of worn muscles.

Inside, the store smelled like peppermint and pine. He paid for a large cup of coffee and a granola bar, stepped outside again, and breathed in the cool air before returning to the truck. The heat of the coffee slid down his throat as if new life was being poured inside him and revitalizing his body.

Damion started the truck and was just about to pull out when another vehicle rolled into the far end of the parking lot—a cargo truck eerily similar to the ones leaving the compound. Damion didn't react at first. It was a common enough model, and he knew better than to let paranoia jump into his head too quickly, especially when he was this tired.

Two men climbed out and lazily walked inside. They didn't look panicked or suspicious—just a couple of regular guys making a late stop. Damion was about to put the truck in gear, but something in his gut twisted. The old instinct and situational awareness that had kept him alive on too many faraway operations were ringing bells right now.

Wait.

He stayed put, sipping his coffee and slowly chewing the granola bar as the minutes passed by. Suddenly, the two men burst out of the store in a hurry. The driver was talking on his cell phone and gesturing wildly with his other hand. The passenger looked panic-stricken, his head twisting towards his partner with clear anxiety etched onto his face. The two quickly crossed the parking lot and hopped into the cargo truck. The driver abruptly ended his call; his face was tight, and he was clearly upset. As the truck began to back up, he glanced at Damion quickly before turning away. The truck rolled another three feet before he snapped his head back towards Damion again, his eyes narrowing into small slits.

Damion's stomach sank. Recognition was a predator, and it had just found him. He didn't know if the man recognized him from the compound, recognized the truck he was driving, or simply sensed something wrong, but the cool air shifted instantly as they locked eyes with each other.

Before either vehicle could make another move, a dark grey sedan with tinted windows slid into the parking lot like a flat stone gliding across water. Damion recognized it instantly—an unmarked police cruiser. The uniformed Farmville police officer parked and exited her vehicle on Damion's passenger side, scanning the lot with the calm alertness of someone used to operating in a quiet, small-town environment.

Damion shifted to put the truck in drive as the passenger in the cargo truck disappeared from Damion's view, leaning down inside the cab. The driver accelerated toward them.

Oh crap. They're going to attack.

Damion didn't waste time. He killed the engine, shoved the door open, and sprinted toward the officer.

300

"Gun!" he shouted.

The officer instinctively reached for her weapon, pivoting towards Damion with narrowed eyes. Damion jabbed a finger toward the oncoming truck.

"Gun! Take cover!"

The passenger suddenly leaned out of the cargo truck's window, shotgun braced across the hood. The blast tore through the air like a thunderclap. Buckshot hit the officer in the chest and shoulder, hurling her backward to the ground. Damion dove behind the patrol car as the cargo truck came to a screeching stop in the middle of the lot, tires burning against asphalt as more shots rang in the air.

The officer lay on the ground, shirt shredded and blood slowly staining through the fabric, but she was conscious — and angry. She unholstered her service weapon with shaky hands and was looking for a target, while Damion dragged her to cover behind her patrol car.

"You good to shoot?" Damion asked quickly.

The officer inhaled sharply. "Left hand only."

"I'm Navy military police," Damion said quickly — close enough to the truth. "Backup weapon?"

"Right ankle," she hissed while grabbing the small radio microphone attached to her shirt.

"Signal 13 — Signal 13! Shots fired, Country Store!"

Damion reached under her pant leg and retrieved a black Sig Sauer P320 Nitron Compact 9mm pistol. The familiar weight of the weapon felt perfect in his hands.

"How many?" the officer groaned.

"Two," Damion replied, sounding surprisingly calmer than he actually felt.

He glanced under the patrol car, hoping for a clean leg or ankle shot on the attackers, but the truck's wheels blocked any usable angle. He needed a better position. Then, he heard it—the flat tapping of shotgun shells being reloaded.

"Déjà vu," he muttered.

Damion rose above the car's trunk, sighted on the first man, and fired off two shots. A blast from the shotgun followed a split second later, but his rounds only impacted off the ground. The attacker staggered, looked up in shock, then attempted to raise his weapon again.

Damion fired two more shots center of mass, and the man's lifeless body collapsed to the cold ground.

Damion pivoted, searching for the second shooter, when two sharp cracks echoed behind him. He spun around to see the officer, pale with pain, firing with her left hand. The second attacker dropped face-first, as his shotgun clattered on the ground.

Damion rushed back to the officer and helped her sit up. "We need to check the truck," he said urgently. "There's a good chance that people are in there. Kidnapped migrants."

The officer gritted her teeth and nodded. Together, they approached the cargo truck, each taking one side. Damion yanked open the rear door.

The smell hit them first—human sweat and grime, days without bathing. A cluster of exhausted migrants stared up at them, eyes wide with fear, as sirens wailed in the distance, growing louder. Customers in the store began rushing out, drawn by the sound of silence after the gunfire. Locals swarmed around the wounded officer, offering jackets and first aid assistance. Damion slipped her backup weapon back into the ankle holster.

"Looks like you're in good hands. I need to go," he said firmly as she studied his face.

"Stop. You're involved in this," the officer rasped, clutching her bleeding arm. "You can't—just leave a crime scene."

"Sorry, I don't have a choice," Damion said. "Someone I care about is in grave danger, and I really need to leave. Now."

The officer turned away and sat on the edge of the truck as he disappeared into the gathering crowd. He climbed back into the truck just as two more patrol cars barreled into the parking lot with flashing blue lights and sirens blaring.

Damion pulled out slowly and eased back onto the road without drawing any attention to himself. He knew he had broken laws—several of them in fact—and more might come before sunrise, if he made it that far. But none of that really mattered now. He had to get back to Bishops Creek. And he had to do it before Donovan realized just how much of his empire was burning, and retaliated.

Chapter 25– The Weight of Two Wolves

Damion rolled back into Bishops Creek long after the town had gone still, the hour so late it felt stolen from the world. His body ached with the kind of exhaustion that settles into the bones after too many hours of danger and too many hours on the road. The headlights washed over familiar bends and rusted mailboxes, each one sharpening the awareness that he was finally—if only temporarily—back on home turf. He called Jacob before pulling entirely off the road. His voice came out rougher than he intended, but Jacob didn't need explanations; he gave him an address where they could meet up and debrief.

Damion met him at a small trailer tucked deep into the woods, where the windows glowed faintly as if the lights inside didn't want to disturb the quiet night. The two men updated each other on everything that had happened, including Damion's unexpected encounter in Virginia. The only thing left on their hit list now was the processing plant, and a chance to intercept the van transporting more migrant workers. If it did, liberating those people could cripple what remained of Donovan's operation.

They chose their approach with the simplicity of men who had undergone numerous operations and knew the problems that overcomplicating an operation could cause. They would rendezvous near the plant after Damion checked on Del.

He drove to the trailer park with the lights off in the last stretch, ghosting between shadows. He checked Del's trailer first—quiet, lights off, all still. Relief eased the tension in his chest, but only a fraction. He slipped inside his vehicle and changed into fresh MIO gear — the black clothing, gloves, mask, boots, and his personal weapon from the locked gun case in the tire well. When he stepped out again, fully prepared for battle, he paused in the dead quiet, listening for anything out of place. Nothing.

Minutes later, Damion parked his car well off a small gravel side road behind a cluster of thick trees. Jacob's silhouette was already waiting, leaning against a stump with the patience of someone who wasn't as relaxed as he looked. Nothing about Jacob ever was. They moved like wraiths through the woods, barely brushing the undergrowth. A pair of military-grade night-vision goggles changed hands between them. Damion didn't ask where Jacob had gotten them, and Jacob didn't volunteer the information. Their camaraderie didn't work on explanations - it worked on dedication and readiness.

As they reached the tree line overlooking the processing plant, the sight stopped both men cold: Three black SUVs, a sheriff's patrol cruiser, and not another soul outside. The building sat in near-total darkness except for a single light glowing on the poultry processing floor — the same level with the catwalk Damion had used during his first infiltration.

"Something's wrong," Jacob murmured.

"Yeah," Damion replied, eyes pinned to the unmoving parking lot, "and it's not Donovan. He's already fled south."

Which left one question: who did those vehicles belong to?

Damion touched Jacob's arm and pointed. "You keep a watch on the perimeter while I take a look inside."

Jacob nodded once without hesitation, his eyes never leaving the scene before them.

Damion fitted the Bluetooth earpiece, then dialed Jacob on the new burner phone Jacob had provided him. He checked his gear, adjusted his posture, and moved fast, crouching low across the open stretch. The security door he'd used before was untouched, the code unchanged — a small detail that made the hairs on his arms lift. Sloppy. Or intentional?

Inside, the silence was cavernous, the plant's massive machinery looming like dark monuments. He weaved through aisles of dormant equipment and skirted every angle of every security camera, now wary of what he had missed the last time. When he reached the catwalk, he positioned himself deep in the shadows, angled perfectly for both visibility and cover. Voices drifted up first — calm, elegant, feminine. Then the sight below came into view, and Damion froze.

A tall woman stood in the center of the room, her auburn hair pulled into a neat bun and her lips painted a shade of red that made blood look dull. Her full-length, sequined gown shimmered even in the dim light, each slow step measured and smooth. Around her stood six men, each armed with semiautomatic rifles, evenly spaced like highly trained professionals. At the center of the circle were two chairs, with two men tied to them. Sheriff Douglas — bloodied, bruised, his head drooping. And next to him —

Sebastian Donovan.

Damion blinked once, steadying the surge of adrenaline-fueled disbelief.

Donovan looked like someone had wrung him out and left him to dry. His face was a swollen map of damage—splits in the skin, a bruised socket sealing one eye shut, his white suit soaked so thoroughly with blood that it resembled a butcher's rag more than clothing. With every few breaths, a violent cough sent a streak of red spilling down his chin.

Damion's attention shifted back to the woman in red. The elegance in her stance made the armed men look like crude tools. Her movements were fluid enough to be beautiful, yet precise enough to be lethal. And when she spoke, the mellow tone of her voice made Damion's stomach tighten. It was the sound of someone accustomed to never needing to speak louder than a whisper, to control an audience or command a room.

Damion began quietly relaying every detail to Jacob, like a professional sportscaster giving play-by-play reports on a boxing match. Jacob's reply came back low and tense when Damion paused between comments.

"Six more men just exited the building near the loading dock - all carrying automatic rifles. They're doing a sweep."

Damion's breath tightened. *"Copy. Twelve heavily armed men for one attitude-adjustment meeting? Who is this woman?"*

Damion continued to watch the scene playing out below him as the woman turned towards Donovan.

"Did you think that you could run, Sebastian?" she asked, her velvety, accented voice warm, yet radiating a quiet intensity that made Damion shudder unconsciously.

"You cost me twenty million dollars. Entire operations burned to ash. Workers lost. Networks compromised by Federales. Can you even grasp the magnitude of your failure?"

Donovan jerked against the ropes. "No, Jefa! I wasn't running. I was going to Miami to secure your waterside acquisitions and return with additional men to deal with this threat to your businesses."

"A small-town policeman is your problem?" she asked, glancing at the battered sheriff.

"No," Donovan panted. "No, it's this other guy—Jackson. He's the one who caused all of this. He's the one who caused the loss of your money and your property."

"And where is this Jackson now?"

"We had him at the compound… but he escaped."

"So, he is a ghost – someone from your imagination?" she murmured, lifting her eyebrows with slow amusement. "And you expect me to believe that?"

The heavily armed men circling the room chuckled just loud enough to show their support for their boss's inquiry.

She pivoted slowly towards Sheriff Douglas.

"And you?" she asked softly, her warm eyes hiding the vicious nature he knew lurked behind them. "Do you know of this…Jackson?"

Sheriff Douglas knew that the chances of him walking out of this room alive were slim to none. If he was going to die alongside this evil man, at least he could make sure that Donovan got the worst of it first.

"I only provided my deputies as extra security for Mr. Donovan's processing plant. I don't personally know anyone named Jackson, Ma'am," he replied while shaking his head slowly and looking at her with all the sincerity of a starving man begging for scraps.

Donovan gasped and snapped, his eyes wide with horror as his ragged voice exploded in fury.

"Liar! I will gut you like a—"

A rifle butt cracked against the back of his skull, silencing him mid-threat. He slumped, groaning, as more blood spilled down his collar. He lifted his head only when the lady in red turned towards him again. Donovan apologized to his boss for raising his voice in her presence, then quickly lowered his head in submission.

Damion is stunned watching the scene unfold. All this time, everyone thought that Donovan was the one calling the shots, when in fact, it was this unassuming-looking woman who controlled everything and rained down terror on the so-called mafia boss. Damion quietly took out his camera and took photos of the scene. Whoever she was, someone somewhere probably needed to know about her. Her heels clicked softly on the tiled floor as the woman continued pacing slowly back and forth, glancing at Donovan.

"Who are you?" she asked quietly.

Donovan blinked. "Jefa?"

"Who," she repeated, "are you?"

"S-Sebastian Donovan."

"And what are you responsible for?"

His chin trembled. "North America regional operations," he whispered.

"You," she agreed, "are responsible. Not this policeman. Not this phantom Jackson. *You*, Sebastian."

Tears rolled down his face, cutting clean streams through the layers of dried blood. Damion's chest tightened. He was watching a wolf get reduced to a trembling mutt. Damion watched as Donovan's shoulders began to shake uncontrollably as the tears running down his face increased, washing more blood on his already soaked suit.

Just days ago, this man was a feral threat to everything and everyone in and around Bishops Creek, as well as other parts of the country. An untouchable force of nature. Now, he was sitting there, crying like a small child who had lost their favorite toy. The change was utterly uncanny.

The woman's attention soon drifted to Sheriff Douglas. A gleaming red dagger appeared in her hand as if conjured out of thin air. She slipped it under his chin and lifted until his eyes met hers.

"What is your name?"

He swallowed hard. "Sheriff J.T. Douglas, Ma'am."

She glanced at Donovan, offering a small, serene smile.

"You see, Sebastian? *This* is how you show respect to your boss."

Donovan sobbed even harder.

"Tell me...do you wish for you, your family, and everyone else you love or care about to live, Sheriff J.T. Douglas?" she asked in her velvety voice, as if there were any doubt to the answer that would follow.

"Y-yes, Ma'am," he replied nervously.

"Then, you are working for me now. When the new... *manager* of the Feather & Fork arrives, you will provide them with the same excellent, uninterrupted security services as before, and there may even be an increase in your allowance for that service if I am satisfied with the results. What do you have to say about that?"

"Yes, Ma'am!" Sheriff Douglas blurted out.

The blade vanished as quickly as it had appeared. One of her men cut Douglas loose. He stood, shakily rubbing his wrists, thanked her, and hurried from the room.

Damion whispered into the earpiece, "Sheriff's coming out. Looks like he's got a new boss."

Jacob: "Copy."

Jacob watched as Sheriff Douglas exited the building and stopped, looking fearfully at the armed men outside. One of the men points towards his vehicle, and Sheriff J.T. Douglas quickly gets in and drives away, kicking up a cloud of dust and spitting gravel.

"Sheriffs clear," reported Jacob over the phone connection.

Inside, the woman stepped aside as her men lifted Donovan from the chair. He sagged between them, limp, barely able to stand. As they began to file out, Damion slipped deeper into the dark shadows.

"Roger that. Looks like they're moving," he whispered into the earpiece. "They're taking Donovan with them."

"They've got a lot of firepower, brother," Jacob replied. "Are we tailing them or letting them disappear with that dirtbag, back to whatever sewer they crawled out of?"

"We call it in and tail 'em," Damion replied. "Maybe the Troopers or DOJ will have a solid ID on whoever this woman is. She must be seriously connected to make someone as evil as Sebastian Donovan squeal like that."

Jacob exhaled sharply. "Copy. Meet me at the tree line."

Five minutes later, Damion sprinted out of the same door he had entered and climbed into Jacob's Bronco. As Jacob starts to drive away, he tells Damion that Donovan didn't come out of the building with the woman and her crew. Damion nods in understanding. The man known as Sebastian Donovan would no longer be a threat...to anyone.

Jacob tells Damion that he had called the same FBI agent as before and reported the 3 SUVs, the illegal detention and interrogation of the sheriff and Donovan, as well as the mysterious woman commanding 12 heavily armed men.

The agent said that they would contact local law enforcement for assistance, since it would take 4–6 hours to send a task force to the area. As Jacob races to catch up to the SUVs, Damion uses the burner phone's built-in camera to take snapshots of the back screen of his digital camera. He texts the photos to the number Jacob used to contact the FBI agent earlier.

Three minutes later, the burner phone rang.

"Who are you," the agent demanded, "and where did these photos come from?"

Damion refuses to give his name but says he is with the man who contacted him earlier and that they are following the unknown woman in the photos. A long silence followed on the line, heavy with the kind of dread career lawmen didn't show easily. Then the agent spoke, his voice suddenly shaky from excitement or fear - Damion couldn't tell.

"Listen carefully. That woman is on the FBI's Top Five Most Wanted. She is wanted by at least seven federal jurisdictions and several international ones. You do not approach her under any circumstances. You do not engage. Stay far behind and report locations only. Understand?" The agent tells Damion to stay on the line while he makes some calls.

Damion and Jacob exchange a grim look.

Two minutes later, the agent returned, demanding their exact location. Damion gave it—northbound on US-258, past Murfreesboro. The SUVs were driving aggressively, unconcerned with any police presence. He reminded the agent that the vehicles were carrying at least twelve heavily armed men. The agent acknowledged the information and ended the call, telling them to keep updating locations until otherwise instructed.

Jacob grunted, eyes narrowing. "Jeez, they're moving fast. I'll try to catch up."

"Just get them in view," Damion reminded him.

They drove flat-out for nearly five minutes until they saw the SUVs' taillights. The three vehicles had slowed down and were driving just over the speed limit. Jacob had been driving almost 80 miles per hour to catch up on the narrow road, and reacted more slowly than either of them was comfortable with as he slowed behind the group of trucks. He had unintentionally closed the distance to within five car lengths before easing on the brakes. Jacob and Damion held their breath, expecting a hostile response from the rear vehicle, but none came.

The SUV ahead of the one they were following put on its turn signal and slowed to make a right turn onto a dark country road, just as the second SUV's turn signal flashed on. After the second truck completed its turn, both vehicles quickly increased speed. Damion and Jacob looked at each other with concern etched across their faces.

"Where's the third?" Jacob asked out loud.

The answer arrived in a brutal instant.

Blinding white lights lit up the inside of the truck's interior, and the Bronco jolted violently as the third SUV slammed into them full force from behind. The rear window shattered, spraying glass into the cab as automatic gunfire tore through the back panels, each impact ringing like a hammer on an oil drum. Jacob stomped on the accelerator, pulling away with his knuckles turning white on the steering wheel.

Damion twisted while unholstering his SIG Sauer P320 10mm pistol, and rapidly fired a volley of shots, unloading the powerful weapon through the blown-out rear glass frame. The impacting rounds caught the driver of the pursuing SUV off guard, forcing him to swerve violently as he instinctively backed off. Still, he quickly recovered, steadied the vehicle, and surged toward them again.

Damion slammed a fresh magazine into the pistol just as Jacob shouted, "Behind you — on the floor!"

Damion reached down, grabbing an AR-15 assault rifle that was lying there out of sight. He braced himself between the seats, leaned towards the back of the truck, and unleashed a full volley of the 5.56mm NATO rounds.

The SUV fishtailed, lights jerking wildly — then suddenly veered left and rolled, flipping onto its side in a storm of sparks.

"Hooah!" Jacob whooped, punching the ceiling. "That's what I'm talking about!"

Damion almost smiled, but his eyes stayed locked onto the empty road behind them, searching for any sign of the other two SUVs. Seeing no additional threats, Jacob eased off the gas as the Bronco's engine quieted into a smooth rumble. A little further down the road, they rounded a long bend — and saw blue lights blooming in the distance.

A police roadblock.

Damion exhaled. "Looks like your FBI guy came through."

When Jacob didn't respond, Damion turned toward him — and felt his stomach drop.

Jacob was staring forward, unmoving, blood soaking through the right side of his shirt.

"Jacob!"

Damion lunged across the console, grabbing the wheel just as Jacob's foot slipped off the accelerator. The Bronco veered, tires screeching, and before Damion could correct it, the big truck slammed into a tree with catastrophic force. The world became a kaleidoscope of colors as Damion flew forward and impacted with the windshield. Metal crunched and screamed piercingly, the Bronco flipped, and everything went dark.

When Damion's eyes fluttered open, he saw only shards of motion—flashing lights, blurred silhouettes, the echo of frantic voices. Hands dragged him onto a stretcher, and he was lifted into an ambulance. His limbs felt cold, numb, and impossibly heavy.

He tried to sit up, but his arms barely moved as he looked down. Handcuffs.

A voice near the doors muttered into a radio.

"Driver, Signal-7. Passenger, suspected person of interest in the Farmville, Virginia shooting."

Damion closed his eyes against the harsh lights, his head pulsing with hot, throbbing pain. As the paramedic reached for the ambulance doors, another transmission crackled through the airwaves:

"FBI priority-one suspect apprehended. Secure transport in progress."

The doors slammed shut as Damion Jackson succumbed to the darkness.

Epilogue

Damion lay on the jail cell bench in the Hertford County Sheriff's Station, eyes closed, hands behind his head, drifting between thoughts and memories. If he'd only left town the night he dropped the girl off with Deputy Mack, he wouldn't be here, staring at the ceiling and walls, watching his life slip through the bars. And, Jacob - Jacob would still be... But he knew, deep down, that walking away would have resulted in a multitude of more innocent dead people in an unmarked pit; nameless, gone without a trace.

The hinges of the cell block door groaned open, and the loud sound of heavy boots echoed down the hall. Damion sat up as Deputy Mack came into view. She silently studied him for a moment, then stepped aside. The young girl walked in, her small frame dwarfed by the large deputy next to her.

For the first time, Damion saw her clearly. No shadows, no dirt, no fear masking her features. Her eyes were a lively brown, flicking with curiosity and life he hadn't thought he'd ever get to witness in her. Her skin, a warm, medium tone, caught the thin shaft of sunlight slipping through the barred window, and her wavy dark hair tumbled loose around her flushed cheeks.

She crossed the space without hesitation, as he stretched out his hand through the bars, and she slipped her tiny hand into his. Her small fingers curled tightly around his calloused ones. For a brief moment, everything else fell away—the stink of the cell, the weight of charges waiting outside those walls, even his Navy career circling halfway down the drain.

She smiled. Not timid, not broken, but wide and certain, like she already knew she was safe. It hit him harder than any punch he'd ever taken. He held on for as long as Deputy Mack allowed, memorizing the brightness in her face. When the deputy finally cleared her throat, Damion let go, slowly, almost reluctantly.

CPS had arrived late, four days late; just before a television news crew also unexpectedly arrived, but Damion was thankful for it. He'd seen the girl as she truly was, alive, whole, smiling—and that was the only proof he needed that the decisions he had made, and his impending punishment, had been worth it. He didn't know how a regional news channel got the story of a found migrant girl, and he didn't care. No one could touch her now. A slight smile formed on his lips at the thought, *"B.B. would've been proud of me."*

Another thirty minutes passed after they had left before the loud thump of the steel door's lock cut his thoughts in half. A different deputy entered the detention area and opened his cell door, beckoning him to get up.

"Jackson! On your feet. You're outta' here."

Damion opened his eyes and stared at the deputy without moving. *I know this script. Cops fake a jailbreak, and there's an evening news headline about a sailor who resisted arrest — shot while trying to 'escape.'*

The deputy tilted his head with a smirk on his face, as if he were reading his mind. *"Seen that movie too.* Relax. Your lawyer's here to make sure you're released. Let's go."

Damion pushed to his feet, slow and wary, then followed him out. He was given a form to sign, and all of his personal belongings were returned to him. A buzzer sounded from a hidden speaker as another door opened to the reception area.

Damion passed through the door, and there, in the center of the room, waited a young man in an expensive charcoal-gray suit that looked like it belonged on Wall Street, not in a town where tractors outnumbered sedans. He didn't greet Damion so much as sneer at him, eyes dragging up and down like he was appraising a junk car with too many miles.

"Well, well. You don't look as bad as I expected," commented the man, his voice slick with disdain. "Though this place..." he wrinkled his nose, glancing around the room, "smells like stale fertilizer and despair."

Damion's brow furrowed. "I was told that a Public Defender wasn't available, and that the Judge won't see me until Monday."

The man scoffed, flicking invisible lint from his cuff. *"Public defender?* Please. Do you honestly think someone with a wardrobe like mine works for free?" He smoothed his hair, inspected his manicured nails, then curled his lip. "This suit alone costs more than the combined monthly salaries of everyone in this sad little building."

"Then who are you?" asked Damion, his voice a little more impatient than he intended.

The man leaned in, dropping his voice to a sarcastic whisper. "I'm your one *get-out-of-jail-free card*. That's what I was told to say. All pending charges dropped. *For doing the right thing*, whatever that's supposed to mean." He rolled his eyes as if the phrase itself bored and disgusted him.

Damion's mind raced as he stood there speechless. Who had gotten him released, and how? He knew that he had blood on his hands – *a lot of blood*. People had died because of him; he shouldn't be standing here as a free man. Then, the cryptic message relayed by the flamboyant, little man reverberated in his head like an air raid siren: *For doing the right thing.*

"Your name tripped some wire in a database," the man went on. "Someone with *real* connections made a call. Don't thank me—I don't even want to be here. My firm doesn't usually send me to handle..." He gestured around the sheriff's office with a theatrical flourish, "—backwoods, Mayberry drama."

He then abruptly turned on his heels without another word and quickly headed for the door.

Damion called after him. "So, what do I do now?"

The man didn't stop or look back. "I don't care what you do. Just so long as I don't have to breathe this town's dusty air for another second."

The insult hung in the silence, as heavy as an early morning fog. Deputies and locals alike glared angrily as he swept out the door. Damion could almost feel the room simmering.

Taking his cue, Damion slipped out the door and into the bright sunlight, blinking against the blaze. For a moment, he just stood there, lost in thought, until the deep-throated rumble of a muscle car engine grabbed his attention.

His 1970 Ford Mustang Boss 429 rolled up next to the curb, paint shining bright in Grabber Orange. The window lowered, as a pair of green eyes caught him first—emerald and mischievous—half-hidden behind copper-red hair.

"Hey, sailor," Del's voice slid out like smoke, smooth and teasing. "Need a lift—or are you just gonna' stand there lookin' pretty?"

Damion grinned despite himself. "How'd you get my car? And don't tell me this is a coincidence."

Del winked. "Coincidence? Sugar, there ain't no coincidences in Bishops Creek. The Sheriff impounded your baby. Lucky for you, Deputy Mack - my cousin - called and told me you were walking out. Thought you might need a ride."

Damion tilted his head, suspicion written across his face. Del bit her lip, then shrugged with feigned innocence. "Why me? Maybe...I let your name slip once or twice after you left. Can't help it if people know I've got a taste for trouble and fast cars."

Damion dangled the keys in front of him. "Then, please tell me how you're driving it when I've got the keys?"

"Oh, that." Del leaned her arm on the window frame, eyes glinting. "Cletus started it with a skeleton key. Told me not to turn her off until I gave her to you."

Damion blinked. "What Cletus? *Not the gas station guy*? The one scratching himself more than he scratches lottery tickets?"

Del burst into laughter. "Yeah, that's him."

"You're telling me that *Cletus* found a skeleton key *and* beat my car's security system?"

"Sugar, he *made* the key. Cletus may look like he fell out of a tackle box, but he's a genius. Used to work for the government with computers, something secret. Never talks about it—unless he's drunk on moonshine. He's probably the smartest guy in town."

Damion shook his head in disbelief as he reached for the driver's door handle, but Del's voice stopped him cold.

"Not so fast. The Sheriff only let me take her if I promised not to bring you back to Bishops Creek anytime soon. Told me to pack up all your things in the trunk, so that you didn't have a reason to waste time coming back. So, round you go. Passenger side."

Damion arched an eyebrow, but reluctantly circled to the other side, sliding in beside her.

"Well, that's convenient," he remarked. "There is one small thing you may have missed when you packed my things. It's hidden at your place. You can run in and grab it so that I don't have to get out of the car. And then, I guess lunch is on me."

Del smirked, revving the Mustang until the engine snarled, then leaned closer, her perfume slipping into the air between them.

"Lunch *and* dinner. And if you're lucky, dessert. Then...*maybe* you'll get your car back."

Damion relaxed into the seat as the Mustang growled into motion, a grin tugging at his lips. "You sure drive a hard bargain, *Delilah*."

Del threw him a sideways glance, her emerald green eyes sparkling.

"That's the *only* way I drive, sailor."

ALSO BY MORGAN KEYES

The Red Light District is a *romantic suspense* that explores the price of military honor, the weight of secrets, and the dangerous pull of forbidden love.

Chief Petty Officer Damion Jackson has built his career on discipline, loyalty, and the Navy's Core Values of Honor, Courage, and Commitment. To his fellow sailors, he is the man who never bends the rules. But beneath the uniform lies a past he's tried to bury—one that is now rising to the surface, threatening to shatter the life he has worked so hard to protect.

When fate draws him to the one woman he cannot have, temptation ignites in the shadows of foreign streets. She is off-limits by regulation and reputation, yet every stolen glance, every secret moment, pushes him closer to the edge. Torn between the oath he's sworn to defend and the passion he can no longer deny, Damion faces an impossible choice. If he follows his heart, he risks his career, his honor, and the fragile grip he has on his past. If he walks away, he may lose the one chance at love strong enough to burn through the darkness.